AF230165

BRUISES

KURT NEWTON

Printed in the United States of America

Lycan Valley Press Publications
1625 E 72nd St STE 700 PMB 132
Tacoma, Washington 98404
United States of America

ISBN-13: 978-1-64562-005-1

INTRODUCTION

They say write what you know.

Bruises come in many shapes and sizes. There are bruises to the skin. Bruises to the heart. Bruises to the psyche.

I like to think I've lived a relatively normal life, with ups and downs, successes and failures. I've experienced unpleasant things, been witness to unpleasant things. I've had to find a place for those unpleasant things to exist alongside what's been good.

The writing helps. But the bruises remain.

I can site the many instances, growing up, developing into the person I am today, where there was an assault on my senses...

The time my mother shot a "tiny bear" off the stonewall when I was little, only to discover it was a woodchuck, its body ruptured, its insides out... displaying the blue and purple meat of death...

The time my father literally picked me up and slammed me into the wall, leaving the impression of my shoulders in the plaster, for what reason I don't know to this day...

The time my brother rolled me up inside a braided rug drying on the grass, and left me screaming, unable to move, feeling I was about to die...

The embarrassment, the shame, the rejection that comes with adolescence...

The heartache and heartbreak that comes with divorce...

The death of parents... the death of siblings...

All of it, bruising, painful, inconsolable in the moment but, eventually, survivable.

The writing helps. But the bruises remain.

From what I've seen, I've lived a relatively normal life. I can't imagine the extent of the bruises some of us endure in the aftermath of unspeakable tragedies or at the hands of people more violent, more sadistic. Like our skin and muscle, the elasticity of the human psyche is something to behold. It's an amazingly forgiving tool in our defense. Survival is in our nature.

This collection is more than just a series of stories by a writer looking to approach a particular subject from every possible angle. It's a series of stories that, over years and years, has helped me find a place for all those unpleasant things I've witnessed or experienced firsthand.

They say write what you know.

I say the writing helps. But the bruises remain.

—Kurt Newton
Woodstock Valley, CT
24 April 2023

CONTENTS

The Pit

THE PIT CAME INTO EXISTENCE several days ago. But, for me, it had probably been there all my life.

After a particularly dispassionate argument with my wife, I drove to work feeling angry, adrift, and disillusioned with the fact that life could never be the way you want it to be. I passed cars unnecessarily. I drove too fast, asserting myself, taking control of the road as if it were my life. If only it were that easy.

I flew past the usual scenery, the narrow windiness of Route 6 leading me out of town and onto the wider up and down hill straight-aways heading west—a stretch that hosts the occasional patch-house or trailer whose dirt drives and muddied lawns are hemmed in by chicken wire or wooden fences, weather-bruised and wind-beaten. A no man's land of rural decay. I admired the trees that stood tall along both sides of the road and hoped that one day they would be rewarded for their patience and reclaim this space.

As I came down one of these long hills, thinking about the trees and watching the sun brighten the day, I felt a twinge in my brain as if someone had placed a tuning fork in the middle of my forehead—not on the surface, but inside.

Up ahead, the road leveled out and the tree-line gave way to a gravelly area once cleared for development but left unused, except for the dumping of clean fill. I noticed a pickup truck had pulled off and was parked on the empty lot facing the woods. Beside the truck stood two men.

At first I thought the men had decided to forego proper social etiquette and were urinating in the broad daylight. But they appeared to be standing motionless, as if their attentions were caught by something in front of them.

I would have given it more thought then, but the car in front of me had slowed to a near stop and I had to brake hard to avoid hitting it. The car put its signal on, almost as an after-thought and slowly pulled over. I watched this from my rearview mirror as I sped past, cursing the near-miss.

I drove the rest of the way to work in a strange preoccupied funk. I began searching the faces behind the wheel of every red two-door that drove by, my heart creeping close to the surface of my chest each time. I hadn't thought about Cindy in quite a while, and I wondered why now? Could it have been the close call that triggered these unexpected thoughts? The near miss that we ourselves had experienced?

By the time I got to work I had completely forgotten about the pickup and the two men standing in the empty lot.

Until that night.

As I drove by the empty lot on my way home I could see the same pickup still sitting there in the waning daylight, only now it was accompanied by a car—the same car I had nearly rear-ended —and two other vehicles. A small crowd was now gathered near the edge of the woods. They all stood, still as statues, staring at some point in the ground at their feet.

Perhaps someone had fallen into a well, I wondered, and these people were simply spectators watching the rescuers at work. My foot automatically eased off the gas and began to lift towards the brake. But a quick flash out of the corner of my eye—the digital clock on the dash changing numbers to double zero—distracted me long enough to look at the time.

I was already late coming home. My wife would still be angry from that morning's silent feud, and I knew she wouldn't appreciate watching my dinner grow cold.

So I continued on home, not realizing until I was halfway up the hill that the tuning fork feeling was back again, this time strong enough to rattle the fillings in my teeth.

"Do you have any idea what's going on down on Route 6?"

Beth looked at me as if I were sitting across the room instead of right next to her at the dinner table. "What are you talking about?"

"I thought maybe you'd heard something."

"No. Nothing."

She didn't even ask for me to explain. Not only didn't she know, she didn't care. My wife of six years, no children, nothing truly in common. I told her anyway.

"It was strange. Some cars were pulled over down by that clean fill area just before you get to Chaplin. Everyone was standing around like it was some kind of town meeting. Only nobody seemed to be doing anything. I almost got into a stupid accident because of it."

"Oh, my God," gasped Beth, her eyes growing large and eager, "you just reminded me. I almost got into a head-on this morning. You know that curve down by that house that always has the big postal truck parked in the yard..."

I could hear my wife's voice, but her words defied meaning. My thoughts kept repeating, *She doesn't care... She doesn't care...* The tuning fork feeling had returned. I touched my forehead and my fingertips tingled.

I remembered how it used to be. Beth and I were so intent on each other's words and movements, our eyes needed only to lock once to lift the weight of a bad day off our shoulders. We found each other the way lost puppies find their mother. There was a sense of the familiar, a need for satisfaction that attracted us into each other's arms. We were young. Perhaps naive. We reveled in the simple fact that we were in love, skipping atop the waves of lust and wonder without truly exploring what lay beneath. And when life came crashing down upon us in the form of careers and mortgage and talk of starting a family, the depth of our feelings—or lack thereof—began to bubble up and make themselves known. We now seemed caught in a holding pattern, a no man's land of memory and habit and little else.

"...I couldn't believe that asshole!"

I looked at my wife as if she were sitting across the room.

"Hmm," I said and finished my dinner, and tried not to wince as the tuning fork dug deeper into my brain.

The next day it rained. Drizzle and fog blanketed my thoughts as I drove past the once empty lot.

The cars had doubled; the lot now hosted a family-sized gathering. No raincoats, no umbrellas. Just a rain-darkened crowd of solemn spectators gazing at something I couldn't see. Memories of my father's funeral cut through the vibration in my head. My father—whose life consisted of attempts at life. Near-misses, valiant efforts. All ultimately futile. I swore I'd never be like him, but found myself following in his slow and soggy footsteps.

I passed by the gathering without incident—or accident—and made it to work on time.

I spent the day working on my latest project—a PowerPoint presentation on *The Cause and Effect of the Chernobyl Nuclear Disaster.* There are better jobs than Graphics Coordinator for a radiation safety training company, but there are far worse.

Like a dream loop I viewed and reviewed mini-movies of radioactive release clouds, photos of burn victims and reactor meltdowns. I read of the heroism of Russian firefighters who knew they would be exposed to lethal doses of radiation, but sacrificed themselves just the same for the health of humanity.

I nearly wept. And as I sat at my desk, growing older, growing fatter, the sludge of my inactivity settling like a reactor meltdown that turns hardened metal into taffy-like blobs, the pictures only confirmed how safe and comfortable an existence I'd led, never once placing myself in a situation that could, for better or for worse, indelibly alter my life.

Once again, on the drive home, I could feel the tuning fork come alive in my head as I approached the empty lot. In the damp dusk the cars and vans had multiplied upon the uneven landscape of gravel and weeds. The pull was much greater this time, an unexpected blinding of thought and action, the one overriding impulse—to stop, to see, to join the ever-growing group in their mysterious circle.

There came a thump off my front bumper and I slammed on my brakes. A dog lay writhing in the middle of the road behind me, illuminated in the blood-red glow of my brake lights. It struggled to regain its feet, but its back was broken. It wore a collar with tags, appeared well-groomed. I realized it probably belonged to one of the parked vehicles, set free as its owner took part in the strange ritual by the woods.

I wanted to get out and help the dog, at least pull it off to the side of the road, but I knew if I got out of my car I would never get back in again.

So I drove on, speeding on the rain-slick roadway, driving as if something were chasing me.

Beth was in the living room when I arrived home.

"How was your day?" I asked her. The dining room table was unset. I looked in the kitchen and saw no food was prepared. Beth stared ahead in silence, at a television that wasn't on.

"Did you want to go out to eat tonight?" I asked her.

She turned and looked at me. "I'm sorry, I don't feel much like eating."

I looked around and noticed the house was unchanged since that morning. I wondered how long she'd been sitting there. Her job at the bank allowed her to leave the house later than myself and brought her home an hour earlier. The bulk of the cleaning and cooking chores fell upon her shoulders. "That's okay, I can make something for myself."

Beth reached for the remote and clicked on the television set. She put the remote aside, not caring which station came up first. It was the Weather Channel—a special on hurricanes. Thick cloud formations with clearly defined eyes swirled across the screen. The voice-over explained how this year was going to be particularly active. Beth stared emotionless at the circular movements.

I thought she was angry at me for one reason or another, but I was too tired to broach the subject. I left her to her sulking, made myself a sandwich and went to bed early.

That night I dreamed of Cindy.

Cindy was a girl I used to work with. We were at her father's house. It was a nice house, with a screened-in porch. It was the middle of the day and we were in the kitchen. Cindy wore a colorful wool sweater. She stood while I leaned against the kitchen table. We were talking about our future and all the reasons why we should be together, but knowing even as we spoke that we were hopelessly locked in a triangle between ourselves and the circumstances that would inevitably keep us apart. In the dream I wanted to reach out to her, pull her into my arms, hold her, tell her that everything would be okay, that we owed it to ourselves to try and make it work... and all the other things that sound so right and honorable in dreams but are laughable when we wake up.

I woke up then, but I wasn't laughing. Instead, I had an ache in my chest the size of a hundred pound weight, and a cold slice of pain in my forehead that got me up and into the shower and ready for work before my usual time.

I couldn't explain it, but there was some place I had to be—beside work. And it was calling to me.

I left the house without saying goodbye or taking a lunch.

Even before I came up over the rise of the hill, I knew it would be a mess. The cars were lined up as if for a police spot-check. There were in fact a couple of police cars in with the now two dozen vehicles pulled off the road and onto the vacant lot. But instead of directing traffic or trying to clean up the mess, the uniformed officers stood ineffectually among the clot of people near the edge of the woods.

I felt myself pulling over. Something was telling me that I had to see what was going on, I had to know. But as I slowed, an unexplainable fear crept up inside of me. There was something about the way the people looked—those stepping out of their cars and walking toward the crowd. Something mindless. Something controlled. I was reminded of a time I waited in a crowd of shoppers standing outside a supermarket that was going out of business. When the doors swung open, the people poured in trance-like and grabbed whatever was available, whether they needed it or not.

I wove through the haphazardly parked cars, hoping I wouldn't be forced to stop by a pedestrian or another vehicle. I was afraid that if I became stationary I wouldn't be able to get moving again.

After I reached work, I sat at my desk idly tapping the keys of my computer, making lists of things I needed to do, places I'd like to visit before I die. Nonsense things like favorite foods, TV shows, music CDs I had yet to purchase. It was a way of filling my mind, keeping it busy.

"You don't look so good," the secretary told me as I pulled a magazine from my mail slot.

I turned around and paused, forgetting why I had come to the front office in the first place.

"I hear there's a bug going around," her voice continued. "They say it starts in the stomach."

The lobby was only a few steps away. Beyond that, the parking lot. I could just walk out, get into my car and drive, I thought.

"Are you okay?"

"Huh?" The secretary's persistence had finally paid off. "I'm fine, thanks." I looked at her. She wore a pair of earphones. I thought she had been listening to the radio. "Have they said anything about what's going on over—"

She held up a finger and began to talk into a miniature mouthpiece I hadn't seen. "Hi, this is Sharon at RSA, I'd like to place an order." She smiled at me, and then turned her attention to the catalog in front of her.

I left her to her business and walked back down the hall and sat in the silence of my office—silent except for the tuning fork humming its long, mournful song of loneliness between my ears.

It was dark by the time I left work. I had put off leaving as long as I could. I had intended to stay until Beth called me to find out where I was. Worried, mad, elated—it didn't matter, as long as she called. But she never did.

I drove along Route 6 numbed by the day's relentless monotony. There had to be some other way of living this life. Once again I thought about Cindy.

Although circumstances never allowed us to get past the stage of heavy flirtation, I knew Cindy was the one—the big love, the love that dwarfed all others. But there were just too many obstacles in our way. There was our age difference, the fact that I was married—though not happily. It would have hurt too many people. So we let it go. We just unchained our hearts and set each other free.

But I could never completely let go of those feelings we shared. A feeling of true understanding. A feeling that, afterward—after Cindy had left the company—convinced me that, by not pursuing our relationship, regardless of the consequences, I had made the biggest mistake in my life.

As I drove, the road began to blur and I realized there were tears in my eyes. When my vision cleared I could see the cars up ahead. Many were nosed off into the thick brush. Some had their doors left open, others still had their headlights on. All were abandoned. The road was nearly impassable.

I drove as far as I could until the feeling became too powerful. The tuning fork was now a full-body sensation. I could imagine what it would feel like to be a hundred feet below the surface of the ocean, the weight just pushing me down.

I pulled over, turned off the ignition, and stepped out of my car.

The night sky held a beautiful clear dome of stars overhead, the air was crisp. I had never felt so insignificant and yet so special in all my life.

There must have been thirty to forty vehicles. The empty lot was no longer empty. In the distance, a tightly-packed circle of people were gathered around the mysterious spot near the woods. In the dark I could see a yellowish glow beneath their feet.

I stepped over tufts of grass. I could hear the crunch of the gravel. My whole body was vibrating as if in tune with a certain natural frequency inherent in the earth. I don't remember breathing or thinking. My only desire was to be with them, to stand among their number, and be a part of whatever it was that had drawn them there.

I reached the group and shouldered my way to the inner circle. There was no resistance from those whom I displaced. I stood in awe staring at the ground before me.

It was a pit as large around as a swimming pool; only instead of water, it contained a liquid yellow light. The light seemed to swirl and eddy, rotating with a slow, hypnotic movement. If I leaned forward, I could follow its tapered geometry as it descended in an endless attenuation.

My senses must have become heightened, because I became suddenly aware of the people around me, aware of their needs, their desires. Upon their faces I could read the stories of why they were there. One: a child lost to disease. Another: a dream of stardom stolen. And many like myself: a heart unable to let go of a love that could never be. It was all the same. Each of us had arrived there—were drawn to this place—by something missing in our lives, and the blind hope of finding it.

A shadow of movement to my right and a body suddenly plunged into the pit. It was a man. He toppled head first with what sounded like a cry of joy. We all watched as his body rotated like a skydiver, growing smaller and smaller below until it was indistinguishable from the yellow light.

Another body followed. This time a woman.

I looked around, alarmed, and saw my wife standing on the other side of the pit. Her eyes were a kaleidoscope of terror and fascination.

"Beth!" I shouted, terrified, but her gaze was unbroken. Perhaps inside the pit she could see a more attentive husband, someone less judgmental, less disapproving. Someone who loved her, flaws and all.

She began to lean. I wanted to scream, "I love you," but I could not bring myself to lie anymore. Her body tipped over the edge and I watched her fall. The pit swallowed her, enveloped her like a cloud. She had a smile on her face as it took her down.

I've been standing here now for what seems like an eternity. Many more have joined our number. It is getting difficult to stand so near the edge without losing my balance, but I manage to hold on. Many have made the leap into the pit, some with shouts of joy, others with expressions of fear still etched upon their faces. There is beauty and horror in this life and the pit claims it all.

As for the rest of us, still waiting, the world has stopped. There is a reason why we are all here. Some of us just take a little longer to come to terms with it. I feel I'm close.

The man next to me leans forward and falls, leaving a vacancy that is quickly filled.

I watch the yellow light rise and fall, spin first in one direction and then the other, its movement nearly slows to a stop, then speeds up again. The more I stare into its depths, the more it becomes like an eye staring back at me.

I feel its gaze as it sees me for the first time.

I lean forward to get a better look. This time I don't pull back.

Puppies For Sale

W**HEN IT WAS TIME FOR** E**LLIE** to kiss her husband goodbye, she tried to hold his lips against hers longer than their usual stay, keep them there by sheer force of will. But they departed too soon. Always too soon.

"Bye, Daddy."

"Bye, Daddy."

Two voices from behind, shouting in unison. Two blonde, smiling-faced boys, age three, pushed through Ellie's legs to get at their father. Awaiting them were the big hugs, the big kisses, the big voice that told them he was just going to work and that he'd be home as soon as he could to play with "You two rascals." All of this went on like ritual as Ellie stood by, smiling her patient smiles, happy for her husband's happiness. Although, over the past three years, the ritual had worn thin. Seeing her husband's face twinned and then tripled was a bit much at times, like standing in a crowded hall of mirrors with no avenue of escape. Ellie longed for the days when it was just her husband's face she saw, those long, wonderful looks he used to give her that were hers and hers alone.

"...and Mommy will help you with the puppy sign. Right, Momma?"

At first, Ellie didn't understand what they were talking about, but she quickly realized her husband was referring to the For Sale sign they were going to make to advertise the puppies their dog Jenny-girl had had.

"Right Momma?" A tug at her bathrobe on one side.

"Right Momma?" A tug on the other.

Ellie glanced at her two boys, their curious faces wondering what her answer would be. "Why, of course I will," she said with mock gleefulness, her eyes growing large, her smile wide. And the two boys matched her expression exactly. "Well, I have to go," Ellie's husband said, backing down the front steps. "Now, you two boys be good for your mother."

"We will, Daddy."

"We will." Again, like stereo.

Ellie waved as she watched her husband's car leave the driveway, and the smile on her face wanted to go with him, but she held it tight.

After breakfast, Ellie dressed herself in jeans and a sweatshirt, and she helped the two boys get into their own clothes. Outside, the weather was bright and unseasonably warm for October, but the sun occasionally disappeared behind a bright puffy cloud and the chill of autumn reminded Ellie that winter would soon be upon them. Overall, a nice day for the puppies to spend a little time outdoors advertising their cute, furry faces to whomever should drive by.

There were six all together, Golden Retriever pups, all a picture-perfect tawny brown, the color of butterscotch pudding with a little whipped cream on top. Jenny-girl had outdone herself, her first litter and, according to Ellie's husband, her last. Out of the six, there were only two males, but they were identical, right down to the white circular tip on their tails. These two they intended to keep. Ellie's husband said it couldn't have been more perfect: a perfect puppy for each of their perfect boys.

But, right now, there was a sign to make. There remained four other pups, unspoken for, that needed a good home.

As Ellie searched the garage, the two boys followed close behind, hanging on her every word and movement. Each tried to help Ellie when it was best that they just stay out of the way. For Ellie, the world was just too small sometimes. But what could she do? The man she loved had given her twin reminders of his love and adoration.

Finally, she found a piece of plywood large enough to make the sign, and she hauled it out and laid it flat on the cement floor of the garage.

The boys crowded in.

Ellie had some old ceiling paint left over from when she and her husband had first moved into the house, and as she knelt over the blank piece of plywood she thought back, remembering the fun they had had, just the two of them, paint-splattered and arm-weary, but still finding enough energy to make love among the still unpacked boxes. Life had never been better...

"Let me..."

"*No, let me...*"

"I can..."

"*No, I can...*"

Twin voices burrowing into her ears.

Ellie tried to paint the letters as neatly as possible, but with the two boys "helping," her letters came out crude and child-like. The only thing missing were the misspelled words and backward letters. But it was important for the boys to feel like they were helping. Always for the boys. "Think of the boys," Ellie's husband was fond of reminding her, as if she herself were a spoiled child.

"There!" Ellie announced, trying to summon some brightness back into her mood.

"There!" the two boys repeated, their competitiveness momentarily forgotten. The three of them stared down at the sign:

PUPPIES FOR SALE
AKC GOLDEN RETRIEVERS

...and below that their home phone number. Simple, straightforward. Four years spent educating herself in the field of marketing didn't all go to waste, Ellie thought dryly. But then it was her choice not to seek a career, choosing instead to start a family, wasn't it? She did know her husband had wanted children right away, didn't she?

"Now, who's going to help Mommy carry the puppies?" Ellie spoke in a perfect nursery rhyme voice.

"I will!"

"I will!" came the dual responses.

"Well, go ahead and get them!"

And around the house the two boys ran. Ellie followed after them, breathing the fresh morning air and admiring the splendidness of her property. Maybe she was selfish—look what she had: a beautiful home, on two beautiful acres, surrounded by tall shade trees which, at this time of year, were the envy of the neighborhood. She could have anything she wished for in the way of jewelry or clothing, all she had to do was ask. What else was there?

Ellie supervised as the puppies were transferred to the front of the yard, making sure the boys handled them properly. Awaiting the puppies was the old playpen the two boys no longer needed. What better display case? Ellie thought when she saw it in the garage, proud of her resourcefulness. Jenny-girl paced nervously the entire time, perhaps wondering what was going on. Why were her babies being removed from her custody? What was wrong with the perfectly suitable hay-lined doghouse she had given birth to them in, had licked their blood-wet bodies clean in?

Ellie wondered what Jenny-girl would do when it came time to hand over one of the puppies to a total stranger. Would she chase after the car? Worse yet, would she try to bite the offending intruder? How would any mother react? Ellie decided then it would be a good idea to bring Jenny-girl out back and tie her up. She didn't want a lawsuit on her hands.

With Jenny-girl safely out of the way, Ellie sat on the front steps and focused her attention on the two boys as they played in the autumn sun, chasing leaves and each other in lazy circles. She watched as their faces giggled and frowned, displayed rapt concentration and careless abandon. So much like their father. But it wasn't enough. No, it wasn't enough.

It was a good thing Ellie had tied Jenny-girl up when she did, because it wasn't long before the first car slowed, then pulled over in front of the house.

It was an elderly couple. Retired, comfortable, Ellie thought. When they got out of their car, Ellie got up to greet them, ready to answer any and all questions regarding Golden Retriever pups. But as they approached, Ellie noticed the camera around the woman's neck.

"Hello," the woman said, her voice possessing a strong, grandmotherly tone. "We were passing by and I couldn't help but notice. Would you mind if I took some pictures of your two boys?" The woman's husband stood sheepishly behind her, looking embarrassed by his wife's forwardness.

"Oh, no, not at all," Ellie said, smiling. "Go right ahead."

The woman wasted no time in approaching the two boys. She talked to them briefly, then squatted into a photographer's crouch and began snapping off picture after picture.

"Beautiful day, isn't it?" the elderly gentleman said, standing alongside Ellie.

"Yes, it is," Ellie replied, watching the woman's immediate rapport with the two boys. The click and whir of her camera was distracting.

"Ever since we've retired she's had that thing around her neck," the elderly gentleman said, trying to make conversation. But Ellie wasn't listening. Instead, she watched as the two boys soaked up the attention like two professionals. First one would throw a handful of leaves into the air, while the other one sat waiting to be covered.

The first one smiled innocently, the second one acted surprised. Ellie saw the rest of her life laid out before her in those twin faces, always the proud mother, always the patient wife, the nurturer, the care-giver, each camera click a snapshot seizing a piece of her future...

"Any luck with the pups?"

Ellie blinked. She realized she had been smiling all along, and her face hurt. "Oh, no, you're the first to stop."

"I'm sure they'll go quickly."

"I hope so."

"People need pets, nowadays... helps to take their minds off the world and its problems."

Ellie turned her head to where the puppies sat in the playpen. All six faces peered out from between the nylon mesh as if through a pet shop window. They too watched the two boys as they shrieked and wrestled in the leaves, receiving all the attention.

The camera finally stopped. "Well, I thank you very much," the woman said, breathing heavily as if it were she who was diving in the leaves. "I bet you have your hands full with those two."

"Oh, they're a handful all right." She heard herself then and realized she sounded every bit the dutiful mother.

"Well, I hope we didn't impose on you too much."

"No, no, it was my pleasure." *Anything for the boys.*

Ellie watched as the couple returned to their car. "Good luck with those pups," the elderly gentleman called to her before getting behind the wheel. "Thanks," Ellie shouted.

They waved as they pulled away, leaving Ellie almost in tears.

When lunchtime arrived, Ellie called the boys in and made them both peanut butter and jelly sandwiches, and gave each a tall glass of milk. She even made a sandwich for herself, but didn't finish it. She just sat and watched quietly as the two boys hurried through their meal, eager to get back outside. This time, Ellie brought a lawn chair with her and sat beside the playpen as the two boys resumed their play.

The day was still warm, but the sun was now making fewer and fewer appearances, sending whispery chills across Ellie's skin. The puppies slept peacefully, one atop the other, their little bodies heaving with each quiet breath. Ellie rested her chin on the edge of the playpen and stared down at them. *Animals are so adaptable*, she thought. So trusting of the life that went on around them. Ellie knew if she were to pick up one of Jenny-girl's pups—one of the perfect males, perhaps—and gently squeeze the life from it, the others would carry on as if it were something that was meant to happen, like a brief spring rain, or a sudden gust of wind.

The two boys whooped and paraded beneath the showers of leaves. They used their hands and feet to shuffle the leaves back into a pile, then they burrowed like sweatered animals, burying themselves and giggling with each newly invented game.

Ellie leaned over the pen and ran her hand along the puppies' soft fur, caressing their thick ears and muscular legs. One stretched, all four legs straightening; its open mouth revealed a tongue curly and pink like a piece of ribbon candy. *So soft. So trusting.*

"I'm tired, Momma."

"Me, too."

The two boys came over to where Ellie sat and nuzzled up against her. They had leaves in their hair, twigs stuck to their clothing. She unfolded the blanket she was sitting on and laid it on the grass for them, and they climbed aboard. In a matter of minutes, the warming sun and the fresh, scented air worked to put them both to sleep.

The afternoon turned late, the sky grew overcast. School buses came and went, but no one else slowed as they drove by. The two boys slept. Ellie watched, and waited. Only another hour and her husband would be home, pulling into the driveway, getting out of the car with that face she loved so much. Soon, her day would be complete.

The telephone rang.

Ellie was nearly asleep herself when she heard it. She slipped off the chair and hurried into the house, taking a quick look over her shoulder to see if the two boys were still asleep.

It was her husband. He was going to be late tonight.

How many times did that make? She had lost count. Didn't he know how much his absences hurt her? Couldn't he see the yearning in her eyes when he left each morning? Didn't he know that it wasn't the same just to have his face in miniature staring up at her wherever she turned, pulling on her, asking her questions; that it only served to remind her of his absence? Couldn't he see that?

"No, no, that's okay... I'll be fine, really... I love you too... Bye..." *Goodbye.* She closed her eyes and pressed the telephone receiver to her lips and thought of the kiss he had given her that morning. One one thousand... two one thousand... three one thousand... She could almost feel it. When she opened her eyes again and looked through the picture window, she saw that a long black limousine had pulled up alongside the road in front of the house. Near the playpen a strange man stood.

Ellie dropped the phone and rushed to the front door, her heart thumping in her chest. She tried to walk calmly out to the playpen.

"Puppies for sale... how charming," the man said. His voice carried an air of sophistication. He was dressed in a dark, expensive-looking suit, and his hair was black and neatly trimmed. An older man, but of an age Ellie couldn't guess. He gripped the edge of the playpen and appeared to be staring down at the puppies.

"Can I help you?" Ellie asked the man, closing the gap between them. Jenny-girl's barks could be heard in the back yard, but the two boys slept undisturbed near to where the man stood.

"I'm sure you can. You see, I'm in the market for some... company." He looked up. His eyes were like two black pools. "It gets lonely where I reside, and I thought..."

"The puppies—yes, they make excellent pets," Ellie offered.

The man smiled at this, leaning his head to one side, as if weighing the validity of what Ellie had just said. He inhaled deeply, then sighed. "Beautiful creatures, aren't they?"

Ellie looked down into the playpen. Most of the puppies had awakened and were staring up at the man. Ellie hadn't realized it at first, but all the puppies had backed off to one corner. "Their mother—the one you hear barking out back—is AKC registered. Their father was supplied by a local stud service, also AKC. He has championship bloodlines," Ellie recited, remembering what her husband had told her to say. She had no reason to fear this man. But then why did she feel so ill-at-ease?

"I'll take them," he said suddenly, as if he had had his mind made up all along.

"Oh! That's wonderful! But first, you should know, we're asking two hundred and fifty dollars—"

The man waved his hand in a gesture that meant money was no object. He reached into his coat pocket and pulled out a billfold. He handed Ellie five crisp one hundred dollar bills. Ellie took them with a wide smile. Wait until her husband got home...

"Have you decided yet which ones you're going to take?"

The man grinned. His eyes locked onto hers. "The two boys," he said. His voice was almost a whisper, but Ellie heard it as if it were voiced from inside her own head.

Ellie hesitated. "The two males...?"

"Is there a problem?"

"Oh, no..." She wasn't thinking straight. Her mind seemed slow to comprehend. The two boys... the two boys... What was it about the two boys she needed to remember?

"No, everything's fine," she heard herself tell the man.

"Good. I'll just need a receipt and I'll be on my way." His eyes... his eyes seemed to penetrate her very soul.

"If you'll excuse me for just a minute, I need to go inside."

"Take your time," the man said, smiling charmingly.

Ellie turned and walked toward the house. She felt the man's eyes on her back, and with each step she knew she was risking something. The hairs on the back of her neck bristled, her stomach fluttered; it was a feeling she remembered from her childhood—the pond behind her house—walking out on the first ice of the winter with a nervous excitement that told her that what she was doing was dangerous.

She gripped the bills in her hand, their thick papery feel rough between her fingers. Five-hundred dollars! It was like found money. What some people will pay...

Jenny-girl still barked out back, perhaps sensing that two of her offspring were about to be taken away. If only Jenny-girl understood the value of money, Ellie thought, maybe she wouldn't be so quick to protest.

Once inside the house, Ellie filled out the necessary papers. Male #1. Male #2. Distinguishing marks: white-tipped tail, etc. Ellie signed her name. She also took a blank piece of paper and wrote up a receipt, then realized she hadn't asked the man's name. But it didn't seem to matter. What mattered was that she take her time.

When she stepped back outside again, the long black limousine was pulling away. Ellie, stunned, simply watched it go, her arm not even attempting to flag it down. Her heart began to race in her chest and she grew suddenly weary. Slowly, her eyes scanned the yard until they came upon the blanket beside the playpen. She knew it would be empty. She walked on numb legs down to the chair beside the playpen. She had to sit down.

The sky was now completely overcast; it would be dark soon. The puppies lay sleeping, all six of them cuddled together as before. Ellie kept expecting to hear shouts and shrieks and little boy laughter coming from the pile of leaves off to her left, but she knew there would be none forthcoming. She still had the five one hundred dollar bills in her hand and she began counting them. One hundred, two hundred, three hundred... over and over. She kept counting even as shadows crept across her vision, and the air turned cold. One hundred, two hundred, three... What some people will pay...

She kept counting even as her husband pulled into the driveway. She couldn't wait to tell him, to turn to his face—that face, the one she had always wanted, the one she couldn't wait a lifetime (or two) to have all to herself again; that tired, lovely face—she couldn't wait to see the happiness that was sure to blossom there once she told him the good news.

BRUISES

THE WATER GLASS FLEW ACROSS the room and shattered against the wall.

Jared stood in the middle of the living room, his fists clenched, his heart hammering. He drew in a deep breath and counted himself down, letting his anger subside. He could hear his wife, Samantha, crying in the next room. After all the promises he had made to himself, knowing full well the consequences, he had done it again.

He went to the bedroom door. "Samantha, open up."

He said it softly, gently, easing himself back into the present.

His wife replied with more tears.

"Samantha, please, the sooner you calm down, the less painful it will be."

My daughter's the sensitive type. You be good to her, or else.

The sound of his father-in-law's backwoods Kentucky voice echoed in his ear. The small wily-looking man had said that to him the moment after he and Samantha had been pronounced husband and wife. If it weren't for the laughter that followed—

from both Samantha's father and her slack-faced, speech-impedimented brother, Cliff—he might have taken the threat seriously.

"Samantha, please, let me in. I'm so sorry. I know it hurts. It hurts me, too."

He hated how that sounded. It wasn't fair. There were men who did much worse things to their wives than he did. Why did he have to be the one stuck with such a—

Freak?

No, he couldn't let himself think like that. He loved his wife, for better or for worse. In sickness and in health. For richer, for poorer.

"Please, honey, sweetheart, open the door. I'll make it better. I promise. It won't happen again."

As her sobbing continued, Jared could only think of one thing to do. He cleared his throat and began to sing.

"Hush, little baby, don't say a word... Mama's gonna buy you a mockingbird... And if that mockingbird don't sing... Mama's gonna buy you a diamond ring..."

It sickened him, but like an incantation, it worked its spell. Her sobbing slowed to a sniffle, and soon the door unlatched. She stood there, tears still clinging to her eyelashes. He held his arms open for her and she crawled in.

He hugged her and she winced. "Sorry," he said. "Here, let me see." He sat her on the bed and lifted her nightshirt. His heart sank.

The entire surface of her back was mottled with bruises, a stormy mass of purplish-red shot through with lightning strikes of yellow and green. No matter how many times he saw them on her skin, it still amazed him.

"I'm so sorry." He kissed her. He could see that she was already sleepy. The endorphins were kicking in and God knows what other strange chemistry her body employed. She closed her eyes and he eased her head down onto her pillow.

"And if that diamond ring turns brass... Mama's gonna buy you a looking glass... And if that looking glass gets broke... Mama's gonna buy you a billy goat..."

Jared stroked her hair. He wished there was something he could give her—a cold compress, a magic pill—but all his medical training couldn't fix what he had done. She needed time now. Time to heal. And the worst part of all was that he never laid a finger on her.

"Six weeks with a rural physician practicing in an Appalachian community."

That's what the flyer had said, tacked to the bulletin board labeled "Opportunities" in the downstairs hallway of the Life Sciences building at Thomas Jefferson University. And the name of the place—Wellness, Kentucky. It sounded ideal.

And while some small part of Jared Easterhouse had actually wanted to help his fellow man—give of himself for the greater good—a larger part just needed to get away. After a bitter breakup with his girlfriend of two years, Katrina, he didn't want to spend another summer in Philadelphia as a daily reminder. He was looking for a change of scenery. He wanted to feel good about himself again. And what better way to do that than to surround himself with simple-minded people with simple needs who would appreciate him in ways Katrina never understood? Besides, it would look great on his resume when he applied for grad school.

At least that's what he thought when he had set out on that warm June day and drove south along Route 95. But, unlike its name, Wellness was like a bruise on the back of the Kentucky hills. Through no fault of their own, the people of Wellness were isolated. Jared had no idea how isolated until he found himself seven hundred miles from home, setting his bags down on the weather-worn porch of what was once a church hall. *Hell, even God has abandoned these people*, he remembered thinking that first day as Walt Handley, the "rural physician" and soon-to-be septuagenarian, came out and greeted him with a firm yet leathery handshake. Before heading inside to begin his new job, he stood looking out across the rolling green hills, an hour from the nearest pay phone, more than three from the nearest hospital, and resigned himself to the longest six weeks of his life.

But two days later he met Samantha and everything changed.

Jared picked up the pieces of the broken water glass and dumped them into the wastebasket—a basket Samantha had made herself out of native wicker. He glanced at their wedding photo above the fireplace mantle. Its frame was made of four bent pieces of willow. It looked like it belonged in a Manhattan studio. Samantha's touch was everywhere: in the wild flower bouquets that brought a colorful and fragrant life to each room; in the "sculptures" that decorated the walls and filled the empty spaces—pieces constructed from hollowed-out gourds, knotted tree branches, seed pods and pinecones. Samantha had a talent for taking the plain and ordinary and making it beautiful—a gift given to her perhaps by the same gods responsible for the ugliness of her condition. To offset an unnatural wrong with an unnatural right.

But Jared's patience with these gods had worn thin.

He stared at their wedding photo and thought back to a happier time, when his heart was as full as his mind was naive, and patience was as virtuous as the smile on a young woman's face.

She walked into the clinic wearing a simple flowered dress. A dress made by her mother, Jared would later find out. Her shoulder-length blonde hair was tied back with a shiny blue ribbon, the kind of ribbon given for first prize at state fairs. She appeared nervous as she sat in one of the wooden fold-up chairs borrowed from the local meeting hall, her innocent blue eyes staring at the clipboard in her hand and the information form attached to it as if she didn't know where to begin.

"Who's that?" he asked Walt.

Walt looked up, squinted, returned his attention to rummaging through the box of meds for a packet of Tylenol. "Samantha Lee

Gentry. Mom died a few years back. Awful sad." He looked up and squinted again. "Looks pretty healthy."

"You can say that again."

Walt gave him a nudge. "She's all yours. I mean, as a patient, of course."

"I know what you mean, Walt. Thanks."

Please, God, don't let her be pregnant, Jared thought. It was his second day on the job and he had already heard, "My Daddy gets lonely sometimes. 'Specially after he's been drinkin'. What else am I supposed to do?"

Let it be something simple, like a bladder infection. Or better yet, nothing at all. And while I'm praying here, God, let her at least be eighteen.

His wish had been granted on all accounts.

But every bright and shiny new piece of fortune has its dark side. For when she stepped into the makeshift examination room—a semi-private screen made of sheets hung over lines of baling wire—and with eyes that never left his, untied the back of her dress and slid her arms out of the sleeves, he knew then that God was indeed a cruel son-of-a-bitch.

Bruises. Bruises the size of fists across her chest and on her stomach. At first, Jared thought it might be a birthmark, a port wine stain, but the addition of green and yellow to the coloration was unmistakable. That's when the anger began to well.

"Samantha, who did this to you?" he asked.

"No one." Her eyes grew wide, as innocent as daisies.

Back in Philly they were required to report things like this to social services. He pried further.

"Who do you live with?"

"My father, my brother," she said.

"Does your father ever hit you?"

She shook her head. "He might yell now and again."

"What about your brother?"

She shook her head again. The bruises were deep. It was a wonder she wasn't doubled over in pain.

"Samantha, it's okay, if someone is abusing you I can help."

Her face contorted into a complex puzzle of pain and fear. "I told you, it's no one. It just... happens. Can you make it stop?"

Jared struggled with his conscience. Sometimes there was no getting through to people. He let it go.

"I can give you some iron pills to help build strength in your capillaries," he told her. "But please take my advice instead. Whatever did this, just stay away from it. And if you need someone to talk to, I'm right here." He tried to be as professional as possible, even though his heart was pounding and his eyes didn't want to leave her face.

And suddenly there were tears at the corners of her eyes. "My mother would have liked you," she said.

Jared felt the moment squeeze. Everything that surrounded them seemed to fade away. "And how does her daughter feel about me?"

She smiled a smile as sweet as summer corn. "She likes him too."

And call it fate or serendipity, he knew in that instant, for better or for worse, they would be together.

Jared felt the floor for the last piece of glass and a tiny sliver entered his skin and bloodied the pad of his finger. "Shit!" he mumbled under his breath and slammed the wastebasket down. He heard a crack but didn't look to see where he had damaged it. If anything, the twenty-four hour watch on his temper was putting him more on edge. He was human for Christ's sake, he was going to lose it now and then. In any normal relationship there are disagreements, arguments. Voices will rise, blood pressures will spike. Love is a tug of war, a constant give and take. But anything closely resembling a difference of opinion brought a grimace of pain to Samantha's features, and a blot to her skin.

Come with me to Philadelphia. I'll introduce you to a whole new world— my world—the way you introduced me to yours. You could bring some of your artwork. I know some people in the art department. Who knows, maybe they could help you get your work into a gallery. How does that sound? The Folk Art of Samantha Lee Gentry. It's got a nice ring to it.

And, like always, she would look at him, her delicate hands picking nervously at her fingernails, her eyes as blue as the sky that hung above the surrounding hills.

Jared, I can't. People are just too hurtful in the city. I don't think I could ever leave. Everything I need is right here.

Then she would put her arms around him and nestle her beautiful face close to his chest. Only this time it didn't work. He let his frustration slip and the anger spilled out.

What you need? What about what I need? I need things to be normal again. I can't take this anymore! It's like living in a fucking prison!

She seemed to shrink away from his voice, cringing with every word. He imagined every syllable hitting her with the force of a slap or a punch.

And it felt good.

And he felt sick for allowing himself those few moments of relief in exchange for her pain.

But it wasn't enough.

He needed a break. He needed to yell. He needed to pound his fist through a fucking wall!

He sucked his finger instead, the taste of blood souring his insides.

He went into the kitchen and began to prepare dinner. Samantha would be awake soon. She would walk out of their bedroom sleep-drunk and tentative. Her face would carry an expression almost apologetic, as if she would just soon forget the incident had ever happened.

But the bruises would still be there. A glimpse here, as she reached up to grab a cup from the cabinet, her nightie top lifting above her waistline. A grimace there, as she turned too quickly to clear the table. Like normal bruises they would need to run their course, each day a dark reminder, a troubled stain of guilt upon his conscience. There had to be an answer.

And as he filled the tea kettle for some nice relaxing tea, for the first time since settling in Wellness, Jared found himself thinking of home.

"Am I gonna die, doc?"

Jared turned to the old man, a sixty-year-old farmer with an abscessed tooth. "We're all going to die someday, Mr. Pickering. But I'm afraid you and Mrs. Pickering here still have many healthy years ahead of you."

"So what's the good news?" The old farmer guffawed. He then received a solid-sounding slap from his wife, who stood dutifully nearby.

Work acted as a temporary relief as last night's incident was pushed to the background of his mind. Jared grabbed a packet of antibiotics from the assortment of medicines the state supplied him every month and handed it to Mrs. Pickering. "Make sure he takes one of these each day for the next ten days. It ought to make him as good as new."

"Is that that Viagra I've been hearing so much about?" The old man grinned as he pinched his wife's rump.

"Stop that, you senseless old mule!" The farmer's wife smoothed her dress, her cheeks reddened. "Thank you, doctor," she said. "And say hello to that beautiful wife of yours."

"Will do. Take care."

"Thanks, doc." The farmer winked.

Jared watched the old couple as they stepped out into the August heat-haze. Dust motes floated in the open doorway. The whisper of the ceiling fan overhead made not a bit of difference in the temperature, but its steady rhythm provided a soothing sound. Jared missed having Walt there. When the older man retired in the spring, it was natural that Jared step in to fill his shoes. Jared received his license to practice from the State of Kentucky, and a modest salary. It was ironic that he found the fast-track to becoming a doctor in such a slow-moving part of the country. But then things were kind of backward here, in more ways than one.

Before returning his attention to the business at hand, Jared spotted the tall, hunched figure of Samantha's brother, Cliff, looming on the porch stoop.

Jared's next patient: a woman and her young daughter. The child had red circular welts upon her arms and legs, an obvious case of ringworm. "Nice to see you again, Mrs. Godoy. Hi, Emily. You want to grab a seat and a lollipop? I'll be right back, okay?" The little girl smiled as he ruffled her hair. Jared headed for the door.

"Good morning, Cliff. Anything wrong?"

His brother-in-law looked at him, face slack, eyes exhibiting about as much emotion as a river-plucked catfish. "Dah wons tuh say you."

"Your father wants to see me?"

Cliff nodded. The young man's size and unreadable expression always made Jared uncomfortable. But then he thought that that was probably normal when talking to the brother of the woman you were having sex with. Particularly in these parts.

"Is it an emergency?"

Cliff actually considered this for a moment before he shook his head no. "Jus come."

Jared had a few more patients to take care of. "Tell him I'll stop by in an hour. Okay?"

Cliff turned then and walked away, his size fourteen feet scuffing the hard-packed dirt of the road.

"Did he say what it was about?" Jared called after him.

Cliff merely kept walking.

The Gentry household was even sparer than their own, Jared observed. There were touches here and there of a woman's influence, but they were remnants long since faded. If only Mrs. Gentry were still alive, he would have so many questions for her.

Mr. Gentry sat in his recliner gripping a beer. Brother Cliff sat on the lip of a rocker nearby, playing footsies with one of the many cats that wandered through the household. Jared sat on a hardwood bench, a glass of iced tea growing warm and sweaty in his hands.

"Well, there's no sense in beating around the bush." Mr. Gentry leaned forward, eyes focused on Jared. "Sammy Lee stopped in to see me this morning, as is her usual. She was wearing one of them halter-tops the girls wear. I guess I don't have to tell you, I seen the marks."

"Mr. Gentry, I didn't touch her. We got into this stupid argument about taking a trip to Philadelphia—"

Gentry put up a hand. "Now, I don't want to hear it. We're talking about my baby girl. I told you she was the sensitive type. Just like her mother, God rest her soul. You don't need to be talking about no trips neither. You know she can't leave here. This is her home. You just need to be more careful-minded."

"But, Mr. Gentry, maybe I can get her some help. You of all people should understand—"

"No buts, you hear me?"

Jared stared at the floor in frustration. The drips from his iced tea had created a miniature puddle at his feet. The drops looked like tears. He tried a different approach.

"Sir, is there anything you can remember that actually helped your wife's condition? Something in her diet? Something she ate? Anything that might have helped speed the healing process?"

Gentry tipped his head back and took several gulps of his beer. After a wet belch, he thought for a moment, then shook his head.

"Can you remember a time when she didn't bruise so easily and it was a surprise to you?"

The small man's brow knitted together. He rubbed at the stubble on his chin. He shook his head, again too soon. "Nope, not an instant. You see, Jerry—"

"Jared."

"Huh?"

"It's Jared. My name is Jared. It's been Jared since we first met. J. A. R. E. D. Jared." Jared could feel his blood pressure rising.

"Same difference," his father-in-law said, which inflamed Jared's anger even more. The man took a swig of his beer, eyes unwavering. "You see—Jared—my Jeannie and I were married for twenty-three years. I treated her like a saint most of the time. But like any young fool, I'd get in a mood that liquor or sex couldn't fix. That's when I'd start yelling and my Jeannie would start crying. I didn't mean none of it, of course. It's like that song—'You only hurt the one you love.' I guess that's true. And I hear what you're saying. I do understand. That's why when you two got married, I told you to be careful. Didn't I tell him to be careful?"

This was directed at Cliff, who looked up and grinned. The young man grunted an affirmative.

"Now, I've heard all I want to hear," Gentry continued. "My baby girl deserves better. Don't make me have to make things right."

And there it was again. That tone in the older man's voice, a glint in the eye, like the strike of flint against a fieldstone. It sent a chill up Jared's spine.

"Show him what we gonna do to him if he don't smartin' up. Go ahcad Cliffy, show him."

Cliff scooped up the cat at his feet and studiously wrapped one of his big hands around the mangy cat's neck and squeezed. The cat's eyes bulged and its tongue stuck straight out like a cartoon character. The cat tried but couldn't swallow. Gentry was laughing now, spilling beer down his already stained shirt. "Go ahead Cliffy," he prodded, and Jared watched as his brother-in-law grabbed the cat's head with his other hand.

"Please, you don't have to show me. I know what I have to... do."

Between "to" and "do" there came a muted snap, like the pop of a knuckle. Gentry kicked his legs up in the air with glee. Cliff merely grinned; he continued to pet the cat even though the animal now lay limp in his lap.

Jared got up and walked numbly out the door before he did something he would regret.

"Don't make me have to make things right!" called Gentry after him. Then more laughter. Laughter that followed Jared all the way home as he tried to figure out what he was going to do next.

Samantha was making another one of her dried flower baskets when he came in through the door.

"Why, you're home early."

Her smile was like sunshine, her voice as soft as summer rain. Jared walked up to her and without a word gently kissed her. She tasted of strawberries.

"My, what's gotten into you?" she said.

"I missed you, that's all." He went in for more. His hands traveled up and down her back, careful not to press too hard. He began to untie her halter-top.

"But, honey, I'm not finished with my basket," she said coyly.

Jared grabbed her hands. "I'm sure it won't mind waiting a bit."

She giggled as he backed her toward the bedroom.

He made love to her more gently than ever before. He slipped into her with a slowness and ease, it was like lying on a raft floating downstream on a lazy summer afternoon. Each caress was a whisper direct from his heart. With each brush of his lips he tried to kiss away the portions of her pain he may have inflicted upon her since that first day they met. Every little stupid thing he may have stubbornly clung to, every complaint he may have voiced too loudly, too directly, too hurtfully. *You only hurt the one you love.* And now he knew why. It was because they are the ones who will forgive you most. But how much is the price of forgiveness? He looked at her.

Her innocent blue eyes were only inches away, like two cobalt-tinted looking glasses—eyes he never wanted to see carry that look of hurt again.

The hardened nubs of her breasts gently tickled his chest as his rhythm increased... as the current began to take him more swiftly. Sweat began to bead upon the soft down of her skin—skin that was never meant to bear the blood brocade of anger, the tell-tale colors of carelessness. He wanted to make everything better. He wanted to hold onto this moment, make it last as long as a dream.

He felt her hands grip him more tightly, her fingers digging into the skin of his back, sinking him deeper. The current swept him along as he rushed headlong toward the waiting cataract. He could feel himself plunging over the edge. She cried out as his love poured into her—love that was only intended to nurture and heal but instead bruised her in so many ways. And as he lay beside her, growing soft in her arms, he knew that the most difficult task in his life would be to leave the woman he loved.

Jared let a week pass. Just knowing he would be leaving instilled in him a leveling sense of calm. The days at the clinic passed uneventfully, nothing worse than a young boy with a broken collarbone and an infant with a case of the croup. He would need to inform the State Health Department of his decision. But not until he was on his way back to Philly. He didn't want the Harlan County sheriff showing up and telling him he couldn't leave.

The hardest part was meeting Samantha's eyes each night as they sat down at the dinner table.

The night before his departure—he didn't like to think of it as an escape—he looked up from his plate and noticed that Samantha was studying him. *Reading* him.

"What is it?" he asked her. He was afraid he was being overly self-conscious or guilty or both.

Her face relaxed. She stared a moment longer. "You're leaving me, aren't you?"

His heart fell from its moorings and sank into the pit of his stomach. When it returned to his chest it was pumping double time. How the fuck does she know? he asked himself. And then he realized that if her body was sensitive enough to bruise at the mere suggestion of pain, what kind of perceptive tricks was her mind capable of?

He tried to think. She didn't seem upset. Just curious. Perhaps her intuition didn't allow her to "see" the details. Maybe a trip back home and to the nearest divorce lawyer was the same as a trip into town.

"You're amazing, you know that. You're right, I am going on a little trip. It's time for my annual recertification. I need to drive to Pikeville to take a test, to see if I'm doing my job right. I was going to tell you."

"I know." She smiled, proud of herself. "It's okay. You'll be back. That's all that matters." She stabbed at a piece of ham on her plate and placed it in her mouth. She giggled then, as if in possession of some untold secret, and this time it reminded Jared of Cliff—

Go ahead Cliffy, show him.

—and the young man's imbecilic grin as he twisted that cat's neck as easily as twisting the cap off a beer bottle.

Don't make me have to make things right!

Jared smiled back at his wife. But for the rest of his dinner he tried not to think about leaving. He tried not to think about anything at all.

The blood was streaming from her eyes, her ears, thick runnels ran from her nostrils like flu snot. So much blood. "How could you?" she screamed, her voice shrill. He felt the weight of his suitcases in his grip and put them down. He tried to console her, but he couldn't touch her. Bruises had mottled her exposed skin, blossoming one upon the other until every inch of her had blackened. And still it continued, past the point of discoloration as her arms and legs began to erupt in minute fissures at first pink and then a deep crimson. "You promised me," she mumbled through lips split like boiled meat as she sank to the floor, her eyes no longer capable of sight. "In sickness and in health... For better or for worse... You be the passenger, I'll drive the hearse," she said in sing-song fashion. She was laughing now, a maniacal grin spread across her ruined features. He stood by in horror and watched as her finger stretched out and, in the blood that now pooled around her, she scrawled out the word "COWARD" in tall, child-like letters...

Jared's eyes flew open. Samantha's sleep-still face greeted him in the morning light. Her blonde hair lay thickly upon her pillow, some wrapped itself around her chin. Behind that smooth, unblemished forehead she was probably dreaming of wildflowers.

And in that one moment he wanted to tell her the truth, wake her up with kisses and let her know that it was for the best. He didn't want to hurt her anymore. Just witnessing her pain left him with bruises on his heart.

But she wouldn't understand. Her reasoning was much simpler than his own, her needs more basic. He wouldn't be able to explain his actions without her interpreting it as rejection. And with rejection would come tears, and with the tears, like a litmus test, her skin would display the colors of his deceit.

He pushed a lock of hair away from her forehead and her eyes opened. She batted his hand away. "What was it, a spider?"

Jared laughed. "No. Just you. Your hair is so beautiful." He gently cleared it from her face.

She relaxed and nudged closer to him. "What else?"

"Your eyes. They're like those forget-me-not flowers you put in those pretty baskets you make."

She smiled and nudged even closer, resting her cheek upon his chest. "What else?"

"Your smile. Your lips." He ran his fingers across her lips and she kissed them.

"What else?"

He wrapped his arms around her and slid her body on top of his. "Everything." He could feel himself growing hard.

"You're silly, you know that." She moved her hips down until she rubbed against him. "That's why I love you."

"I love you, too," he said. And it was all he could do to keep the tears out of his eyes.

As Jared prepared for his "trip to Pikeville," Samantha made some sandwiches, two of which she loaded into a paper bag along with an apple. It was his lunch for when he got hungry taking his test, she told him. She also made a large pitcher of lemonade and, like Little Red Riding Hood, packed it all into a large basket for her weekly visit to see her father and brother. Her absence would allow Jared time to backtrack and pack his belongings. He had planned it that way.

When they pulled up in front of the Gentry house of horrors, Jared kissed his wife for the last time.

"Good luck," she said, her sweet smile preserved in one final snapshot.

His heart squeezed. "Be back before sundown," he lied. Gentry and Cliff were just stepping outside when he pulled away.

Although he felt like the worst kind of human being, Jared knew his simple plan was enough to convince his wife. But it was foolish of him to think that Gentry would buy the story that easily.

Once home and packing, that foolishness was born out when Jared heard a pick-up truck roll up out front with a backfire and two rusty door slams.

"See, what did I tell ya."

Gentry held Samantha by the elbow as they entered the house. There were tears in her eyes. Several boxes filled with Jared's books and other belongings sat by the door. Jared stood like a deer caught in headlights in the middle of the living room, the suitcase he had just packed still in his hand.

"Don't look like no re-certify-cation day to me, right, Cliffy?" Cliff stood in the doorway, that sickening cat-killing grin on his face.

Jared was scared. He put the suitcase down and pleaded with Samantha. "I can explain." But the bruises were already beginning to show. Her eyes had begun to puff and redden on their way to two black eyes. Her lips began to swell. A trickle of blood ran down one nostril. It was not as severe as the nightmare he'd had, but it was a hundred times worse, because this was real. He might as well have taken his fists and did it himself.

Samantha ran past him into their bedroom, like all the other times before, only this time before she slammed the door shut she said, "I'm sorry." And it wasn't so much what she said, but the way in which she said it that made Jared wish he had planned his escape better.

"Samantha, please, let's talk about this."

"Looks like she don't want to hear it, *Jared*," Gentry said mockingly. Both Gentry and his goon son took a step forward. They both smelled of alcohol.

Jared stood his ground. "I suggest the two of you leave right now. This is between me and Samantha. I don't want any trouble."

Gentry laughed. "No, no more trouble. We're here to help, aren't we Cliffy?"

Cliff kept coming toward him and Jared prepared to throw a punch, but the tall, gangly monster was quicker than he expected. And a lot stronger. Like a snake he ducked past Jared and grabbed him from behind.

"That a boy. Hold him, son."

Jared prepared for Gentry's onslaught. A good ol' backwoods Kentucky ass-whooping. But Gentry reached into the pocket of his overalls and pulled out a jackknife instead. As he slowly pried it open, displaying a dirty yet sharply-honed blade, he said, "I warned you. Didn't I warn him, Cliffy?"

Jared felt Cliff nod behind him. He couldn't believe this was happening.

"I'm sorry it has to be this way." Gentry drew closer.

"No, wait! You can't do this! *Samantha! Tell them it's not my fault!*" When she answered only with tears, he pleaded his case to Gentry. "It's her. She's doing it to herself! It's not normal."

"But it's your words."

"We'll get a divorce. I'll go back to Pennsylvania. You'll never hear from me again."

Gentry smiled and shook his head. "Death till you part, remember, son? Besides, this town needs a doctor. My daughter needs a husband. And you... Well, you just talk too much."

One of Cliff's hands reached around and grabbed Jared by the forehead and bent his head back.

"Cliffy here was always talking back to his momma. My Jeannie, God rest her soul, is in her grave because of him."

Jared stared up into Cliff's open, grinning mouth. Inside was the jagged stump of what was once a normal tongue.

"You see, *Jared*, medicines aren't the only remedies we have here up in these hills," Gentry said as he leaned in. "Now open wide..."

Jared's screams could be heard clear into the next county. But, to most, it sounded like the screech of a hawk, or the cry of a bobcat in the middle of mating season. Like a secret truth, the sound simply buried itself into the folds of the mountains.

"So am I gonna die, doc?"

It was a familiar question, one asked jokingly, but still one never knew. Another old farmer—these hills were full of old farmers. Jared inspected the old man's foot. The old man's toenail was so badly ingrown, his big toe was nearly twice the size and he could barely walk.

Jared grabbed his notepad and began writing. He tore off the sheet and handed it to Samantha, who stood there beside him dressed in that simple flowered dress her mother had made for her.

"He says to soak it in a bucket of hot water and Epsom salts. He'll give you some pills to help bring the swelling down."

Jared pointed to his ear and then to Samantha. You listen to her, he intimated.

The old farmer smiled. "Sure thing, doc. And sorry to hear about your little accident."

Jared shrugged his shoulders and nodded an appreciative thanks. *Shit happens.*

The old man eyed Samantha. "You're a lucky man, doc."

As the old man limped away, Jared reflected on his life. It wasn't so bad, after all. He lived in the beautiful blue hills of Kentucky, in the bucolic-sounding town of Wellness. He had an important position in the community. He had a beautiful wife. One who loved him, cared for him—cared enough to find a solution to the problem that nearly destroyed their marriage.

As Samantha put away the meds and checked the chart for the next patient, Jared stared at the back of her lovely head and said, "I love you," in a voice that now only he should be able to hear.

Samantha turned then, an innocent smile upon her face. She reached out and curled a finger under his chin, and said, "I love you, too, silly."

Under the Bridge

Every night at sundown the birds flew. They flew up, above the busy rotary intersection, above the traffic, silhouettes against the fading light, distracting drivers with their manic sky patterns; then down, in great diving swoops, underneath the bridge, disappearing for a time to skim above the cold river water below. Then up again, lilting, tilting, shifting in waves of particle black.

Wade watched their movements from the footbridge. The birds reminded him of a huge, intricately operated Chinese kite—the way they rose and dove, as if controlled by one master pull string drawn through each of their bodies. He listened to their collective cry, calling high above the traffic drone, and wondered only mildly what brought them all together here like this.

He could ask himself that very same question. Why did he come back to this spot? Did he leave something behind? Some unfinished business that needed to be resolved?

Wade leaned against the railing and looked down into the black, smooth-running water, the warm spring air carrying the dank odor downwind, and remembered another time, an overcast day, three months earlier, before winter came and clogged the gutters and buried the ground with ice and snow... a day when all he wanted to do was to get out of the rain...

The embankment gave way beneath his feet, and he nearly fell. Instead, Wade skidded, one hand dragging behind, until he reached the stony river bed below.

The cars rushed overhead, around the rotary, black tires twinging against the cold tar. Gray skies hung low, draining the life from the day, squeezing it until wet pebbles of rain began to fall. Wade pulled his army coat collar tight around his neck, and walked over the rain-streaked stones toward the bridge. When he got there he realized he wasn't alone.

An old man—gray scruffy beard, red flannel shirt tucked beneath a sleeveless parka—thrift store ensemble—was sitting on a wooden kitchen chair, elbows on his knees, thick hands splayed over a makeshift fire. The fire's smoke sent a gray curl up into the underpinnings of the bridge, unseen, blending in with the exhaust fumes overhead. The old man regarded Wade through tired eyes.

"I just want to get out of the rain," Wade told him, approaching slowly with his hands in his pockets.

The old man still looked at him; his eyes were hard to read: red-rimmed, liquid blue eyes once now faded to gray. The old man reached behind and hefted a wooden crate. He brushed its surface with a callused hand. "Have a seat," he told Wade and placed the crate across from him. He then returned his gaze to the fire and the backs of his hands.

Wade looked at the crate, at its close proximity to the stranger, decided it was better than sitting on cold stone, and settled in beside the fire.

"Name's Joe," the old man said and held out his hand once Wade sat. Wade fumbled a hand out of his pocket. "Wade—" He hesitated. "Just Wade." The old man's grip was warm and rough, like shaking an old sneaker left out in the sun too long. Wade stared into the fire.

"I don't have any food, if that's what you're after."

Wade's head snapped up. The old guy sounded just like his father, always making him feel like he was trying to get something for nothing. "I just wanted to get out of the rain, that's all."

"Uh, huh." A grunt. The old man picked up a stick off a pile of driftwood beside him and placed it on the fire.

The rain came down harder, pelting the bridge overhead with an audible force. Wade looked downriver toward the open sky and saw clouds the color of ductwork. The river flowed more choppily now, disrupted by the downpour. A cold breeze hurried past and Wade clutched his coat tighter around his chest to ward off the shivers.

"You got a home?" the old man asked Wade.

Do I have a home? Funny question coming from a homeless guy, Wade thought. "Yeah, of course I do."

"Then why aren't you there?"

Always poking, always prodding, always knowing what's best...

"Maybe I don't want to be there. Maybe I'm not welcome. Look—if you want me to leave, I'll go." Wade rose, face twisted with a sudden contempt. *You think you know so much... You think you can run my life like you run that stupid business of yours...*

The old man: unmoved, gaze fixed upon the fire. Staring so long, Wade followed his gaze into the fire, wondering just what he was looking at. Then, finally, the old man's voice: "Maybe you should take it easy. Not jump to so many conclusions," and a piece of wood snapped, sending a column of embers spiraling up into the air before them.

Wade felt suddenly fatigued, his legs drained. He sat back down with a bad case of the shivers; a pang of hunger squeezed his stomach. Taking quick inventory, he remembered he still had a candy bar in his coat pocket. Maybe if he ate something, put his body to work, he wouldn't feel the cold so much. Wade ripped open the candy bar, and was about to take a bite when he offered it to the old man. "You want some?"

The old man shook his head, patted his chest. "I'm all set." His eyes squinted slyly.

Wade finished the cold, brittle chocolate in three quick bites and tossed the wrapper onto the fire and watched it burn. "So, you live down here or something?" Wade noticed an area up under the bridge, just under the rise of the girder, up high and tight and dry beneath the shelter of the arching steel: the bulk of a plastic bag overstuffed with belongings, and a couple inches of cardboard bedding.

The old man twisted his neck, coughing as he did so—coughing so hard his face turned purple in the orange light. A lump of yellow phlegm, veined with red, like a nugget of gold panned from some deep, viscous river, surfaced to the old man's lips and he spat it to the ground.

"Are you all right?"

"Damn damp," the old man said, still clearing his throat. He reached inside his parka and pulled out a thin bottle. Shaky hands unscrewed the cap, but before taking a swig he offered it to Wade. Wade shook his head and the old man guzzled the bottle, winced, then returned the bottle to its place of origin.

"How old are you, Wade?" said the old man, one eye squelched shut.

"Nineteen. Why?"

"*Nineteen*." Spoken as if it were a woman's name. The old man pulled out a handkerchief and wiped his mouth. "Got a girlfriend?" He folded the handkerchief and stuffed it back into his pants pocket.

"I'm working on it."

"What's her name?"

Wade didn't know what to make of this old guy. What the hell did he care if he had a girlfriend or not, or what her name was? Why was he being so... *nice?*

"Her name is Lorna. She works over at PJ's." Wade stared at the flames as they licked around the driftwood looking for a place to bite. "But I think she's already taken."

"Pretty name. Lorna. *Lorna Doone*. Ever see that movie?"

Wade shook his head.

"No, of course you haven't. Black and white. That was back when they made movies right. The women were beautiful then. Gene Tierney. Susan Hayward. Didn't even need color to know what color their eyes were. Or the color of their hair." He looked at Wade with a grin. "Sometimes you could even smell their perfume right through the screen..."

Wade grinned back, but only to satisfy the old man, like the way he used to satisfy his father whenever he didn't want to start trouble.

Wade let his eyes roam around the cold empty cathedral of the bridge, bored with the cold, bored with the rain, bored with life itself. If this is what it led to—this lonely old man, lonely but for memories of some old movie actresses Wade had never heard of—then he didn't want it.

But then, he didn't know exactly what he wanted either. A fact his father never let him forget. *What are you going to do with your life, boy? Waste it on that loud music and riding that deathtrap motorcycle of yours? You should be thinking about getting an education, that's how you get ahead in this world. You think that job at the mill is going to get you what you want? Not in your life, boy. Not in your life.*

The fire snapped again, making Wade jump. And out of the silence came the old man's voice.

"Boy, you've got no reason being down here."

Wade didn't know what to say. Who the hell did this guy think he was? "I was just trying to get out of the rain."

"I know what kind of rain you're talking about. I've lived sixty-six *hard* years, made some mistakes—even spent some time in prison. But you have to understand one thing, boy. Rain's gonna find you no matter where you are. Even under here."

The old man's eyes were like pale limpid disks; the fire danced in their lifeless gaze. Wade was chilled by what he saw.

"Look, the minute it lets up I'll be gone. And don't call me 'boy'." Wade rose to his feet and walked to the edge of the dry rocks and looked out at the sky.

It was dark now; the rotary's lampposts glimmered a pale blue overhead and the bridge was slippery with headlights from the passing vehicles. Wade reached into his pocket and felt the jackknife that lay nestled against the coarse fabric of his army jacket like a hornet asleep beneath a heavy stone.

Wade turned to the old man sitting beside the fire. Joe No Name. One of life's derelicts. Wade wondered whose life—or *lives*—had the old man screwed up besides his own? Who sat at home waiting for *him* to show on countless occasions? To show him their homework or to play a game of catch? Or to talk—just to talk? A bottle of alcohol, a business meeting—it's all the same. It all boils down to one thing: a lack of love. And when love is absent, in rushes hurt and resentment, and then fear. Then anger. And, finally, rage.

You'll never measure up, boy...

Wade gripped the jackknife in his hand

never measure up...

and thumbed the blade release.

Joe sat as before, seemingly content to die by this fire, underneath this bridge, on this cold and rainy day. Content to not know what hit him. Or why.

Wade's ears were ringing, his heart pounding so strong in his chest he thought the old man might be able to hear it.

Two steps closer and the sound filled the night, obliterating the rain and the street noises.

A few more and Wade pulled the knife from his jacket, gripping it as if it were an extension of his arm, feeling the power surge, the blade like a lightning rod sucking the fury from the sky...

But something was wrong. The old man was doubled over, his face constricted, a hand pulled into a fist jammed in front of his face.

The sound of the old man's coughing finally broke through the siren raging in Wade's ears. Coughing worse than before. A heavy, wracking, agonized cough, like choking on life itself. Wade folded the jackknife and pocketed it, and rushed to the old man's side.

"I'm okay—" the old man attempted to say. This time blood was smeared across his lips and his face was a color like Wade had never seen: a ghostly pale lavender in the firelight.

Panicked, Wade looked around and spotted a coffee can and rushed to fill it with river water. By the time Wade was at his side again, the old man had retrieved his bottle of cure and had downed the remainder of what was inside.

"Better... better, now..." The old man regained some of his original color and struggled to place a couple more sticks on the fire. He was visibly shaking.

Wade stared at him in horror, unable to speak. The rain was letting up now, but it was cold and getting colder.

"Maybe you ought to see a doctor."

The old man looked up, eyes indiscriminately sharp. "Maybe you ought to run along now. Show's over."

"What do you mean by that?"

"I mean, you can go home now. You've seen all you need to. The show's over, boy."

Anger raged in Wade once again. "Yeah, well maybe I don't want to go just yet! Maybe you don't know me like you think you do! Maybe I'm the kind of punk kid who gets his kicks pig-sticking old bums like you... just to put them out of their FUCKING MISERY!" Wade's eyes sparkled with fear as his voice echoed in the night.

The old man stared at him, calmly. "I guess that's what the water was for." He motioned to the coffee can still in Wade's hand. "Do what you will." Another cough, this time brief, restrained.

Wade looked at the coffee can in his hand, and let it drop. He wished he'd never met this old man. But now that he had, he couldn't just leave him like this. What the old man needed was a hospital bed and a warm night's sleep. Three meals a day. Someone to look after him.

But what was the use? Once restored, he'd probably be back out walking the same dead-end streets, living the same dead-end life.

"Look, PJ's is right up the street. I could get you a coffee?" Wade offered. It was the least he could do.

The old man shook his head. "That stuff will rot your gut."

Wade suppressed a laugh. Stubborn old bastard. "Well, I could use some. You sure you don't want anything?"

The old man just nodded. He coughed once and closed his eyes against the fire. To Wade it appeared as if he were dozing.

"Okay, then, I'll be right back."

Wade stuffed his hands into his pockets and climbed the embankment to the street above. He crossed the intersection and walked up Main Street to PJ's and bought two large coffees and a couple Danish. Lorna was working behind the counter and she waited on him. When he said, "Thanks," she smiled genuinely and said, "Come again." He walked back to the bridge, his spirits lifted. Maybe there was a chance after all. When he returned to the river bed, the old man was gone.

Or so he thought.

The fire had died down and it was hard to see. More than once Wade stumbled, nearly falling on the jutting rocks. Only the rush of the water could be heard, and the far off sounds of traffic.

"Joe?" It was the first time he'd called the old man by his name. "Joe?" The name reverberated against the steel hollows of the bridge. Wade squinted. Up under the rise of the girders, where Joe's belongings were stashed, a larger form lay there as well. As Wade approached he realized the form was too still, too quiet.

Wade sat down beside the body of the old man and told him he'd brought him some coffee and a Danish, and wouldn't it be nice to have some company for the night... And for the next hour Wade talked to the old man like he'd known him all his life.

"Remember that vacation in Vermont in that cabin on the lake? You came running out and took a dive off the dock in those stupid looking plaid swimming trunks of yours, and we all laughed. Remember? Or the time you taught me how to shoot—'Keep your arm steady, breathe out, just squeeze the trigger...' Remember that,

Dad? Or all those times we spent tossing the football around or hitting the softball, before the business came first and all the trouble started. Before you had to go and die and leave me here all alone..."

And when he was done remembering, Wade remembered to move Joe's body down to the edge of the river where he dug a shallow grave and covered it with stones...

Now the birds flew, sweeping up into the sky, pivoting, momentarily still, before swooping back down again...

From the footbridge, Wade stared at the river below, past the sleeve of his army jacket—a jacket that was now for real. Eight weeks of bootcamp and he was home again, home to visit. Home maybe just to come down here and do what he had to do, see what he had to see.

The spring thaw had melted the ice and snow, raising the level of the river, and Wade watched as the birds swept down beneath the bridge and came back up again, nourished by what they found there: newborn fish and freshly hatched insects, and something else, a memory, buried, so long ago it seemed, loosened from beneath the shifting rocks along the river's edge.

And as the sun set like a red teardrop in the sky, and the street lamps began to flicker on, illuminating the swirl of traffic making its way through the busy rotary intersection, Wade left his post and plodded up lower Main toward PJ's—for a cup of coffee, and maybe a friendly face.

'Thumbin'

INSIDE HIS '77 BUICK REGAL station wagon, George Bennett drove along Route 44. The mist-enshrouded night was reason enough for him to keep the speedometer hovering near 30 mph, but there was another reason.

George yanked a can of beer away from its neighbors on the seat beside him, held it between his knees and popped the tab; white foam ran down the side of the can and onto his pant leg. The night was warm, the can sweaty in his grip. A cold beer tasted good on a night like this; it helped to keep reason from bobbing its unwanted head to the surface of his mind.

So many young girls, he thought. Each one the same. Each looking for something other than what their small town lives had to offer. Each risking their pretty young faces and pretty young bodies for the sake of something better. Only to find, if they were lucky, that the world was the same no matter where they went. And if they were unlucky—that the world could be far more terrible than they could ever imagine.

George focused on the mist ahead, the headlights penetrating as if through a murky lake. A road sign floated by identifying a town by the name of Harlan, twenty miles distant.

God, how many towns had he traveled through since he began this "mission"? How many more before he was done? The religious aspect of his deeds didn't escape him. In his previous life, he had been accused of playing God on more than one occasion. But that was so long ago it seemed. Too many miles, now. Too many young girls, too many small towns. What was important was to keep moving, keep spreading the word...

He took another guzzle from his beer and belched loudly. The noise was low and close in his ears, inconsistent with the monotone thrum of the road beneath him. He weighed the beer in his hand and decided to finish it off, chugging it dry. He tossed the can into the back of the station wagon, where it clanked against the others. As he was wiping his mouth with his forearm, he saw her: arm out, hand cocked, thumb pitched in the direction of town; impatient half-lean into the road kind of determination that said, "You better pick me up or else!"

George's heart geared into a nervous idle as he slowed the wagon. He cleared the passenger side, swinging the half-polished six-pack into the backseat. When he pulled over, the girl quickly danced to the handle, opened the door and slid in.

"Well?" she said. There was bubblegum on her breath; the rest of her smelled fresh like shampoo. "You heading into town or what?"

It was her all over again. Blue jeans, white blouse, denim jacket. Bracelets—a whole collection of them—on one wrist; the other wore nothing but a thin gold watch.

"C'mon, let's go. I haven't got all night!"

George checked his mirrors and pulled the station wagon out into the fog again. As his heart settled back into his chest, regaining its previous rhythm, he felt that familiar twinge of purpose hardening his thoughts. Too late to stop now. The wheels were already in motion.

"Miss your ride?" he asked her.

She had red hair, wore dangling earrings, teardrops that caught the light; her eyes were big and brown. She was humming some invisible tune in her head. Pretty girl, as near as George could tell. Why do they do it?

"Yeah, something like that," she said.

"Harlan, right?"

"Yup." Her eyes were focused on some point beyond the mist, her mind somewhere beyond the present.

"So what's in Harlan?"

"You're not from around here, are you?" She eyed him suspiciously, jaw exercising the gum in her mouth.

"Just passing through."

He could feel her eyes on him, sense the swivel of her neck as she checked her immediate surroundings. Then her head began bobbing once again to that internal radio station of hers.

"Jimmy's," she finally said. "It's a dance club. Hey, can't this boat go any faster?"

George increased his speed another five miles per hour, but in the mist it was as if they were barely moving, as if they were caught in some soft cushion of time that existed for just the two of them.

"Don't you think it's dangerous?"

The girl's jaw stopped momentarily, throwing off the beat of her chewing. "It's just a dance club!"

"That's not what I mean," George said. "I mean a young girl like yourself, out here alone, accepting rides from total strangers... Aren't you afraid?"

"To hitch? Naw—" She put her feet up on the dash; George hated when they did that. "It's like I've only got one life to live, right? I mean, I'm not going to sit around being afraid of every little thing. Besides, you look pretty normal to me. I can usually tell. You kinda remind me of my English teacher."

"What about your parents? Do they know you're out here thumbin'?"

"You're kidding, right? My parents? God—my father would freak if he ever found out. And my mom... well, Mom's in another world. They're so uncool it's not even funny. I mean, we don't even have cable. So, what do you do?"

George glanced at her. Talking to this girl was like switching TV channels. "I'm a physician," he said.

"Wow, a doctor, cool! So where's your car? I mean, all doctors have great cars. It's in the shop, right?" She turned halfway in the seat, pulling one leg up under the other. "I bet you got a Mercedes or one of those fancy sports cars or something, right?"

George only shook his head. "I don't have a practice any more."

"Oh. What happened?" Her voice went low. "You're not one of those abortion doctors, are you? I mean, I think abortion's okay. You know, in certain circumstances. I mean, if a boy got me pregnant and I didn't want it... well, you know."

"No, nothing like that. You thirsty? You want a beer?"

For the first time the girl hesitated.

George's heart began to race a little. Did he ask too soon? This was always the critical moment, the moment when it was either: "Okay, that's it, pull over and let me out" or—

"Sure," she said. "Why not."

George reached over his shoulder into a cooler in the back seat and pulled a fresh six-pack into the front. These were the bottles, the ones with the twist-off caps. They also twisted back on.

He selected a bottle and handed it to the girl. "Hey, wait a minute," he said, pulling it back.

"What?"

"How old are you?"

"Eighteen. Why?" Defiant.

She wasn't a day over seventeen, George figured. "Here; just kidding." He handed her the bottle. She grabbed it, twisted off the cap and took a deep mouthful, watching him the whole time.

"By the way," George said, taking a swig from his own, "I believe the drinking age in this state is twenty-one."

"So? I won't tell if you won't."

George gave her a grin, but it was more a grimace. Why did

they have to talk like that—all tough and adult-sounding? What the hell was their hurry?

She was watching the road ahead, staring out at the mist that enveloped the night. "You know," she finally said, "you're not so bad for an older guy. My dad would go ballistic if he ever caught me drinking a beer... he sure has enough of them himself. You married?"

George nodded. "I used to be."

"Yeah? I'd like to get married someday, have some kids, you know, all that regular stuff. But most guys are real jerks. I mean, you seem nice enough. Besides, you're older. I mean... guys my age..." She shook her head. "God, my luck I'll still be living at home when I'm thirty." She took another drink from the bottle.

"I had a daughter, too."

"Huh?"

George kept his eyes on the road ahead. The fog seemed endless, fathomless...

"A daughter. She would have been eighteen-years-old next month."

"So, like, what happened to her?" Another drink, slower this time.

George turned to look at the girl. "She was hitchhiking."

The girl stared at him—this girl with no name. All of them had no names. It was better that way. Better not to know who they were —like his own daughter. As she continued to stare at him, her eyes grew half-lidded. George knew she could barely hear him now.

"The coroner said she'd been raped several times... before she was shot. Once in the head. Somehow she still managed to crawl up out of the ditch onto the side of the road. That's how they found her. Otherwise..."

"Wow," was all the girl could say. The half-emptied bottle of beer slipped from her fingers and fell to the floor. Seconds later she lay slumped against the seat. George reached down and picked up the bottle to keep it from spilling onto the floor mat.

Secobarbital—sleeping pills—a capsule in each bottle. A left-over prescription from earlier in the year, prescribed to help George cope with his tragic loss. He still had twenty capsules left. Ought to last him all the way to California. Until then...

Up ahead, another sign loomed, indicating a side road was coming up. When he reached it, George turned onto a narrow secondary that wound its way through open fields, then thick woods. He hated this part the most. He hated to be lumped with all the psychos and sickos—the rapists and the serial killers—but he knew that's what they would tell each other. The parents. But parents never learn. It's the kids you have to teach.

A half mile later he slowed, then pulled over. He kept the engine running. The young girl mumbled something unintelligible as he removed her from the seat. "Shhhh," George whispered as he laid her in the thick grass along the side of the road. He had to do this quickly—no telling when someone might happen by. Although, out here, the odds were slim.

From the back seat he retrieved his bag, the only part of his previous life he managed to retain—and put to good use. He worked in the bright beams of the wagon's headlights. First came the antiseptic wash. Then the novocaine injections—enough to deaden the median nerve. Tourniquets applied around each wrist. Then came the scalpel... and the bone snips...

Two days later.

It was night again. George drove south along Route 283, looking for her. He pulled a cigarette pack out of his shirt pocket and withdrew a smoke. He had another pack in the glove compartment, but those were laced with chloral hydrate powder. His "patients" either chose one or the other. Small vices. But even small vices eventually kill.

He pushed in the cigarette lighter on the dash and waited. It popped out moments later, red hot coil glowing. He touched it to the end of his cigarette and inhaled deeply, examining the lighter before putting it back. Not the best thing to cauterize a wound, he thought to himself, but it served its purpose. As he believed he served his purpose, guaranteeing at least a handful of young ladies will never thumb again.

As he watched the road ahead, smoke snaked into his eyes and he rubbed them with the heel of his palm. When he could focus again, there she was, like a vision through the eye of his windshield: cut-off jeans, tank top, blonde hair long and flowing; arm out, thumb cocked—swollen, diseased.

George put on his signal light and pulled over to offer her a ride, and, perhaps, provide a cure.

Something Profound

IT'S THE REASON WHY PEOPLE sit through funerals, attend weddings, wait expectantly outside delivery rooms—that unnamable presence that accompanies death and birth and the consummation of love. They're all hoping for a glimpse at the infinite. They're all looking for something profound.

At least, that's what I had hoped to find when I went to visit my dying father at the hospital. But instead of finding an old man ready to breathe his last breath and release the reigns of torture he had inflicted upon our family, I walked in and found demons pounding on his chest.

But a lot has happened to get me to this point. First you need to understand what would make a relatively young man still cling to the hope that all could be forgiven, that even the most tainted of souls could somehow be redeemed. Let me go back.

I was the youngest of four children, and, at first, growing up, I didn't recognize that the man I called father, the man who my mother lovingly referred to as "Pug", was a monster. I didn't tense up the same way my older siblings did when he shouted out in anger. I hadn't seen what they'd seen. Not yet.

My father was a big man with big hands. He was a magical, mythical creature who possessed the power to control the universe. He had a voice like thunder, a stare that could stop you cold, and a personality that could drown a room in laughter just as easily as stun it to silence. To say I looked up to him was an understatement. I was his bouncing baby bunting boy. His son. His model. I could do no wrong. He favored me, and my older brother resented it. This was another thing I didn't realize until much later in life. My brother hated me. But that's a whole other story.

Like I said, in my father's eyes I could do no wrong. But one day I must have. That was the day he almost put me through the wall.

I don't remember much about what led up to the "big slam"—I only remember that my mother was in the hospital having an operation and it had been the end of a long week, or two, or however long one stayed in the hospital back then when one was having a hysterectomy. But to me, at six years old, it seemed like forever.

For years I have made excuses for my father on that day—the day things *changed*. I must have been whining or fussing or throwing a tantrum. I must have said something that tipped my father over the already precarious edge he had been tight-roping since my mother was away—making meals, washing clothes, putting up with the day-to-day kid's stuff times four. And being the youngest, perhaps I asked for something, or did something so irrational, it just blew my father's mind and he had to react, he had to DO something, or self-destruct.

So he let out a controlled burst. And that's when I saw it, that flash of... otherness. Something raw came forth from inside his large frame and showed itself—if only for a moment, the moment it took for him to pick me up, lift me like a bag of groceries, and slam me into the wall, leaving an impression of my head and shoulders in the plasterboard. I saw it in his eyes, the embodiment of pure machine-like terror. And then it was gone. But during the few seconds it appeared, the damage was done. Like the exposed core of a nuclear reactor, its effect was devastating. Stunned and frightened, I believe from that day forward I retreated into myself and tried not to do anything that would trigger such a reaction again.

But, inevitably, circumstances would align against us. Something at my father's work would initiate a sequence that wouldn't launch until he arrived home. By now the four of us kids had learned to complete our chores or settle our disagreements before we saw his car pull into the driveway. But it didn't seem to matter. There was always something left out, overlooked. An empty soda can on the end table. A bad report about school work. It could be something as simple as the wrong response to a question asked at the dinner table. And the sequence would reach its end, the code completed. The monster would smile, and in its maw we would see oblivion.

Those large hands would become missiles. Those who were their targets would be laid to waste beneath a rubble of tears and bruises—both inside and out.

Call it stupidity or just blind faith in the belief that people can change, but no matter how many times I witnessed my father's transformation and experienced the pain he inflicted—upon myself or those around me—I always forgave him. I never let go of the hope that one day my father would rid himself of the monster that crouched inside the dark corridor of his eyes.

For the longest time, that monster took the form of alcohol. My mother often explained it was because my father drank too much that he was the way he was. And, looking back, I can hardly recall a memory of my father where an open beer wasn't within arm's reach.

I remember nights he would come home late and there would be no explanation. Or he would leave soon after dinner and disappear into the dark only to return at an hour of his own choosing. He would enter the house, his shoulders hunched, his mood altered. His voice would be much louder than usual, his laugh not his own, his stare not so accurate. Sometimes. the alcohol would put the monster to sleep. Other times, it made it irritable and more easily roused. On nights like these, we made silent pacts with each other not to speak or do anything to draw attention to ourselves. There was never a pattern to the monster's behavior. It seemed to abide by its own unique set of rules. This was why I was so frightened—and yet curious—the night my father asked if I wanted to go with him.

My father collected guns. He bought and restored old rifles. He had a small room to himself at the end of the hall where he worked, sometimes late into the night. Inside the room—which was off limits—I had seen glimpses of a workbench, a gun case and shelves of unnamed paraphernalia. When he went out alone at night, he sometimes said he was going gun hunting. One night, when he grabbed his coat, he turned to me. His eyes stared as if he were trying to fathom whether I could be trusted or not. Then he spoke. "You want to go?" I was ten years old.

My mother tried to step in and give him a reason why I couldn't, but his eyes began to change. "But he wants to go." A large hand fell upon my shoulder like a vulture's claw. "Don't you, son?"

I nodded in agreement.

My mother quickly pulled back, but not before kissing me on top of the head and making sure I was dressed warmly.

As my father and I rumbled off into the night, I could see my mother's face in the living room window staring as if she would never see me again.

That night, I was introduced to my father's world. It was a world of darkness and solitude, of cold metal and long, winding roads. We stopped at several houses that operated shops out of their basements or converted sheds. They were all the same. Guns hung from every available space. There were cigar boxes and coffee cans filled with brass casings and lead bullets. Trays of tiny primers and cardboard canisters of gunpowder. Animal heads gazed down from the walls. While my father talked business, I picked through the odds and ends. When I saw something I liked, my father would throw it onto the pile and pay for it with a grin. "Starting him early, I see," the gun shop owners would invariably say. And my father would nod. "They're never too young." And the shop owners would laugh, not knowing fully what my father had meant.

As the night wore on, my father began to stop at more than just gun shops. We would pull up alongside curbs in front of neon-lit buildings and he would disappear inside for ten to fifteen minutes at a time while I stayed in the car and played with my new toys— three old copper-cased civil war cartridges, each the size of a pack of gum and as heavy as a pocket knife. Each time my father returned to the car he was more animated than before, talking to me as if I understood what he was saying, or talking to no one in particular. At one of the many small town intersections we passed through, he changed his mind and made a last-second turn that sent the car spinning around like an amusement park ride. He laughed and I laughed with him, scared and thrilled to the point of nearly pissing my pants. I enjoyed it when he laughed. It was a rare treat.

I wanted to spend all night with him, but it was getting late and I knew my mother would be angry that we hadn't returned home yet. And as we drove under the streetlights of a town I didn't recognize, my father's mood quieted. He seemed to be scanning the night. Hunting for something that couldn't be found in a field or in the woods.

The streets were empty except for a woman pacing back and forth beneath one of the street lamps. She was dressed as if she were going to a party. My father pulled over. He put the car in park. Without a word, he got out and approached the woman. My only thought was that they somehow knew each other and he was just saying hello. But instead of a quick "Hi, how's it going?" the two of them began to walk away. They entered an alley and were suddenly gone.

I sat in the car. I was nervous and I didn't know why. I didn't know what was going to come out of that alley. I counted the times the corner streetlight changed from green to yellow to red, transforming like the eye of an animal, from kind to cruel, from being at ease to being afraid. I must have dozed off thinking about it because I heard the trunk open and shut. By the time I opened my eyes my father was getting into the car and placing the key in the ignition. He didn't look at me at first. His hands shook slightly and he leaned over and reached into a paper bag down by my feet. His fist came back gripping a beer. He pulled the tab and took several long gulps. When he finally turned his attention my way, I noticed he had perspiration on his forehead. His eyes were like two bullet holes. "You ready to go home?" he asked.

We drove back through the night a different way than we had come. It took a long time. I didn't recognize many of the roads. One was nothing but stone walls and woods, not a house for miles. We pulled over and my father got out. He opened the trunk and lugged something off into the woods. When he returned I could feel him pause. My skin began to burn as his monster's eyes stared at me, but I pretended to be asleep. He put the car in gear and we drove home.

He never took me again.

Until this day, I wasn't sure why he had taken me that night. I now believe, like any proud father, he was trying to pass on a kind of legacy. But he either deemed me not worthy or not ready to accept what he wanted to give. Perhaps he realized I would one day find it for myself.

So the illusion persisted. As I grew into adulthood, I gave my father every benefit of every doubt. I defended him as if he were accused of a crime that everyone was convinced he had committed but only I knew he wasn't guilty of. He just needed one person to take the time and effort to understand who he really was, and I was the one who was going to do it, and then everything would make sense.

I believed this as I watched my siblings abandon him one by one, finally growing old enough to slip out of our dimly-lit household and into whatever light they could find on their own.

I watched my mother deteriorate into an old and withered shell of her once vibrant self.

I watched my own marriage dissolve, my wife more strong-willed than what I would have preferred. I married her because I needed her to be who *I* wanted to be, but in the end couldn't.

I watched my own world become one of darkness and solitude, much like that endless back road night when my father took me gun hunting.

I watched until I had nothing left except the one hope I had clung to since I was old enough to know what hope was.

I had prepared myself for this moment and didn't even know it.

My father's drinking had reached the point where he was no longer coming home. And when he did, my mother tried not to let him in, but her guilt was perhaps as strong as my faith and she would eventually succumb. After she died, he took up residence in a moldering pay-by-the-night hotel on the lower part of Main Street in town. I learned all of this from the officer who was the first on the scene when they found him in his room, unconscious from an apparent fall. It was two o'clock in the morning when the phone roused me from sleep and I made my way to the hospital.

It was the first time I had seen my father in over four years. Tubes entered and exited his body like worms. His head had been shaved, a half-moon incision cut into his skull. The sheet barely covered him, and as I approached the hospital bed I could see the bruises—a panoramic purplish blue—covering his chest. The doctor had said that my father's heart had stopped on the operating table when they were inside his brain removing the clot, and I wondered if having a heart attack could cause this kind of bruising

—a constriction of muscles so violent it looked to be the equivalent to being thrown against the steering wheel in a car accident, only from the inside out.

Standing there, looking down at the man who was both a source of menace and admiration throughout my life, I was thankful that I was the one they called. Although I had dreaded this day since my own mortality began to seep into my consciousness and weigh upon my thoughts, I wanted to be here if anything should happen. I needed to be here. I had earned that much.

And so I waited.

And with each day that came and went, the bruises got worse.

On the second day, as the doctor performed routine responsiveness checks on my father's comatose body: tickling the palms of his large—now impotent—hands, pinching the base of his yellowed fingernails, massaging the jut of his bony sternum. I asked what was wrong with his chest.

"Your father has been through hell," he explained. "Trauma to both his head and his body. We don't know what extremes he has suffered, but they are severe. If it is any comfort, his condition is surprisingly steady."

And, yes, I was comforted. But at the same time I was also worried. I needed him awake. I needed him lucid. I hadn't waited all these years to at last be cheated from my just reward.

You see, my goal in all of this—my mission—was that I was going to save my father. I was going to save him in my own mind from torturing me for the rest of my life. I was going to look him in the eye and tell him that I forgive him. That I had absolved him of his sins. That I understood that he had lived his life the best he was able. And he was going to thank me. Not in words or tears, but with a nod perhaps or a gentle sigh, an acknowledgement that, finally, someone had accepted him for what he was and not what he could be. And then he would close his eyes for the final time and I would be rid of him at last.

I wasn't going to leave his side until that happened.

I slept in the waiting room when I was tired. I ate vending machine junk food when I was hungry, drank bitter black coffee when I needed to stay awake.

On the third day his condition was unchanged, the bruises however continued to bloom.

On the fourth day he began to stir, movement twitching at his extremities. A good sign, the doctor admitted, though he still seemed puzzled by the persistence of the bruising.

On the fifth day my father began to mumble.

This was it.

I hadn't showered or shaved in days and the hospital staff was beginning to give me sidelong glances. By now I had become a fixture in the hallway outside the ICU at night. They probably didn't understand why I was holding a bedside vigil for a dying old drunk. For their benefit, I drove to a local pharmacy and bought a disposable razor and some shaving cream. I washed up as best I could in one of the hospital restrooms.

It was after midnight, the staff reduced to a skeleton crew. I couldn't sleep. Not when I was so close to fulfilling my duty.

I slipped past the nurse at the desk, who was watching a late night talk show on a small portable television. I could hear my own heartbeat pounding in my chest as I approached my father's room. Then I realized the sound wasn't coming from inside of me. I swung open the door and stood in shocked amazement.

Their clenched fists rained down upon my father's chest. The heavy thump resonated through the floor. It was a wonder that no one else could hear it. Two half-human-sized creatures sat crouched upon my father's bed. They turned to look at me, eyes red, lizard-green skin glistening with a worked-up fury. They snarled and their mouths dripped a thick viscous saliva. They resumed their assault.

My father's chest wasn't moving. The color of his face was a pale cyanotic blue.

I moved then, taking a bold step forward. I was going to beat the two creatures off of him with my own fists if I had to, but they were already scurrying from the bed. They disappeared into an opening in the wall where a heating panel had been dislodged. As the second demon's tail slithered from sight, the panel snapped back into place as if nothing had been disturbed.

I didn't have time to try and understand what I had just witnessed. My only concern was to revive my father. I was about to rush out and get the nurse when I felt the heat upon my face—a familiar burning sensation. I turned then and saw that my father's eyes were open. He was staring at me.

But his face remained blue.

His chest still.

His lips parted. "Thank you," he whispered. He didn't blink.

A strange calm descended over me as I approached the bed. I didn't care how or why this was happening, all I knew was that now was my chance to speak my peace, spill the sentiment I had stored and rehearsed all these years. But as I leaned over and looked into the bottomless depths of those eyes, I saw, not remorse or humility or anything remotely human. What I saw instead was the monster lurking in the shadows, its own eyes the blackened coals of death itself. And the thing that was my father smiled. Its rotted teeth crawled with tiny parasites, its breath reeked of meaty decay. A hand reached up and latched onto my arm and pulled me close. "My son," it said. And then it released its last breath into my face.

I fell back, gasping for air. I was suddenly overcome by visions. I could see what my father had seen throughout his life. I relived every deed my father had done. Deeds so heinous and cruel, it made my stomach retch with revulsion. I relived not only the incidents I was aware of within our own family, but those I was not. Incidents that took place on nights he wasn't home, in places where there were no other eyes to witness except his own and those of his victims.

A flower shop at closing time, the manager, a dark-haired woman, cashing out for the day. Surprised by my father's entrance. "I'm sorry, we're closed for the evening. My assistant must have forgotten to lock the door on her way out." The monster suddenly surfacing, seizing the moment, twisting the woman's neck until it was as red as the roses that filled the showcase.

A young man, his car pulled along the side of the road, out of gas. College stickers on the back windshield. Thankful to see there were still people in this world willing to lend a hand. That hand— large and powerful—the last thing seen, rushing towards his face, about to crush his jaw.

And when opportunities didn't present themselves, my father created his own, entering into dark, shadowy realms where the lost and the destitute meet to swap pieces of their souls. Barflies and prostitutes. Some broken or twisted in back allies for a cigarette. Others murdered for much less. Male or female, young and old, he was indiscriminate in his thirst for death. All of them were disposed of along narrow, winding roads, buried beneath the leaf-rich decay of the woods' floor.

I could see all of this because I finally understood. It made sense to me now. The alcohol that had been blamed for my father's behavior wasn't a cause, but a remedy. It wasn't used to forget what a miserable life he possessed, but to protect us—his family, to subdue the monster that clawed at his insides and keep it from crawling free and destroying us. Like any animal, he did what was necessary to ensure his lineage would survive.

And as I sat on the floor of my father's hospital room, his death only moment's old, I could already hear the whispering. With it came a creak of metal and I turned toward the heating panel. From the darkness of the open duct, their eyes stared out at me. I realized then that they needed a home. Something to protect. Something to devote their lives to.

I nodded and they crawled forth into my arms. I held them like my children and they nudged their bony muzzles against my ribcage and began to burrow under my skin.

It's the reason why people sit through funerals, attend weddings, wait expectantly outside delivery rooms—that unnamable presence that accompanies death and birth and the consummation of love. Tonight I have experienced all three.

The hospital is now miles behind me.

The road ahead looks like a hole shot through the night.

And, what can I say, there's a thirst in my throat that this beer in my hand just can't seem to kill.

THE WHITTLING

LITTLE JOHN STEPPED OUT INTO the cold November daylight with blood on his hands.

He searched the woods around him—white birch, oak, and pine—just letting his eyes roam, using up some of the adrenaline still coursing through his veins.

He needed a place to sit down.

The old wicker chair. It sat in the corner of the porch stacked with newspapers. Little John walked over and shifted the stack onto the floor—torn strips of newspaper clung to his tacky fingers. He sat.

Little John remembered when Grandpa used to sit in this very same chair, huddled over, elbows on his knees, huge gnarled hands working a piece of wood with that short, sharp knife of his—the one with the deer antler handle. Grandpa said his own father had made that knife for him when he was just a boy—killed the deer himself. *For a small boy growing up then, a good hunting knife was as much a companion as an old hound dog...*

Grandpa died when Little John was seven—not even old

enough to help carry the casket.

Little John gazed out across the leafy lawn, and the long gravel driveway that ran down the hill and out between the break in the stone wall... and remembered.

"Little John! For the last time—get away from that window before your father gets in here!"

Summer sits outside, breeze like a warm breath through the window screen. Tiny spider's web in the corner, white paint chipping from the sill, warm wood against tired forearms. Looking, waiting. Getting hungry. Just a little while longer.

"Supper, boy." Poppa's voice low, boot heels heavy on the hardwood floor.

Easing away from the window, off the worn red felt of the couch. Walking to the kitchen table and climbing up onto the seat. Not understanding why no one else seems to wonder, why no one else seems to care where Grandpa went. Nothing but the sounds of knives and forks, and silence. Mashed potatoes, roast beef and gravy, green beans, corn on the cob. Grandpa even had a corn cob pipe. Kept it in his shirt pocket.

"When is Grandpa coming back?"

All sounds stop. Momma's eyes grow deer-like, frightened. She looks at Poppa. Poppa, bread in one hand, knife in the other, finishes what he's chewing, rests the knife gently on the edge of his plate. Looks up.

Dark, coal furnace stare. Exhaustion, resolution in those eyes. He knows what to do. How to fix things. Poppa always knows how to fix things.

Thick fingers on small shoulders. Into the bathroom.

"Why, Poppa! What did I do?"

"Just be quiet, boy."

"John, no!"

"Stay out of it, Jeannie."

Momma's voice gets lost behind the click of the bathroom door.

"But why, Poppa, what did I do?"

"That's enough now. The sooner we get this over with..."

The pants come down. The trembling dutiful climb to get over Poppa's knee. The big, callused hand, as big as a dinner plate, full of lesson and cure and retribution and pain, and anger, oh yes, lots of anger, fistfuls of anger.

"Why, Poppa, what did I do! WhatdidIdo! *WhatdidIdo!*"

The linoleum floor, curled and blurred through unpronounceable tears. *Why! Why!*

And finally:

"Grandpa's dead, boy." Final. Fixed. As the first of the hammer blows comes down. "And when you're dead you're dead." And the echo of these words, each like a nail in Grandpa's coffin.

you're dead you're dead you're dead you're dead

snick!

you're dead.

Little John took a deep breath, lifted his chin to the sky. There were clouds in the distance, the sun was a dull glow behind naked woods. Parched gray skins, skeletal branches. Little John barely felt the cold that was beginning to settle upon his own skin and seep into his bones.

...Used it to skin rabbits, gut fish, take the legs from those big meaty bullfrogs... Yup, now I just use my 'magination. Here, try it yourself. Be careful though. Your momma would skin me alive if she ever caught me teaching you how to use that thing. That's it...

"That's it. Get 'em near the pile. No sense in doing a job twice."

Poppa, sweat on his brow, shirt sleeves, like extra muscles, rolled up above his elbow. Bend, grab, heave. Nonstop like an oil rig. The tree laid out before him like the bones of a dinosaur, all cut up for firewood. Each piece arcing through the air to land with a *clunk thud*. Making it look so easy.

Helping. Need to help. Grateful to help Poppa do anything. Watch. Look. Listen. Grab the ends. Sap, sticky—tree blood—still wet, smells good, even... tastes good.

"Is this what they make maple syrup out of, Poppa?"

A nod, maybe even a smile. Oh, great to help. Swing back and forth, then up, into the air. Like learning how to swim. One... two... three, into the water. Same thing. Got to get 'em near the pile. No sense in doing a job twice.

Poppa. *Clunk thud! Clunk thud!* Crisscross on the pile. Making it look so easy.

Closer then. The smaller ones are up here anyways, lighter, get them right on the pile. Like Poppa. Everything like Poppa.

Bend over. Stand up. One... two... three. *Clunk thud!* That's it.

Over. Up. One... two—

Pow! Earthquake. Atom Bomb. Car Crash. Gripping both ears to staunch the flow of pain, ringing, falling. Falling. Long, slow motion fall, down into the mud and sawdust, and all the world becomes a scream.

Poppa's grip, rough and sudden, pulling hands away, standing the world upright. Pushing hair aside for inspection. Feeling, painful pressing feeling, while little black fireflies swirl against an all-too-bright background.

"Didn't break the skin," Poppa says. Disappointment in his voice. "You're all right." Disgust. "Next time you won't stand so near."

The hands pull away, receding. Back to work. *But I'm not all right!* Poppa readies himself to begin again, hesitates.

"What are you looking at, boy?"

Dull ringing. Bass drum throb. The fireflies take crazy kite swoops around Poppa's head, leaving a halo of black smoke trails like snakes. And everything turns to stone.

"Nothing, Poppa. Sorry, Poppa. It don't hurt no more."

A smile then. Yes, a real smile.

Everything like Poppa...

snick!

It had turned colder, daylight solidifying into night. Little John could feel the memories emptying, good with the bad, draining as if the pores of his skin had grown too large to contain his insides. It all came rushing out in a torrent of past offenses, colliding with the present like a log against his skull—or the thin tip of metal against tendon and bone—until there was nothing left... nothing but the hollow emptiness of the white wicker chair, the worn whisper of Grandpa's memory, and the cold cloak of diminishing daylight around him.

It was time to go inside. Finish the job he'd already begun.

Little John eased himself up out of Grandpa's chair. He felt old, like the way Grandpa must have felt each time he pulled himself from this, his favorite resting place. If only Grandpa were here, Little John thought. He'd be so proud. He taught me well.

The screen door opened with a creak, swinging wide on its broken spring. Little John stooped as he passed through the doorway and into the harsh light of the kitchen. In the ten years since Grandpa's death, the house had slowly folded in around him, doorways hanging lower and lower, the rooms shrinking until, at times, it seemed like he could see the walls move, inching forward like the jaws of a cider press.

(Little John! Get away from that window!)

The rest of Sunday dinner was still simmering on the cookstove —corned beef and cabbage—the three portions that had been served still on the table, untouched, long since gone cold.

Little John stepped over the bodies.

They lay on the floor—Momma and Poppa, their arms and legs asprawl like two ragdolls torn of their stuffing and tossed by a problem child. Little John tried not to meet their eyes, intent instead on finding what he'd come back inside for. But after all these years of dodging their stares, enduring their cold evaluation, he couldn't help but look now, drawn to their frozen expressions like those of dead animals.

Momma's eyes were shut, her face mercifully set, wrinkle free, as if at peace for the first time in her life: love's companion to the end. Poppa—Poppa, whose eyes could reach out and grab him from across the room—just stared, eyes open, fixed on some invisible point between floor and ceiling, two gray glass orbs drained of their power, their menace, their hold, lost perhaps in the translation from this life to the next.

(when you're dead you're dead...)

Little John looked away. His eyes searched the kitchen floor. It had to be here somewhere...

There... just like that...

Grandpa sitting in his wicker chair; Little John on a milk crate alongside, watching, legs hanging down, the toes of his sneakers gathering the thin shavings of wood into a small pile, like hair from a haircut. Listening as Grandpa rambled on. What would it be this time? A lion? A bear? A fox? A wolf? Listening to the *snick snick* of the knife blade as it performed its clever magic...

Did you know, boy, that there's an animal locked up in every one of these? Yup, a little cut here, a little cut there, and pretty soon you uncover what's inside. All it takes is time... that's all... time to whittle it away...

There—over in the corner by the sink, underneath the overhang of the cabinets: the deer antler handle, the gleam of metal shining through.

Little John stepped carefully around the kitchen table, cautious of the thick slippery pools that gathered beneath. He stooped and took hold of the knife. He turned it over in his hand, rubbed the drying blood from its handle. Little John nodded to himself as if everything made sense now, and in the cool brightness of the kitchen light he slowly pressed the short, sharp blade into the meat of his palm. Blood welled up around the thin metal as he looked on in fascination.

From there, the rest was easy.

THE HOUSE NEEDED WORK. Plaster, paint, polish, a light bulb here, a new fitting there. It was a beautiful, old Victorian, emphasis on was, emphasis on old. But Janey Lavinsky knew what she wanted, and there was nothing her husband, Michael, was going to say to talk her out of it.

"Mommy, is this our new house?"

Janey looked at their six-year-old daughter, Jessica, and then at her husband, who simply shrugged his shoulders." I guess it is, Honey," Michael answered for her.

Janey put her arms around Michael and kissed him on the lips. "Let's go sign some papers," she said.

From high above, the attic windows stared down upon the family of three as they got into their car and drove off. Behind the windows, surrounded by age and dust and silence, something creaked.

Moving day.

Janey and Michael enlisted help from their friends with bribes of pizza and beer. It was a long day filled with activity and laughter and only a few broken items. Jessica played ring-around-the-boxes and hide-and-go-seek with Eve, another little girl stranded with nothing to do but watch the grown-ups shuffle in and out of the big house. When it was Jessica's turn to hide, she ran upstairs, leaving her newfound friend with her face against the refrigerator door counting.

The staircase was wide and winding, and by the time Jessica reached the top she was nearly out of breath. The upstairs carpet swallowed her footsteps. She passed by first one door, then another. She remembered these rooms from when her mom and dad first looked at the house with the realtor lady. Jessica kept walking until she reached the end of the hall. At the end was a narrow door that led to another staircase that led to the attic.

"...*nine, ten, here I come, ready or not!*" came her friend's voice from below. Jessica heard tiny shoes running up the hardwood stairs. Jessica opened the narrow door and stepped inside. The door shut behind her.

"*I'm gonna to find you...*"

Jessica stepped up onto the first step of the staircase, her heart pounding in her chest. She felt invisible, as if she were in a closet.

"*It's only a matter of time, Jessie... I'm getting warmer... I can hear you breathing...*"

Jessica didn't really believe Eve could hear her but she wasn't taking any chances. She began to back up the narrow stairs, careful not to make any sounds. When she reached the top, she couldn't believe what she saw.

The attic was huge. And dusty. And dark.

The floorboards seemed to go on forever. There were windows in the shapes of half-moons, like sleepy eyes, dust—and cobweb—covered. Daylight struggled through them. There were thick posts like telephone poles that ran from floor to ceiling. Wide beams ran cross-wise overhead.

It was neat. And a little bit scary.

"*I'm gonna find you...*" Eve called, but she sounded less confident, now.

creak

What was that? Jessica's inner voice whispered. She turned her head in the direction of the noise.

In the middle of the room sat a large wooden chest with gold hinges. It looked like a big toy box. Jessica took two steps toward it.

creak

Maybe it was her own feet making the noise. The floor was old, and old things made strange noises. But she could swear it was coming from the box.

"*C'mon, Jessie... no fair...*" Her friend was tiring of the game. Eve's voice trailed farther and farther away.

creak

There was something special about this place, thought Jessica, and something really special about that box.

She walked over to the chest and stood before it. She waited. Her heartbeat was all she heard. Then—

creak

She smiled. Then she reached down to lift the lid.

Downstairs, Janey saw Eve sitting on the sofa, her arms laced across her chest.

"Where's Jess?" she asked the girl.

"I don't know."

"Where do you think she went?"

"She's upstairs, I think, hiding. I couldn't find her. She doesn't play fair."

"Upstairs, huh?"

Janey put the box of knickknacks she had in her hands down onto the floor. She didn't like Jessica running up and down the staircase, it was too dangerous.

When she reached the top of the stairs, Janey called for her daughter.

There was no answer.

She checked every room, every closet, looked under every bed. She even checked behind the dressers. After all, a six-year-old could squeeze herself into quite a small space.

"Jess, stop playing now and answer me!"

Not a sound.

Maybe she wasn't up here, thought Janey. Maybe Eve was mistaken and Jessica was sitting inside one of the kitchen cupboards waiting to be found.

Janey was about to head downstairs when her ears pinned back.

creak

The sound came from the end of the hall.

But the only thing at the end of the hall was the door leading up to the attic. That door was locked. Off limits. She and Mike had agreed, the stairs were too steep, the potential for danger too great for their curious daughter.

But Janey needed to be sure. She walked to the end of the hall and sure enough, the door's ornate, hundred-year-old knob rattled in her hand but did not turn.

Relieved, Janey headed for the stairwell—

creak

—and stopped. She knew the house was old, she knew creaks in old houses were as common as aches and pains in the bones of the elderly. She also knew her daughter. Call it mother's intuition, but Janey couldn't shake the feeling that something was wrong.

She reached into her back pocket. Maybe the attic door had been left unlocked. Maybe Jess went up the narrow stairs and the door closed behind her—and locked.

But why wouldn't she answer? Why isn't she kicking and screaming and crying to be let out?

Janey began to panic. She couldn't find the key the realtor had given her. It was an old skeleton key, like the ones found at flea markets. A simple, stupid thing to open a simple, stupid lock.

"Jessica!" Janey pounded on the attic door. "Jessica, are you up there?"

She tried the knob again, and to her surprise it turned in her palm. The door opened.

She rushed up the narrow stairway. "Jess?" Her voice sounded shrill and weak in the still, lifeless air.

She saw the chest in the middle of the room and her throat constricted. Tears filled the corners of her eyes. As she walked toward the chest, she remembered the plans she and Jim had for this room: a study for him, an arts and crafts studio for herself, a play room for Jessica, a nursery for the new baby, if and when that time came...

Janey crouched in front of the old chest and slowly lifted its lid... and their lives changed.

Downstairs, Janey's scream was heard by everyone.

After the investigation, Janey and Mike were told to move on with their lives. It was an accident.

Their friends stopped by to check in on them now and then to see how they were coping, to provide an open ear or a shoulder to cry on. But eventually the silence of the Levinsky household became too depressive and everyone just stayed away.

Janey blamed herself for not keeping an eye on her only child. Michael blamed himself for not recognizing the old chest as a hazard. And when they tired of bearing the weight of the guilt themselves, they set it down and blamed each other.

It was an accident.

Babies drown in bathtubs filled with six inches of water.

It was an accident.

Kids are backed over by their parent's cars while playing in the driveway.

It was an accident.

Children crawl into things they can't get out of and suffocate.

An empty freezer. An old wooden chest. It's never easy to understand, but it's a part of life, and for whatever reason these things happen.

Four months after the death of her daughter, Janey Levinsky stopped trying to convince herself that these things *just happen* when she finally made the trip back upstairs to the attic. Her return wasn't prompted by the idea that it would be therapeutically healing, or because she was struck with a sudden sentimental yearning—although Oprah told her that she must and will eventually do these things. No, Janey found herself scaling the steep, narrow attic staircase because in the silence of the afternoon—a silence she occupied all-too-often since her husband went back to work and left her to her unpredictable tears and her daily medication—she heard footsteps. Running playfully. Followed by laughter. Coming from the attic.

Janey cautiously peered up over the top step and into the open space beyond. She expected to see Jessica as she last remembered her, dressed in her little blue jumper, a smile as bright as the sun, getting ready to make another mad dash to go hide from Eve.

But Jessica wasn't there. In place of the previous emptiness, the attic now hosted Michael's computer desk, a bookshelf, a small refrigerator and a recliner. A large braided rug covered the plank flooring in the middle of the room. Michael had also moved his weight bench up here. The old wooden chest was now a coffee table, only instead of coffee cups it was crowned with empty beer bottles.

It looked like a bachelor's apartment, thought Janey. Perhaps that's how Michael felt. After all, she was hardly there for him, locked up in her own one-room world of guilt and grief. And when she did come out, the distance between them was, most times, too difficult to bridge.

She walked over to the chest. A sense of déjà vu washed through her.

She crouched down and ran her fingers along the chest's edges. She caressed its smooth wooden surface and the cold metal corner reinforcements. She cleared the top of empty bottles and lifted the lid.

Her daughter lay inside, her face tinged with blue, her eyes closed as if she were sleeping.

Janey looked away as tears flooded her eyes. When she looked back, Jessie was sitting upright, her face still blue. She had a smile from ear to ear.

"You found me, Mommy. Now it's your turn to hide!" Her daughter giggled.

Janey felt her daughter's breath upon her face. It smelled of fish and sour milk. Janey fell backward and crawled for the stairwell, her heart racing in her chest. Janey didn't look back as she fled the attic, but she could hear the creak of little girl bones chasing after her.

"I saw her, Michael. She's up there."

Michael had come home to find Janey locked in their bedroom. Michael held her as they sat on the bed together.

"Janey, listen to yourself. You must be having a reaction to your medication. I'm calling Dr. Hemmingson."

She pulled away. "No! I saw her. Her face was blue." Janey's eyes grew as wide as Easter eggs. "We have to help her, Michael."

"No, Janey, our Jessica is at St. Columba cemetery. We buried her, remember? She's in the ground. Now, please, stop this."

"It hid her soul. Hide and go seek. Now it wants us to play. Don't you see?" Janey's eyes looked toward the ceiling.

"You want to ruin it all, don't you? You're not satisfied that our Jessie's gone, you have to throw it all away?" Michael grabbed her by the shoulders. "I'm here, Janey. It's just us now. We can try again. We can have more children."

She stared at him. "But she isn't gone. She's up there, Michael. Don't you believe me?"

"I believe you need some professional help."

"You don't believe me." Janey looked away, a veil of

disillusionment descending over her features. Maybe she didn't see what she had seen. Or heard what she had heard. Maybe this was all a dream that she would soon wake up from.

"Janey, listen to me."

"I'm tired, Michael. Can we do this some other time?" She lowered herself onto her pillow.

Her husband sat in silence. "I love you, Janey," he said finally, "but I won't sit by and watch you destroy yourself, and our marriage in the process."

He got up then and walked out. When he closed the door behind him, Janey closed her eyes and drifted off to sleep.

Michael sat in his recliner, two beers emptied, a third ready to join them. His nerves were calm now, settled into a comfortable bath of ennui. Outside, the night pressed against the attic windows. The house was still.

Michael liked it up here. It was high and away from everything else. It was almost as if he were floating above the world and all its problems. Michael didn't believe in evil spirits. The old chest beneath his feet was just an old chest. And if Jessica's spirit were trapped inside of it, the result couldn't be anything but beautiful and sweet. Because that was the kind of child she was.

So when he heard the floor creak and saw his daughter standing in the corner hand-in-hand with a young woman, he was more surprised than shocked, more intrigued than fearful. Jessica was smiling. The woman was also smiling. The woman was beautiful. She wore a long flowing gown, white as window curtains and just as sheer.

As they walked toward him, Michael didn't think it strange that he could see the shadows of furniture behind them—through them. All he could think about was the way his life used to be, when Janey was Janey, and Jessica was there to leap into his arms when he walked through the front door after a long day's work. The way he wished it could be again.

His daughter led the woman over to where he was seated, almost as if to introduce her to him. The woman proceeded to push the recliner back.

creak

Michael closed his eyes as the woman pressed her lips against his. He felt a strange sensation and realized he couldn't breathe. His eyes flew open and what was staring at him was hideous.

The woman's skin clung to her face in dry leathery strips. Gray strands of hair sprouted from her bony skull. Her eyes were black pools of nothingness. Her lips crawled with tiny movements.

Jessica giggled at her side, her face now a pale blue.

Michael couldn't move. All he could feel was the life escaping him as if something had stuck a spigot into his heart and had opened it up full.

Janey entered a fitful dream. Her body struggled to pull her awake, but inside her sleeping consciousness she was an unwilling spectator to a domestic squabble.

The man was shouting. "I married you so you could bear me children. Not babies born without a breath of life in them!"

"But we can try again," the woman replied, sobbing.

The house was the same, only newer. Beautiful hardwood furniture surrounded them, cherry and mahogany. Lace doilies sat beneath crystal lamps which sat atop marble end-tables. Patterned wallpaper adorned the walls. A large Persian rug lay perfectly on the floor. The man was dressed in a fine suit, the woman in a beautiful flowing gown. Each bore hairstyles that hadn't been worn in over a hundred years.

The woman clutched at her husband's arm. "I love you. Won't you hold me?"

"Love?" the husband looked at her with disdain. "I hold the livelihoods of two thousand families in my hands, and I can't even have a family of my own. Do you know how that makes me feel? It's a disgrace." He turned away from her. "Leave me, now."

"But Phillip."

"Get out!"

The woman ran from the room in tears. She rushed upstairs. Janey followed her.

At first, the woman entered the bedroom. She looked around desperately. Finally, she stared at herself in the mirror. Janey could also see herself in the mirror standing behind the woman. The woman rushed past her and out into the hallway, and up to the attic.

The attic was stacked with moving crates. Some had fallen and excelsior had spilled out onto the floor. Amid the jumble of items sat the chest. It was new and shined a golden honey brown. The woman kneeled before it and opened its lid. Inside were linens, small knitted clothing, a silver baby's rattle, a music box. It was a hope chest created in anticipation of the arrival of a newborn.

The woman closed the chest. Tears stained her cheekbones. She set about unraveling some wire used to secure one of the crates. She stood the chest up on end and climbed on top of it. She looped the wire up over the top attic beam and wrapped the two ends around her neck and twisted it tightly.

Janey watched in horror as the woman then kicked the chest out from under her and fell with a sudden jerk, the wire sinking deep into her throat, cutting off her airway. The last image Janey saw before she woke was the woman's eyes staring hopelessly into space, her face turning a light shade of blue.

Janey rushed up the attic stairs. "Michael!" she yelled. She reached the top step—

"Michael, we have to get out here."

—and stood in disbelief.

Michael was fully reclined, his neck was bent, mouth open, his face a now familiar cyanotic hue. He was absolutely still.

Janey numbly walked over to him. She wanted to cry but tears no longer seemed to hold much meaning. "Now you believe me," she said as she reached out and caressed his face.

creak

Janey turned.

The old wooden chest sat at her husband's feet. It was touching him. It shouldn't be touching him, she thought and shoved the chest away.

She heard a giggle. Her heart sank. What if Jessica was still inside? She reached down and lifted the lid.

The chest was empty.

creak

Another giggle, this time accompanied by a grown woman's laughter.

Janey looked up. Her daughter was standing just three feet away. Standing beside her was the woman from the dream.

creak

They looked the same as the day they both died. Then they changed, their faces transforming into the hideous death masks they presently wore.

Janey stepped back in horror—

— into the arms of her husband, who picked her up and forcibly placed her in the open chest and shut the lid tight.

The young couple stood on the front lawn of the old Victorian and admired its stateliness. The woman turned to her husband. "Are you sure we can afford this?"

"Not a problem," her husband said. "I've got it all figured out."

"Did you figure in junior here?" She pointed to her stomach, which bulged beneath her dress.

"He or she will be in diapers and formula up to his or her kneecaps," he said.

"That's not very deep."

"You know what I mean."

They gazed at the old home.

"Why do you think it sat empty for so long?"

"Probate probably. But whatever the reason, it's a steal."
They turned to each other and decided with a kiss.
"Let's go tell the realtor the good news."

From high above, the attic windows stared down upon the expectant couple as they got into their car and drove away. Behind the windows, surrounded by age and dust and silence, something creaked.

Angels of Mercy, Angels of Grief

T HE TEENAGE GIRL STOOD ALONG the roadside, her car idling on the shoulder, a small bouquet of yellow daffodils in her hand. The ground at her feet was gouged, the marks formed by a straight-line pair of tire tracks that ended abruptly at the foot of a large tree. The tree stood defiant, only a small patch of bark torn from its trunk. A clot of flowers and plastic hearts and handmade signs covered the ground beneath the wound.

"WE LOVE YOU, JULIE."
"WE MISS YOU, JULIE."

"Excuse me."

The girl jumped. She turned and took a nervous step back into the grass as the stranger approached. There were tears in her eyes.

"Huh?"

"You knew her, didn't you?" the man asked.

"Uh, yeah... from school. Julie was my friend."

"Are these all from her friends and her family?"

"You mean the flowers?"

"Everything."

"I guess so."

"What about that one?" The man pointed to a circular object attached to one of the tree's exposed roots. It looked like a pretzel made of wood. "The cross. Did you see who left that one?"

The girl looked. She didn't see what the man was pointing to. "I don't know. It could have been anyone. Are you from Julie's family?" Her eyes searched the man's face.

"I'm sorry to bother you," he said, and walked back to his car. The girl watched him leave.

The man took one last look at the memorial beneath the tree. Something seemed to glow between the flowers. He tried not to shudder as a chill rushed over him.

Nathan Webber had not rested since his wife passed away, killed on a narrow stretch of road a mile from home. No other cars involved. A high rate of speed was ruled out. There was no blood-alcohol. Sherry didn't drink. A deer, perhaps, the police offered. She might have fallen asleep. It happens more often than you'd think.

Their attempts at explaining away his wife's death were not comforting. And the knowledge that it happened often was even more distressing.

Especially after he discovered the cross.

It looked handmade, carved from a single piece of hardwood. A simple design, really. Just a cross within a circle—not a plus sign, but a cross. Harmless. Thoughtful, in fact. A heartfelt offering to the memory of his wife.

Like most fatal car accidents, Sherry's coworkers, friends, and family had created a makeshift memorial at the scene, marking her memory with flowers, handwritten prayers, and other tokens of their appreciation. It warmed Nathan to see how many lives Sherry had touched. He was thankful for the two years he had been allowed to be her husband; loving her, cherishing her, abbreviated though it was. As a professional photographer, he had taken many pictures of her. They adorned the walls of their apartment. Her smile was the essence of joy. The roadside memorial was so beautiful, he had to photograph it, capture its memory. For Sherry. For himself. It was therapeutic.

But his photographs not only captured a moment in time, they captured a glimpse of what would become a living nightmare. There was an object in the pictures, nearly hidden by all the flowers.

He went back to the scene.

There was a wooden cross nailed to the base of the tree Sherry had hit. Nathan stared at it for a long time. Sherry had not been a religious person. Their wedding was the last time they had seen the inside of a church. But the cross appeared damaged. Its circular edge had been crushed, as if it had been there *before* the accident.

The police sirens were wailing again, on their way to another accident. Nathan's heart began to race. He had to beat them there. He had to hurry. Then he opened his eyes and realized it was just his cell phone ringing. Like coming up from beneath a watery undertow, he pulled himself out of a restless sleep and grabbed the phone.

"Hello?"

"Nate, it's Dan. I got that package you sent."

"Dan? Shit." Dan was a good friend of Nathan's, an old college buddy. He worked as a chemist for a biotech company.

"Sorry, Nate, did I wake you? Is this a bad time?"

Nathan looked at the clock. It was 11:00 am. He had missed his morning appointment. "No, that's okay. So, did you find out what it's made of?"

Dan laughed. "Nate, the package was empty. Did you forget to put it in the box?"

Nathan sat on the edge of his bed. His head pounded. He didn't want to hear this. He wanted it just to end, have a simple explanation, and then he wouldn't have to think about it anymore.

"I must have forgotten to put it in there. I've had a lot on my mind lately." He knew damn well he had put it inside the box, wrapped it up tight, sealed the box with strapping tape just to be sure. It couldn't have fallen out.

"No problem, buddy. Just send it again when you get the chance."

"You didn't happen to throw the box away, did you?"

"You want it back?"

"It's just that maybe..." How could he explain this to Dan? *The wooden icon I sent you, it might be invisible?*

"Nate, really, there was nothing in the box. I made sure of it. Is everything okay?"

"Yeah, everything's fine. I just remembered I'm late for an appointment. Thanks, Dan, I'll talk to you later."

Nathan ran his fingers through his hair. He got up and sifted through the stack of printouts by his computer: pages from various websites. One depicted something called The Tree of Knowledge of Good and Evil. "It was of a species that could not be viewed with the naked eye... a tree that is seen only by divine insight and not natural eyesight," the caption read. Another printout was covered with symbols, one of which was circled with a red marker. It was an oblong shape carved from a single piece of wood, surrounding a cross, called a *lamen*, which supposedly represented the four natural elements: fire, water, air, and earth. There were other printouts as well, pages on The Cult of the Cross, talismans and amulets, and other topics on the occult and supernatural, which only worked to fuel Nathan's anger and anguish.

He grabbed the stack of papers and threw them into the garbage. *Divine insight. Bullshit!*

He stared at the pictures on his bedroom wall. Interspersed among Sherry's artfully framed photographs were other photos, tacked haphazardly in place. Photos of roadside memorials, each with a red circle drawn around the place where one of those crosses appeared.

He didn't know how or he didn't know why, but somebody was behind all this. Nathan was sure of it.

He looked at his wife's picture. Her smile squeezed his heart.

"I'll find out who did this to you," he told her, tears streaming from his eyes. "I'll find out if it's the last thing I do."

Nathan bought a police scanner.

Over the next six weeks, there were fourteen accidents in the surrounding area, two fatalities.

The first was a young man on his way home from a party; the second, a housewife and mother of three, returning from an errand. As a photographer, Nathan was never much interested in tragedy and pathos. There was already too much unhappiness in the world; he figured he didn't need to add to it. He was a portrait photographer. His subjects were people, families—like the family he doubted he would ever have now. Not twisted metal. Not bored policemen, stone-faced coroners, or nervously grinning spectators. And, least of all, not the on-scene spectacle Nathan was witness to, of a husband and wife returning home from a night out to celebrate their twentieth wedding anniversary, arriving upon the scene of an accident only to realize it is their son who lies lifeless beneath a blanket as rescue workers cut his body free from the wreckage. The cries, the wails of injustice, that followed rivaled even the most piercing of sirens.

Two fatalities. Each, Nathan would later discover, initiated by a harmless-looking piece of wood nailed or lodged in place like a divining rod for death and destruction, placed there before any other memorial tributes could gather.

Two fatalities. Two sets of pictures. The second set much like the first, except a different road, a different curve, a different set of faces in the crowd.

Except for one.

A tall, thin figure wearing a long coat and a wide-brimmed hat, standing inconspicuously along the perimeter of the scene. Hands tucked inside his coat pockets, shadows obscuring his features.

Nathan looked at the twin images. He imagined the smile

beneath the shadow, the sick glee residing in the man's heart. Like a pyromaniac returning to the scene of the fire he had set.

Nathan had his man. All he had to do now was wait.

It was two weeks before the next fatal accident occurred.

Accident? Nathan didn't even know what to call them anymore. Accident sounded too innocuous. Like luck or circumstance. Nathan began to entertain the notion that there were no accidents. Was it an accident when he and Sherry met? Was it an accident that there was a problem at the bank that night and she had to stay a little later than usual to clear it up? Was it an accident that Nathan insisted they change their minds about eating out and instead offered to cook some spaghetti, make a salad, and have it ready by the time she got home?

But she never made it home. And it was three days before Nathan could bring himself to remove the dinner from the kitchen table.

The flicker of police lights lit up the night. A gentle rain was falling and the lights danced across the surface of the road. Nathan sat in his car. He turned the volume down on his scanner. "11-80." Police code for a motor vehicle accident: major injuries.

The ambulance pulled away, sirens off. The crowd dispersed— neighbors, strangers returning to their lives, thankful, perhaps, that death chose someone else this night.

Nathan watched as the tall, thin man got into what looked like a rental and drove off.

Nathan followed him. It was 2:00 am.

The man drove to a roadside motel a mile outside of town, and pulled in. Nathan pulled into a 24-hour gas station across the street and began filling up his tank. He watched as the man got out of his car. His walk was deliberate, measured, as he climbed the stairs to the second floor balcony and entered his motel room. He didn't even turn to see if anyone was watching. Guilt-free.

Nathan asked the station's attendant if it was okay if he parked in the back of the lot. He told the kid he was a private investigator working on a case. He slipped the boy a twenty and said there would be more if he could convince the other attendants to look the other way. The attendant grinned and grabbed the money.

For the next two days, Nathan dined on convenience store snack food. He watched the world come and go. But the rental stayed put. There were times Nathan dozed, and when he woke, the fear would grip him like a pair of cold hands. What if he missed the stranger? It wouldn't take a minute for the man to walk down to his car and disappear, en route to his next victim.

But the car remained in its slot. No sign of the tall, thin man in the long coat.

On the third night, Nathan had his Swiss Army knife in his hand. He was carving the strange symbol, the *lamen*, into the vinyl dashboard, when he caught a glimpse of his own face in the rearview mirror.

He hadn't showered or shaved in a week. He had been in the same clothes for nearly as long. Was he losing it? Had his wife's death pushed him so far beneath the shadow of grief that nothing else mattered but this silly notion that accidents weren't accidents but some kind of unnatural conspiracy?

Once again, he felt tears storming toward the corners of his eyes, preparing to drown him in an uncontrollable wave of self-recrimination. He looked at the knife, how it gleamed in the artificial glow of the overhead sodium lights. How easy it would be to cut a simple line down each arm and just bleed away into the night. No more pain. No more tears.

There was movement across the street.

Nathan put the knife aside and grabbed his telephoto lens.

The tall, thin man in the long coat had exited his motel room and locked the door behind him. He appeared to pull a watch from his coat pocket to check the time. Nathan zoomed in to get a glimpse of his face, but the man turned and proceeded to his car.

Nathan cleared the debris from his lap and keyed the ignition. It was 11:00 pm.

The man traveled west, away from the city, and onto rural routes. Town centers came and went, their blinking-light intersections like ghost towns in an endless night. Nathan made sure to keep far enough behind the rental so as not to draw suspicion. Although he doubted the man paid any heed.

The rental turned onto a narrow side road called Breakneck Hill. Nathan shut his headlights off and followed. He kept close, his eyes never losing sight of the rental's red tail lights. About a mile in, at the base of a long hill, the rental braked and pulled onto the shoulder. The car angled its headlights toward a large tree. A hundred yards back, Nathan rolled to a stop and cut the engine. He stepped out into the dark. It was after midnight.

Nathan didn't know what he was going to do or say. He watched as the tall, thin man first checked his watch, then methodically went about his business. He was crouched in the tall grass before the tree, bathed in the white glare of the headlights, quietly nailing one of those wooden crosses into place with a small hammer, when Nathan confronted him.

"Why?"

The man turned. His face was no longer obscured by shadow, his features suddenly lit by the high-beam headlights. Nathan was expecting something hideous, malevolent, a human embodiment of pure evil. But this man looked like somebody's kindly old grandfather. His eyes were a soft, innocent blue. Caregiver's eyes.

"Oh, my, you startled me, young man."

"Why?" Nathan asked again. His hands were balled into fists at his side.

The man turned to the wooden icon and gave it a few more taps. He stood up slowly and pocketed the hammer. His expression was unchanged. "You would not understand," he told Nathan.

"Try me." Nathan could barely hang onto reality. This was the man who killed his wife. Why wasn't he at the man's throat choking the life from him?

"Why? Because they wish it so, that's why."

"What is that supposed to mean? Who are *they*?"

"Oh, you don't want to know. Please, accept your loss, move on with your life." The man stared into Nathan's eyes. "But that would be difficult, now, wouldn't it?" He reached into his coat pocket and pulled out his watch. It wasn't a typical pocket watch. It was circular, but it had two distinct dials. "There's not much time," the man said, "they'll be coming soon." He tucked the watch back into his pocket.

"Please," pleaded Nathan. "My wife. Why her? Why any of them?"

"Oh, it's nothing personal, believe me. I have no knowledge of who will be next. I just know the time and the place. It is very precise, actually. And it provides structure and order to an otherwise chaotic world."

"For whom?" Nathan asked incredulously.

"I'm sorry. For them, of course." The man's arm gestured to some invisible component in the night sky. "You see, the pain, the suffering these events inspire—they hunger for it. Like you and I, they need to be fed. I merely set the table. Do you recall a mother of three who was killed a short time back? Tragic, wasn't it? They could have taken the entire family, but they chose just her. But it wasn't to spare her children. Quite to the contrary. Her children will grieve for *years* to come."

Nathan became enraged. "But isn't there enough pain and suffering in the world without you adding to it?"

The old man laughed, a cheery, good-natured chuckle. "I don't add to it, I merely participate in bringing it about. As the saying goes, it's a nasty job, but somebody has to do it." A smile graced his lips. His face was warm and loving. "You see, these beings—I call them grief angels—they are as necessary as the air we breathe. You might think it monstrous, but without the horror and the cruelty and the ugliness that exists throughout the world, there would be no jubilation, no delight, no beauty, and absolutely no hope. Without the one you cannot have the other. Shattered youth, broken innocence, the utter senselessness of untimely death—to them it is all just caviar and cheesecake with a white wine chaser."

"You're insane," said Nathan. His voice was weak. It felt like his insides were pouring out.

"No, young man, I am just an ordinary fellow with an extraordinary occupation." Once again, he pulled the strange timepiece from his coat pocket. "Oh my, I really must be going." The man then turned and began to walk back to his car.

Nathan stood on the side of the road questioning everything he had ever believed in. He no longer felt grief-stricken. Nothing was going to bring his wife back, he realized that now, and crying about it only fed the bastards who had orchestrated his pain. He wasn't about to stand by, however, and let what had happened to him happen to another husband, or wife or mother and father. The old man had left him with no other option.

Nathan pulled the Swiss Army knife from his pants pocket and pried the wooden icon from the tree.

"Here," he shouted. "Aren't you forgetting something?" He threw the object at the old man. It hit him in the back and fell to his feet.

The man turned. He didn't look angry. In fact, he seemed... *relieved.*

"So, you're the one," he said.

There came the sound of a car racing in the distance. Headlights popped into view over the crown of the hilltop that led down to where the two of them stood. The old man held his ground. Nathan yelled for him to get out of the way. But the car was traveling too fast. The old man turned to face the oncoming vehicle and spread his arms as if to embrace it. The car locked up its brakes. Nathan watched in horror as the vehicle struck the old man, sending him end-over-end into the air and then back down onto the pavement in a shattered heap. The car skidded to a stop. Nathan rushed to the old man's side, and cradled his head.

"I'm so sorry," he said.

The old man forced a smile. "It's quite all right." He coughed, and his body convulsed. Blood seeped down the corner of his mouth. "It is up to you now," he said. "You must feed them."

Nathan shook his head. "I can't."

The old man's eyes intensified. He grabbed Nathan's arm. "If you don't, there will be chaos." He reached into his pocket and pulled out the timepiece and put it into Nathan's hand. "Now you will truly see."

Nathan felt a strange sensation in the center of his palm as his fingers folded around the circular mechanism. The old man also handed him a set of keys.

"Mister, is he going to be okay?"

Nathan looked up. The teen driver's eyes were shot with adrenalin and fear. But that wasn't the only thing Nathan saw. Behind and above the teen's head, odd shadows were forming. They appeared from out of the darkness like images on photographic paper in a bath of developer—shapeless, diaphanous forms that seemed to grow more substantive as the moments elapsed.

The teen was shaking. Guilt, pain, terror—the essence of each was seeping from his body in multicolored tendrils. The creatures moved in close and began to feed on the dark delicacies.

Nathan returned his attention to the old man. Soft blue eyes stared up at him. The old man's face held a look of peace and contentment. He was no longer breathing.

"Stay with him," Nathan told the teen. "I'll get help." Nathan pocketed the watch and the old man's keys and ran to his car.

Nathan called in the accident. He then headed back to the motel where the old man had been staying.

The room was sparse. It smelled of old books and onions. Clothes hung on hangers in the closet. The bed was neatly made. On the lamp table lay a book. Nathan sat on the edge of the bed and picked it up.

It was a copy of the Koran. A newspaper clipping was stuffed inside, acting as a bookmark. *Woman Dies in Auto Crash*, the caption read.

> *Marie Richmond, 26, wife of Tompkin University professor, William Richmond, died early this morning when her automobile plunged into the Tompkin Reservoir. The cause of the accident is still under investigation.*

The clipping was yellow with age.

Nathan pulled the timepiece from his pocket and examined it in the light. Its housing was made of wood. The two dials appeared to be made of polished crystal, each slightly elliptical. The bottom face indicated a date and time, the top face, a direction. Each dial also had an outer ring that moved independently. Nathan rotated each ring until they aligned. The next alignment would occur in two days. Another fatal accident. Another contribution to the well of pain and suffering in the world.

Nathan wanted to destroy the timepiece, but couldn't bring himself to do it. He could still see Richmond lying in the road, the look of contentment on his face even at the moment of his death. His was a tragic and yet noble life.

Without the one you cannot have the other.

Nathan went to stand, and his heel kicked something beneath the bed. He reached down and pulled out a canvas sack. He uncinched the top. It was full of wooden icons. Enough to last a lifetime.

One year later, Nathan watched the homes slide by as he drove out of town and onto the backroads. There was comfort in the knowledge that his actions preserved a sense of balance in his tiny corner of the world. He was sure there were others like him taking care of their own designated space, just as he was sure there were places without a caretaker, places where chaos ruled the night as well as the day.

He checked his watch. The twin dials glowed an ominous yellow in the night. Their alignment was close at hand.

Nathan whistled a nonsense tune as he drove along the empty country road. He couldn't wait to set the table for them. It gave him such pleasure to see them gather.

It gave him such joy to watch them feed.

Skins

One day, after school, Jeremy Bowen ventured up the long, gravel drive that led to the old cemetery on the hill, because he'd been told the dead lived up there. "You can hear them whispering between the graves," his classmates told him.

What he found instead were a handful of black snakes sunning themselves on the warm gravel, and the whisper of his own footsteps as he walked between the lichen-covered headstones.

Jeremy now sat on a smooth granite slab—which looked more like a long, wide coffee table than a grave marker. He pulled a cigarette from a pack he kept in his coat pocket, lit it and drew the hot, soothing smoke into his twelve-year old lungs. He watched the snakes lying in the sun, their black skins glistening like sequined leather. He wondered if they made their homes in the graves below, their black bodies coiled around chalk-white skulls or inside empty rib cages. He bet they infested the burial vault that was built into the embankment at the top of the hill, its gray weathered door looking like the entrance to the underworld.

"Can I help you, son?"

Jeremy jumped and turned to see an old man standing where, just moments before, there had been nothing but grass and gravestones. "No, pops," Jeremy answered sarcastically. "Just... resting my bones."

The old man chuckled, hiked up his pants and sat on the granite slab beside Jeremy. "Mind if I sit down? Legs ain't what they used to be."

Jeremy shrugged. *Must be a drag getting old*, he thought, and snubbed out his cigarette on the granite facing.

"Will you look at them," the old man said, referring to the snakes up on the hill. "The only company some of these folks have known for quite some time."

Jeremy let his eyes skim over the headstones. He noticed the smooth, sloping nature of the cemetery, and realized it was probably the highest point in town. He could see the school from where he sat. He could also see the town library, and the fire station. He bet if he stood atop the burial vault, he would be able to see clear into the next county.

"So, what are you doing up here, son? Relatives of yours?" A wrinkled hand patted the tombstone they sat upon.

"Just having a cigarette," Jeremy replied. "Ain't no law against having a cigarette is there?"

"None that I know," the old man replied, his voice adopting a grandfatherly tone. "But you are kind of young—still in grade school, I figure. And those cancer sticks you're putting in your mouth there will most likely shorten your life. But, no, I guess there ain't no law against being underage and having a cigarette in this weedy, dry-as-dust cemetery... unless you don't want to share one with a bothersome old man?"

Jeremy turned to him. "Do you want one or what?"

"Don't mind if I do."

Jeremy fished out the pack of Marlboros and handed it to the old man. "The lighter's inside," he told him. The old man fumbled with the pack, got one lit and took a long, slow drag. "Ah, that's nice," he said, handing the Marlboros back to Jeremy. A few silent moments passed between them before the old man spoke again.

"You see, sometimes kids come up here just to cause trouble. They knock over headstones. Tear up the grass. I just like to make sure nothing happens to them."

"To who?"

"The dead, of course."

Jeremy smirked. "What can happen to them? They're dead."

"Ah, but are they? Death isn't just the end of life, you know."

"No?" Jeremy raised an eyebrow. Maybe this old guy was weirder than he thought. He checked the grass to see if there were any weapons nearby.

"Oh, it's the end of life as we know it. But who knows what really happens after we die?" The old man took another drag on his cigarette, a contemplative look in his squinty eyes. "Could be, we end up like that rotted log over there, returned to the earth. Like the bible says: 'Ashes to ashes, dust to dust.' Or perhaps we're more like our friends up there on the hill, just trading in one skin for another." Jeremy glanced over at the snakes. The sun was beginning to dip low in the sky. Soon it would be behind the trees. "Or perhaps a little of both."

Jeremy imagined a whole casket full of snake skins, whispering like crepe paper. *You can hear them whispering between the graves...*

"Hey, look, Mister, it's getting late. I gotta get going—"

"You see, Jeremy, death may not be the end we all imagine it to be."

Jeremy stared at the old man. "How did you know my name? I didn't tell you my name."

The old man chuckled. "When you're old like me, Jeremy, you get to know a lot of things. Like I know that both your parents were killed in a car crash when you were only five years old..."

"How did you know that? Who told you?" He stood and back-stepped away from where the old man sat.

"Like I said, when you've been around as long as I have, you can't help but hear things."

"No, you couldn't have heard that. Who are you? What do you

want?"

The old man calmly smoked the last of the cigarette Jeremy had given him, savoring it, then stamped it out beneath his foot. His wrinkled face looked up at Jeremy. Jeremy didn't notice it before, but the color of the old man's eyes was dark, almost black.

"Look, Jeremy, your parents—"

"My parents are buried in upstate New York!"

"And you thought maybe, just maybe, if the dead whisper to each other here... they just might tell you what's going on over there, am I right?"

Jeremy turned his eyes away. The snakes up on the hill were getting restless and beginning to move. Jeremy could almost hear the dry scrape of their skins on the gravel drive. "I gotta go."

"Now hold on a minute, son. Don't you want to know? Don't you want to hear what you've been waiting to hear all this time? Or don't you think life owes you that kind of favor?"

Jeremy began to walk away.

"They don't blame you, boy. They don't blame you one bit. It's not your fault."

Jeremy stopped. He turned back around. He wanted to be angry, he wanted to yell at the old man for thinking he was so smart. But his eyes betrayed him and tears began to blur his vision. "I didn't even get a chance to say goodbye..."

"Well, listen. Maybe—just maybe, mind you—if you say it here, right now, it might well travel all the way to upstate New York. And they'll hear you. And they'll know."

Jeremy looked at the old man. The old man's eyes seemed to dilate then, like one of those snakes up there on the hill. (Or maybe it was the tears in his eyes playing tricks with his vision.) Jeremy had this sudden impression that underneath the ground lay a vast network of small round tunnels—snake holes—which ran from cemetery to cemetery, state to state, and a word heard here could be relayed on the backs of quick, slithery messengers to be delivered there.

Finally, Jeremy spoke.

"Goodbye, Mom," he said. "Goodbye, Dad... I miss you both."

Jeremy thought he heard movements in the gravel up on the hill, but he was afraid to look. He then wiped his eyes and tried to summon a little hardness back into his youthful face.

"Well, I gotta get going, Mister. I'll see you around."

The old man smiled. "Oh, you will. You take care, now."

Jeremy stuffed his hands into his coat pockets and headed home.

When Jeremy was far enough down the cemetery drive and out of sight, the old man walked up the hill to the burial vault. He took a quick glance over his shoulder, then... *changed*. His legs became one. His arms, hanging at his sides, melted into his body—a body that thinned and elongated in a matter of seconds, eventually coiling down onto the ground like a fat, black electrical cable. Meanwhile, his old man's clothes had become a transparent skin, which he shed as he wormed his way beneath the weather-beaten entrance of the vault, and into the cold, dark, whispering hollows below.

THE BANANA MAN

THE BANANA MAN WAS ON Michael Willis' mind lately and he didn't know why. It could have been because his life was getting just a little bit crazy. His job was feeding him anxiety like so many handfuls of aspirin. His girlfriend had just moved out. And—oh, yeah—his sister, Michelle, was dying.

Michael tried not to think about that. Instead, as he sat at his desk taking a mental break from the paperwork that just seemed to pile higher and higher, he thought about the Banana Man.

It was a character on one of those early morning children's shows Michael used to watch growing up. On the show, the Banana Man would come out dressed in a big baggy suit with lots of pockets, and this strange music would play. He wouldn't say a word; all he would do was pull bananas out of his pockets. Many remembered the *show*, it ran for eighteen years—Captain Kangaroo, Mr. Greenjeans—but no one seemed to remember the Banana Man. And this irritated Michael, this collective forgetfulness. But then—why did it matter?

But it did matter. To him.

Michael's eyes focused on the photograph of his sister he kept on his desktop.

Why, Michelle? Why don't you want to remember?

There was so much left unsaid between them. And now she had cancer. Not only was it slowly eating his sister to nothing, it seemed to have eaten any chance for reconciliation between the two of them.

Looking at his sister's face staring back at him, Michael felt defeated by mere circumstance. His only relief was in knowing in his heart how he truly felt. He loved his sister and he had to hope his sister would know that too, once she passed on.

But why the Banana Man? Another kind of relief?

Maybe that was it. Like the comedic relief he provided on The Captain Kangaroo Show, the Banana Man was acting as a kind of catharsis for Michael's own inner turmoil. Movie-goers tend to flock to a good comedy when the economy's falling apart. But that still didn't explain why no one else seemed to remember.

Maybe they would if they were going through what I was going through? Michael considered. Then he shook his head at the weirdness of that thought. As weird as the music that used to play when the Banana Man used to caper in front of the camera wearing that emotionless clown face of his... and then reach inside one of his many pockets to pull out a—

A gun?

A knife?

Now, why the hell would I think of that?

Michael rubbed his face with his hands. He picked up his coffee mug and downed the last of the morning's coffee. Cold. Bitter. Like the feeling in his heart when he looked at his sister's photograph.

Why doesn't she remember?

Michael shook his head, rattling the Banana Man away into the shadows of his own memory. He then forced himself to concentrate on the endless work in front of him.

9:30 pm. Michael should have been relaxing. Perhaps watching TV or listening to music. Instead, he sat at his kitchen table in his empty one-bedroom apartment finishing up some paperwork from earlier in the day. Take home. When was it going to end? Thankfully, the phone rang, giving him an excuse to put his pen down.

"Hi, Michael, it's me."

"Lisa?" Michael's ex. Her voice sounded like refuge to his ears. How long had it been? "How are you?"

"Fine. Look, the reason I'm calling is I forgot a few things. My leather boots, my curling iron... a couple CDs."

"I'm not surprised. You did leave in kind of a hurry."

"I know, I couldn't help that. Is it okay if I come by tomorrow and pick them up?"

"You could come over now, if you want." Michael tried to keep the sound of desperation out of his voice. But it was hard. Really hard.

"No, Michael, tomorrow, after work. Around six? Will you be there?"

Tomorrow. What was tomorrow? Michael had to think for a second. Lately, the days just seemed to blend into one another.

"I don't know... I guess so."

"I've still got the key. If you're not there, I'll just let myself in, okay? I'll leave the key on the kitchen table."

Michael found himself listening to her voice; he missed the sound of it. He missed the sound of something other than his own tired thoughts spoken aloud. It had only been a week since she left, but it seemed like months.

"And there's one other thing." Lisa's voice softened a bit. "Your sister's back in the hospital."

"What?"

"Remember Janet? She works over at Mercy. She saw the name in billing. Just thought you'd like to know."

Silence.

"Michael? Are you still there?"

"Yeah, I'm here."

"Are you all right?"

Lisa's voice was suddenly distant; it was being displaced by music. "Yeah, I'm all right." Strange music, like the twisted notes spilled from a winding-down calliope. The music of the Banana Man.

"Okay, then. I'll be by tomorrow."

"Okay."

"Bye."

"Lisa wait!"

But she had already hung up.

Michael wanted to call her back. For some reason he didn't want to be left alone tonight, alone with that music playing in his skull. But he realized he didn't even know where Lisa was staying now. She might have told him once, but he probably didn't hear her. Too busy to listen. Too goddamned wrapped up in his own work to give a damn.

Your sister's back in the hospital.

Damn!

Tomorrow, after work, he decided. Tomorrow he'd go see his sister.

That night Michael dreamed of the Banana Man.

He was a small boy again, sitting cross-legged in front of the television set, absorbed in his favorite program. Suddenly, that eerie music began to play and he knew the Banana Man was about to appear. But instead of the feeling of joy he remembered, the sight of the Banana Man struck dread in his chest. Something about the way the Banana Man capered up to the camera, filling the screen... and the hand that went reaching, groping into one of his many pockets. What would it be this time?

Michael woke up before he could see.

Mercy Hospital was over a hundred years old. Made mostly of red brick and stone, and built with the architecture of the period, it looked like a prison. *Did they think they could lock up diseases back then, keep them from escaping?* Michael wondered as he walked through the ivy-grown front entrance and up to the visitor's desk. Michelle's room was in one of the newer wings. Fourth floor. Cancer ward. When he found her room, Michelle's husband, Pete, was there sitting at her bedside. The look in his eyes told Michael he'd interrupted something. Their lives, perhaps.

"Hi, Shelly." Michael held a vase of flowers in his hand. "I got these for you." It was an awkward moment.

"Hi, Michael... thank you..." Michelle's voice filtered out calmly and slowly, happily sedate. She lifted a lazy finger, an IV trailing from her wrist. "Put them over there, okay. They're beautiful." Michael had to walk over to the side of the bed where Pete was sitting. "Hi, Pete."

Pete turned to Michelle. "I'm going to get a soda. Do you need anything?" Michelle rolled her head from side to side.

Pete brushed past Michael on his way out. Michael watched him leave. The rift between he and Pete he could live with. It was his sister he was worried about.

Alone now, Michael stood beside his sister's bed. He had to look at her now. Really look. His heart sunk in his chest. He didn't know what to say.

Michelle's skin was a pale yellow, her face gaunt. Purplish half-moons painted the underside of her large brown eyes. She had probably lost forty pounds since Michael had last seen her, which was over a year ago, not since she had first been diagnosed. Perhaps most shocking of all was her hair. How different people looked without their hair—almost inhuman—as if the only thing separating us from the animals was our hairstyles. Her once long, silken brown locks were now nothing more than a couple month's worth of patchy growth. *Concentration Camp Coiffeurs, Styles To Die For,* Michael thought, his mind playing sick word games with him. Michelle's eyes watched him, held him in a steady gaze.

(glaze)

Stop it!

"It's okay, Michael, really... it's all right."

Finally he could speak. "I'm so sorry, Shelly. I should have called you or something. But things were so backed up at work..."

"Michael, I know, you don't have to explain."

"No, really, I should have kept in touch. But after that last time we spoke to each other, after some of the things I said—I was way out of line. I should have never brought that stuff up until you were ready."

"Don't worry about it."

"What do you mean? I do worry about it. I should worry about it. I worry about you."

"It doesn't matter now."

Michael looked at her. That's what she said the last time he'd spoken to her. Nothing had changed, Michael realized, and a lead weight began to sink down into his stomach. And then he thought of something that might help her. "Hey, remember this?"

Michael backed up a few steps. He then enacted a silly pantomime of a man reaching into his pocket.

Michelle stared at him.

"You remember... the Banana Man... on the Captain Kangaroo Show?"

"Michael, I don't know what you're talking about."

"Yes, you do. We used to watch it together. We used to have to sit real close to the TV just so we could hear it because Mom and Dad were always fighting."

She looked at him. Her eyes told all. Like everyone else, she didn't remember the Banana Man either. How was that possible? Michael could understand her not wanting to remember the fighting or the other stuff that happened—especially the other stuff. But that was no reason to blot out your entire childhood. The Banana Man helped them escape. On countless occasions he was their safe haven when the environment they were in had lost its safety. Not remember? They had made it through, damn it! They should be proud of themselves. Remembering was what helped Michael sort it all out. Remembering was the key that unlocked all those mental mysteries.

"Michael, you've got to stop all this nonsense. When are you going to grow up and take responsibility for your life?"

"But I have," Michael told her. "Shelly, I can understand not wanting to remember what Dad did to you, but——"

"Our father was a loving and caring man! Why do you keep doing this?"

"——but don't not remember us in the process, that's all I'm asking. I love you... and now... now you're dying... and all I want is for you to die in peace, okay?"

Michelle was about to respond but she began to cough instead, and Michael hurriedly poured her a cup of water. Pete must have been just outside the door because he came rushing in and took the water from Michael's hand. Michael stood by, helpless, tears straining at his eyes. When Michelle's coughing fit finally died down, her eyes were closed. She was resting. Pete grabbed Michael by the arm and steered him out into the hall.

"Listen, Michael. Your sister hasn't many more days left on this earth, and I would like very much for them to be as calm and peaceful as possible. I would appreciate it if you didn't come by to see her."

"But she's my sister! I'm trying to help her."

"Michael, stop thinking of yourself for once. It upsets her to see you, can't you see that?"

"You don't get it. You weren't there."

"Look, I don't know what's going on with you, and frankly I don't care. But keep it away from here. If you love your sister, you'll do that——for her sake."

Pete turned and re-entered Michelle's room, leaving Michael alone in the hall. He had stopped listening after Pete had told him not to come by and see her. Instead, he heard the music again——that strange, lilting, sick calliope music. Even more strange was the fact that it sounded as if it were being broadcast over the hospital speakers.

When Michael arrived home he found a note with a key taped to it on his kitchen table. *Michael, here's the key to the apartment. I found all my stuff. Thanks for everything. Hope things work out for you. Lisa.*

He crumpled the paper up and threw it into the garbage, key and all.

Damn you! Damn all of you!

That night, when he went to bed, he tried not to dream. But the Banana Man was there just the same, waiting for him... reaching one of his big, bulky hands inside one of those big coat pockets... reaching in and pulling out...

What?

By the middle of the week, it began to eat at him.

At work, Michael's desk seemed to shrink beneath the clutter, prompting a sit-down chat with his boss who stressed the importance of efficiency and organization, and how time was money, and if one more client was lost due to misplaced paperwork, Michael would need to seek alternative employment...

eat at him

Like the emptiness of his apartment... like the vacancy in his heart now that Lisa was gone...

eat at him

At night, when the city lights dimmed and the dark became a playground for his thoughts, flashing childhood atrocities upon the walls of his bedroom, to be played over and over again, forward, backward, in slow-mo: the cowering shadow of his mother being beaten in the next room, her cries for help drowned out by the volume of the television set; the shadow of his father poised at the top of the stairs—poised before sliding in the direction of his sister's bedroom...

eat at him

Like the dream of the Banana Man, and his hand reaching into his pocket, each time coming closer and closer to revealing what was inside... the hem of a cuff... the first glimpse of a glove... something dark within the palm of that glove... a shape, an implement...

eat at him

The way a cancer must feel, like a piece of yourself broken free inside your body with a mind all its own and a solitary urge to eat, eat its way toward daylight...

By the end of the week, Michael had had enough. He could feel the time slipping, the opportunity for resolve passing him by. He had to see his sister again. This time no questions, no pleas for understanding. Just be there for her, like he wasn't in recent years. To hold her hand before it slipped away. Forever.

It was late when he finally left work. He'd stayed well past seven and still hadn't made a noticeable dent in the paperwork. At this point, he didn't particularly care.

He drove to Mercy Hospital, stopping first to pick up some more flowers—roses this time, only roses. Love everlasting. When he reached the fourth floor and entered his sister's room, her bed was empty.

His first thought was that she had been moved. He walked over to the nurses station and asked the young lady behind the counter where Michelle Richards had been moved to. The young lady turned to an older woman behind her, but the older woman was already on her feet.

"Are you a friend of the family?"

"I'm her brother," Michael said. The expressions on the two women's faces still hadn't registered the way they were supposed to. Then the older woman spoke.

"I'm so sorry, but your sister passed away this morning."

(the words... he understood the words but)

"This morning? Why didn't anyone call me?"

(he heard himself respond, felt the movement of his jaw, but he still didn't understand the first part, the part about his sister passing away)

"I'm sorry, sir. Mr. Richards made all the arrangements. You needn't worry. Your sister's last hours were very peaceful."

(passed away... passed... away)

"Peaceful?" He looked at both women in amazement. "No, no, they weren't peaceful. They couldn't have been." He turned on numb legs and walked away.

Halfway down the hall a voice called after him. "Sir! Your roses——"

But Michael kept walking, his feet gaining speed, past the strangers waiting at the elevator, until he reached the stairwell. He had to get out of there fast, get some air.

Once on the street, he decided to walk, just walk, get some feeling back into his legs. Tomorrow, he'd catch a bus and pick up his car, or whatever, whenever. Right now he just needed time to think.

He walked slowly beneath the street lights, their overhead glow like the cold light of a refrigerator, without pretense. It seemed fitting. All he could see in his mind was Michelle's face from when he last saw her. That look of... of what? Acceptance?

It doesn't matter now.

For her, maybe, he thought. She was his only sibling, and that made the loss all the more irretrievable. With her gone, he was now an only child. She had always been there to share the pain. Now, he was left to face it alone.

But he wasn't alone. He could hear footsteps behind him.

He didn't pay attention to them at first, but something made him finally stop and turn.

There was nothing there.

Across the street, a young couple walked arm-in-arm in the opposite direction. Aside from them, the sidewalks were empty. The streets were empty. Then, suddenly, a taxi blew by, running the red light which had just changed, startling Michael, and everything returned to normal again. He walked on.

He crossed into the west end of the city. Low rent, high crime. The buildings around him deteriorated to tenement housing and graffiti-scrawled store fronts. He had just passed a fenced-in playground area when he heard the footsteps again.

Again, he turned. This time, backlit by a street lamp at the last corner, he saw a shadow looming large and distorted against the brick face of a building.

It was stupid for him to be out here like this; he was just asking for trouble. But a part of him didn't care. It was the other part that turned his legs around.

He cut across the street and picked up the pace, reversing his direction back toward the hospital. After a block's worth of solitude he dismissed the footsteps and began to think about his sister again.

...our father was a loving and caring man...

...stop thinking of yourself for once...

...your sister's last hours were very peaceful...

He shook his head, fighting back the tears that threatened to engulf him. *I could have helped her. I could have been there for her all this time*, he thought.

But he'd let his work consume him. It had consumed his relationship with Lisa, with Michelle, and now it was working on consuming him.

But the work was only a mask for the real culprit. The real culprit was—

Footsteps.

Again.

Behind him.

Only now they didn't sound like the steady gate of a person. They were more like the half-step movements of the disabled.

Or the capering steps of a clown!

That sudden irrational thought raised the hair on the back of his neck, and without looking back Michael broke into a slow jog. Just a few more blocks and he'd be back at the hospital. Back to his car. Then home, behind the safety of his own four walls.

He jogged until his breath became ragged and yet, impossibly, above his own jarring footfalls and the hammering of his heart, he could still hear the shufflings behind him. In fact, it sounded as if they were gaining on him.

At the next corner he panicked and ducked into an alleyway—only to find that it was a dead-end. A large dumpster sat against the back wall; it was his only camouflage. He ran for it. But he didn't have time to climb inside. Instead, he ducked down tight beside it, hoping that if he were very still he wouldn't be seen. He held his breath as he watched the entrance to the alley.

What appeared was like something out of a dream, and it nearly stopped his heart: the stark silhouette of a man in a baggy suit. The Banana Man.

The Banana Man capered down the alley, paralyzing him with fear. Halfway, the Banana Man's hand was reaching into one of those many pockets.

Michael clamped his eyes shut. That's when he heard the music in the air—that eerie melody he used to hear when he was a kid watching television, watching while his parents fought in the next room. He remembered trying to become part of the television set to escape the loud, angry voices. Even as a child of seven he remembered wondering what it would be like not to be living. Not to necessarily be dead—just something like on TV, something other than the living hell he and his sister were going through...

A hand tapped him on the shoulder and his eyes bolted open.

The streetlight was blocked by the body of the figure standing before him. Half-bent, the Banana Man held out his arm in a supplicatory gesture. One bulky gloved hand flipped over and opened up. The Banana Man nodded when Michael took the gift from his hand, then capered away into the night.

The alley was suddenly quiet—quiet but for the dying calliope music that still lingered in the air. Michael stared at the gift in his hand and nearly laughed. No, it wasn't a banana, or a gun, or a knife, as he had feared. It was a long plastic rectangle with a series of buttons on it: a TV remote.

Michael got to his feet and slowly walked back to the hospital, where he got into his car and drove home.

It was late. Michael sat cross-legged on the floor in front of the television set. The room went dark then bright again with each switch of a channel. He was searching... searching. He finally settled upon one channel in particular and put the remote aside, and in the emptiness of his apartment he began to talk.

"I'm sorry I wasn't with you," he said, eyes transfixed upon the screen. "Is everything all right?... That's good... No, things didn't work out between Lisa and I... Too busy... But all that's going to change... I'll find someone else... I know... It's not good to be alone... But I have you now... We have each other... And nothing is ever going to come between us again... I promise..."

He stopped now and then to listen as the blank snow-filled screen flickered before him. He nodded. A smile touched his lips. He talked long into the night.

He had a lot of catching up to do.

DEAD DOGS

HARLEY NEAL OPENED THE SCREEN door and slipped out into the warm June night. Her daddy was asleep—finally—the television flickering and muttering its late night nonsense. She hurried down the porch steps.

The near-full moon hung low, just above the treetops. The high-pitched buzz of crickets and katydids filled the air. She continued down the rutted dirt drive to the main road. There she waited. "C'mon Beau... Where the hell are you?" She chewed her gum, snapping it once in the dark. The tall trees crowded around her.

For a moment she felt alone beneath the moon and the stars. There came the hoot of an owl, followed by the rustle of an animal in the woods. She picked up a stone and tossed it in the direction of the sound. Whatever it was fled. Seconds later, she heard the drone of an engine in the distance. Headlights lit up the night. A black pickup truck slowed and rolled to a stop in front of her; a country beat boomed softly inside. The dashboard illuminated her boyfriend's smile. He winked. She got in.

They drove to their usual spot, a willow grove up near Potters Creek, and parked. Beau turned off the ignition but kept the radio on. They kissed and began touching each other. Just as Harley was about to give herself to him, once again she pulled away, adjusting her tank top to cover herself. "How come we never go anywhere public?" she said.

Beau sat back and took a deep breath. He looked at her. "You know why, Harley. It's because I'm captain of the baseball team. There's a lot of expectations on me... the State Championship... college... the pros. My parents just wouldn't understand me being with a girl like you."

"Because I'm piss-poor white trash? Is that why? You know I don't like it when you ignore me in school."

"Harley, that's *them* talking, not me. You know I love you. I'm risking everything coming out here to meet you. After graduation, it will be different, you'll see. When I go away to college I'm taking you with me."

"You promise?"

"I promise."

"Scout's honor?"

He held up two fingers and gave her puppy dog eyes.

"Hope to die?"

He crossed his heart.

A grin tugged at the corner of her mouth. She felt her heart giving in again. "I love you so much, Beauregard LaFollette."

"I love you too, Harley Neal. Now c'mere and let me show you just how much."

Harley giggled as he pulled her onto his lap. Their mouths met and she let herself melt into him.

Two hours later, Beau dropped her back at her house and took off into the night. She walked weak-legged up the driveway in a euphoric haze. She didn't see the creature perched on the rooftop. At least not until the hair stood up on her arms. She looked up.

For a second, she thought she saw a very large owl perched above the porch, its eyes reflecting the light of the moon. But when she stopped, there was nothing there. It was then she realized there were no insect noises. The night was as still as death.

She hurried toward the house... then fell, sprawling onto the hard-packed dirt of the driveway. Gravel bit into her palms. She looked to see what she had tripped over. It was the body of an animal. A dog. A mangy stray. She kicked at it as she scrambled to her feet.

Again, she stared into the woods, and thought she saw the same twin reflections, this time high up in the branches of a hickory tree. She heard a whisper of a voice that sounded like air bleeding out of a radiator. It was spoken as if close up to her ear. "He's cheating on you," the voice said. Once again, goosebumps danced across her arms.

She ran into the house and locked the door behind her. The goosebumps remained even when she crawled into bed and wrapped herself in a blanket.

When Harley awoke the next morning, the first thing she did was go to the kitchen window and see if the dead dog was there in the driveway. She stared at the dirt where it had been. It was gone.

"Hey, baby-girl, you're up early."

Harley jumped as her father came up behind her and placed a dirty breakfast plate in the sink. She turned to him.

"Dad—have you been outside yet?"

"Nope. Why?"

She stared out the window again. "Nothing. I have to get ready for school."

Woodfield High School's football team usually got all the attention, but this year, with Beau LaFollette as their ace pitcher and leading RBI producer, it was the baseball team getting all the press these days. The Nighthawks were headed for the State Championships for the first time in thirty-five seasons, and LaFollette was the reason why. When Beau walked through the school's hallways, he left a trail of high fives and adoring smiles in his wake. His good looks and athletic physique was desired by most of the feminine half of the student body, and even by some of the males. As Harley stood at her locker with her best friend Leann, she was thinking just that. On the one hand, it made her feel kind of special that Beau had chosen her to be his girl, and on the other hand, it pained her to see all these other girls fawning over him thinking they had a chance. There were many times she wanted to shout out loud, "I'm in love with Beauregard LaFollette and he's in love with me! So, hands off!" But she knew it would ruin things between them. She could still feel his hands on her from the night before, touching her in all the places she liked.

"What are you grinning at?" Her best friend Leann looked in the direction of Harley's gaze.

"Nothing. Just somebody."

"Beau LaFollette? You're kidding me right? Ew."

"What? You don't think a boy like that would like me?" Harley turned to her friend, grin now gone.

"Yeah, he'd like you. For one night." Leann grabbed her books and shut her locker. "Wait, you're not serious, are you?"

"So what if I am? You think he'd cheat on someone like me?"

Leann stared at her. "Oh, my God, Harley, you and him didn't..."

Harley rolled her eyes. "No."

"Oh, my God, you *did*. When? Tell me."

Leann had her by the shoulders now. Harley debated whether to tell or not, but the debate didn't last long. She had to tell someone or else she'd burst.

"Every Thursday night for the past three weeks."

"Oh, my God, where?"

"Out by Potter's Creek. He picks me up, we go there, we park..." The grin was back.

"You little whore! I'm so envious. So how come you guys aren't *together* together."

"It's just our little secret for now. We'll be *together* together after graduation. You have to promise me you won't tell anyone."

"Okay."

"Promise!"

"I won't. I promise. Oh, my God. You have to tell me everything."

"I will."

Leann stared at her, mouth half open, trying to keep from smiling. Harley had a hard time keeping a straight face, too.

Down the hall, Beau was surrounded by friends. They laughed and joked. Harley saw that one of the girls in the group was Nicole Madison. She was standing a little too close to Beau. She kept flipping her blond hair and batting her blue eyes like she was posing for pictures. And laughing way too much. And putting her hand on Beau's chest, and touching his arm. Beau looked Harley's way and frowned. Harley noticed Leann was staring him down and elbowed her.

"Would you quit it!"

"Sorry. It just doesn't look like he's not making much of an attempt to keep Nicole from pawing him up and down. I wonder what else he lets her do?"

"Shut up! I should have never told you." Harley turned and slammed her locker shut.

"All I know is I wouldn't stand for that."

"Well you don't know what we have. That's all show. What we have is real."

"Okay. Whatever you say. My lips are sealed."

Before they could get into a fight, the warning bell rang. Harley and Leann headed off to class with promises of calling each other later. Harley's class was in the direction of Beau's. She watched him walk down the hall, his friends peeling off one by one, until only Nicole Madison was left. They rounded the corner together.

Sitting in History class, all Harley could think about was Beau and

Nicole together... in empty classrooms, out in Beau's pickup, in the Sanders Field dugout.

All I know is I wouldn't stand for it.

Why did she stand for it? While every other couple was proud to be on display for all to see, she was kept invisible. She knew she wasn't anything great to look at, but maybe everyone would finally see her if Beau only acknowledged her. It wasn't fair.

Guys are nothin' but dogs, her momma used to say, cigarette smoke curling up around her dirty blond hair. And when she'd say it her daddy would grin. And if her momma caught him grinning, he'd slink off into the living room, beer in hand, tail between his legs. Harley missed her momma. It was a year ago she was put in the ground, only two months after the doctors told her she had cancer rotting up her insides. Her momma didn't give a damn and smoked right up until the end.

The class bell rang and Harley hurried out to intercept Beau on his way to his Industrial Arts class. She was waiting at the bottom of the stairwell.

"Are you sleeping with her?" she said, confronting him.

Beau told his friends to go on ahead; when they did, he grabbed Harley's arm and pulled her under the stairwell.

"What are you talking about?"

"Nicole and her 'Oh, Beau, you're so wonderful' act."

"Shhhh... keep it down."

"Why? You afraid someone might hear us and actually see us together?"

"Harley! She's just a friend."

"I saw you two. She can barely keep her hands off you."

"Yeah, and what was I doing? Was I touching her back?"

"Well, you weren't telling her to stop."

"What do you want me to do? She likes me."

"And I *love* you... and I thought you loved me. But you'd rather be seen with her. How do you think that makes me feel?"

"I'm sorry. You know it's just you and only you."

"Then tell everyone."

"Harley, you know I can't do that."

"If you won't tell, maybe I will."

"Now you're talking crazy."

She stepped back. "So now I'm crazy? Well, you better watch out then 'cause crazy people do crazy things."

"What's that supposed to mean?"

Harley didn't answer him. Instead, she stormed out through the double doors leading into the rear parking lot. Beau didn't follow her. He had appearances to keep up, after all.

But the minute Harley walked away, she felt sorry she had confronted him. What was she thinking? Instead of anger now she just felt like crying. What was wrong with her?

As she stood in the parking lot, tears obscuring her sight, she felt the hairs on her arm rise. She looked across the parking lot where Sander's Field began. In the distant woods she saw something large and black sitting in the trees.

Guys are nothing but dogs...

It was impossible but the words entered her head as if they were her own thoughts... but the voice wasn't hers.

She quickly looked to see if anyone else was nearby to help confirm what she was seeing. But there was no one. And whatever was in the trees in the distance was now gone.

But the voice in her ear lingered. If she wasn't mistaken, it sounded exactly like her mother's voice.

The weekend came and went. Harley left messages on Beau's cell until it was full. She waited by the phone but Beau didn't call her back. He was angry; she knew it. She had done exactly what he had warned her not to do. But it didn't feel like it was her doing. That thing on the porch that night, and again in the trees at school—it was in her head, twisting her thoughts, making her do these things. She wanted to explain but it just sounded crazy. More crazy than her actions.

Monday she didn't go to school, afraid to see Beau's face. It was noon when she woke up. Her daddy was off to work at the auto repair garage in town. The dishes were piled high in the sink. The house was a mess. When her mother was alive the house was at least kept clean. Now everything was falling apart.

She stood at the sink drinking a glass of cold water. A slight breeze blew through the window screen like warm breath on her face. She looked out and saw a dog walking up the driveway. Another stray. Its tongue hung to the side, saliva dripping off the end.

Harley grabbed a mixing bowl and filled it with water. When she stepped out the front door, the dog stopped in its tracks. It stared at her, panting. The dog didn't move as she slowly approached. She placed the bowl on the ground and backed away. She sat on the porch steps, waiting. The dog finally walked up to the bowl and began lapping up the water.

Harley thought about Beau. She couldn't help but think about Beau. Why hadn't he called her? She figured he would at least have the balls to talk to her, tell her it was over, and not just leave her abandoned like this, like some poor stray dog.

You're not the only one he takes there.

The air was warm but immediately the skin on her arms rippled with gooseflesh. She couldn't move. The thing was back. She felt it watching her, gauging her reaction. It had some kind of control over her she didn't quite understand.

He tells all of them the same lies.

She held her hands over her ears, but the voice slipped right though, like a snake in the grass.

He doesn't love you.

A pickax leaned against the tool shed. She walked over and picked it up. She walked to the dog and hefted the pickax over her head. The dog had stopped drinking. Harley saw her reflection in the bowl of water. In the trees above her shoulder she saw a black blot like a collection of rotted leaves.

"What the hell am I doing?" she said, throwing the pickax aside. She backed up until she sat down on the porch steps crying.

There came a screech in the trees above and something swooped down and grabbed the dog, lifting it up and out of sight, spilling the water. Harley looked to where the dog had been just moments before. Water spilled out of the metal bowl, staining the dried dirt. She heard a distant yelp and the dog came falling out of the sky, hitting the ground near her with a sickening thud.

Harley couldn't move. She stared at the dog. Its legs were twisted and broken; splintered ribs protruded from its side.

Why? It didn't have to kill the dog, she thought. Because she wouldn't kill it herself?

Her paralysis broke and she got up from the steps angry. She shouted at the sky, "What do you want?"

But there was nothing but bright blue. Nothing in the trees. But she knew it was there, waiting, listening. At last, the voice said, *Tonight he'll be there.*

Then it was gone, erased from her senses. The vacuum it created was mind-numbing.

Harley stood in the middle of the driveway, alone, abandoned. She was no longer afraid. She knew what she had to do.

First, she grabbed the pickax and dragged the dead dog into the back yard, where she buried it in a shallow grave.

"So tell me again why we're driving out here this late? And why you brought that pickax?"

Leann drove her parents' car. Harley had called her to ask for a favor. They were on their way to Potter's Creek.

"It's Beau."

"He's cheating on you, right? Parking at the same place you two go?"

Harley's silence confirmed Leann's suspicions.

"What a lying piece of shit."

Harley stared straight ahead. Did everyone know but her? Was she the only one who believed Beau when he said "I love you"?

Harley bowed her head. "That's what I want to find out."

"But Harley, you're scaring me... a pickax? C'mon, don't do anything stupid. He's not worth it."

"I just want to scare him, that's all. I just want whoever else he's doing this to, to know what kind of animal he is." She held the pickax handle between her legs, the echo of the voice she had heard earlier in the day still fresh in her mind.

Leann slowed as they approached the willow grove. The "monster trees", as they were commonly referred to in childhood—due to their tall, hairy appearance, looked silver beneath the light of the full moon. As predicted, Beau's pickup truck was there, its bed sticking out from behind a pair of tree trunks. Leann pulled up right behind it. The car's headlights illuminated two people inside, hurriedly getting dressed. Harley got out of the car, pickax in hand.

What happened next was unexpected. Beau started the engine and the pickup took off, fishtailing around the twin willows and cutting back toward the road. Harley jumped into Leann's car and told her to go after him. Harley wanted to know which girl he was with.

They chased him along Potters Creek Road toward Route 44. The road was narrow. Thick woods gave way to tall grass and scrub pine as the two vehicles raced along in the night. A full moon kept a steady pace along with them. Beau's speed increased, and the gap between them lengthened.

"C'mon, Leann, we have to keep up!" Harley gripped the pickax handle like a divining rod.

"Harley, I'm afraid. Just let him go. He's stupid and a coward. Let's just go home."

It was then, as the two of them watched Beauregard LaFollette's black pickup race away, they saw what looked like a dog run out from scrub onto the road, right in the path of Beau's front wheels. The pickup swerved, hit the soft shoulder, fishtailed for a moment before its wheels caught the pavement and flipped. The pickup rolled several times. A door flew open on one of the rolls and a body was thrown onto the road. At last, the truck came to a stop. So did Leann.

Harley and Leann sat in the car, headlights illuminating the accident. The truck lay on its side, its engine steaming. Broken glass glittered on the pavement. Harley felt a twinge and looked out toward the moon. She caught a glimpse of something large flying in the night sky. The twinge dissipated—or, more accurately, discharged. Harley knew the visits by the thing and its voice were over. At least for now.

"Harley, what should we do?"

Harley turned to her friend. "Go home."

Leann nodded. She shakily backed her parents' car onto the shoulder and made a U-turn.

When Leann dropped Harley back home they promised each other not to say a word. This was a promise Harley knew Leann would keep.

Alone now, the sound of Leann's car fading in the distance, Harley heard the cricket sounds once again. She looked up at the night sky and saw so many stars. The moonlight lent everything an ethereal glow.

Inside the house she could see the television light flickering.

She walked up the driveway, her thoughts on her mother.

She no longer felt so abandoned, so alone.

Trunk Story

WILLIAM WARD CRAFT SAT AT the back of the banquet hall, eyeing the trunk on the stage. He was alone at a small table, a drink nestled between his aging hands. Few in the publishing industry had expected him to show up tonight, even though he lived in a large country farmhouse just an hour's drive from the city. And even fewer had expected him to actually contribute a story, let alone help produce the book that would honor the man who ruined his career.

But William Ward Craft was a nice guy, and a damn good horror writer to boot. Once a respected figure in the genre, writing such memorable stories as "Spider House" and "The Well-Wishers," he was called "a master of quiet horror." "Quiet" indicating heavy on mood and atmosphere with a minimal amount of blood spilled. It was the path traveled by all the great writers in the field: M.R. James, Algernon Blackwood, on up through Ray Bradbury, Shirley Jackson, and Charles L. Grant. Where blacks and grays and the whisper of the unknown carried more weight and dread than the color of blood and brain matter. Where poetic grace and a mastery of the language cut deeper than any knife, hatchet, or chainsaw.

Craft had it, and when an upstart publishing company offered to publish his long-overdue first collection back in the late '80s, Craft took a chance and agreed. The young publisher was James Brian Bailey, the publishing house, Fever Dream Books. Fever Dream grew into one of the hottest specialty publishers in the genre, and over the next twenty years launched the careers of many of today's top horror writers—including the tops of them all, Jack Youngblood—while leaving some writers behind. William Ward Craft being one of them.

A young woman stared at Craft from a table nearby. She quickly turned away, whispering to her date and shaking her head. He'd received several of these looks from tonight's attendees, most of whom were twenty years his junior. Curiosity pinched their brow as their brains struggled to place a name with the face. Most ultimately decided that if they didn't know who he was, he must not be very important.

But they didn't know what William Ward Craft was capable of. Until last night, even he didn't know what he was capable of.

The lights went down. Twin spotlights hit the stage. One shone upon the trunk, while the other tracked a man casually walking up to the microphone, the MC of tonight's special event, none other than Jack Youngblood himself, the man who owed the largest debt to Bailey and Fever Dream Books. All stood and applauded. All except one.

"Good evening, folks," Youngblood began, his trademark sweatshirt-with-sleeves-rolled-up image jettisoned in favor of a classy-looking tuxedo. *He could afford it now, so why not?* thought Craft, watching the man who was leading the horror genre toward oblivion.

"In the fifteen years since I've known James…"

Blah, blah, blah. We all love the hand that feeds us. Tell us something we don't know. Craft grit his teeth. The few he had left. He sipped his drink in the dark as Youngblood spewed his well-rehearsed sincerity.

"By the summer of '91, recently divorced, out of work, barely able to scrape enough cash together to pay the electric bill, let alone the postage to send manuscripts out, I had nearly given up writing."

Several audience members elicited groans of disbelief, as if it made them physically ill to think how close they came to a world without Jack Youngblood's stories.

"And then a letter showed up in my mailbox. It was from Fever Dream Books. James wanted to publish my apocalyptic zombie novel, *The Inheritors*."

There was scattered applause and a couple of whoops.

"He had tried to call but my phone had been disconnected."

Laughter.

"And I couldn't call him…"

More laughter.

The rest of Youngblood's introduction was lost on Craft the moment he heard the words "The Inheritors." Craft clearly recalled James Brian Bailey's attempt to explain the rejection of his follow-up short story collection.

The genre is changing, William. Quiet just doesn't sell anymore. The Inheritors is my fastest-selling title to date. It's what the readers want. I'd be foolish to ignore that fact. Try me again with something edgier. Take care, old friend.

The Inheritors was nothing more than Romero's Dawn of the Dead put to words, with shorter sentences and a faster pace. So fast the readers couldn't see the flaws. *Take one part Matheson, two parts Bloch, add a dash of Leiber, now don't forget your blood and filth, shake and stir, and pour over ice picks, hedge trimmers, nail guns, and whatever else you can find at the hardware store, and feed it to the seething, slavering masses...*

Craft stared at the new king of horror, at the attentive gazes on the faces of those seated nearby, their ears tuned like Pavlov's dogs to his every word, and the fire of his ulcer burned so hot in his gut he felt faint.

He squeezed his eyes shut until he saw tiny flashes of light. He needed to lie down, get some rest. But he had to stay awake, or he'd miss the finale. The readers wanted something edgier? Well, tonight they were going to get it.

"And, so, with nothing further to say—I know, can you believe it?—I give you the man of the hour—hell, the man of the decade—James... Brian... Bailey!"

Chairs scraped along the carpeted floor, bodies stood, sharp applause like picture windows shattering assaulted Craft's ears. His heart hesitated momentarily before deciding to beat again. The wall of people remained standing. Waiting. Time stretched and still no James Brian Bailey. The applause began to wane.

Craft remembered the day Jack Youngblood contacted him, a brief letter asking if he'd contribute something to a special twentieth anniversary anthology collecting contributions from all the writers published by Fever Dream Books to be given as a gift to Bailey at a special banquet held in his honor.

"Anything... a trunk story, if that's all you've got."

Craft was stung by Youngblood's insinuation that all he had left were trunk stories. All the years of hurt and resentment and self-imposed isolation came tumbling forth. But instead of an angry rebuke, Craft not only agreed to contribute an original story (the first in nearly two decades), he offered to assist with the book's production. After all, Craft had owned and operated a small publishing venture for nearly five years in the early 90s to help authors like himself, shut out by the industry's move toward more explicit horror. So when Youngblood came down with appendicitis and was hospitalized, with the project in the final stages of production, it was up to Craft to complete the job.

Craft seized the moment as one would a golden ticket. It was his chance to show the world that he still had one great story to tell. It was his idea that the finished books arrive at the banquet hall in a trunk.

Youngblood's amplified voice snapped Craft out of his reverie.

The trunk still sat center stage, untouched.

"Is he in the bathroom?" Youngblood asked, looking toward the wings. The audience laughed. "James? Oh, James? Did anyone tell him it was tonight?"

More laughter. *The kind of laughter that comes from mindlessly adoring fans,* thought Craft, *from zombified fools in love with the fleetingly popular.*

By now, the applause had all but stopped. People were taking their seats again. The crowd obviously suspected that this was part of the show. James Brian Bailey would suddenly descend from the ceiling, or was sitting out in the audience all along, or—

"Open the trunk!"

The shout came from the back. Heads turned but no one could identify from whom the raspy call had come. It was soon followed by others calling to open the trunk. The trunk was definitely large enough to hold a person.

On stage, a smile painted Youngblood's face. "Hmmm..." He eyed the trunk. "Maybe we should all just take a break." He tiptoed over to where the trunk sat. "Obviously James was held up in traffic." He pointed to the trunk and mouthed the words *He's in there, right?* "But because we all have places to go—and time is money—we'll just have to proceed without him. So... It gives me great pleasure to present this gift, in absentia, to James Brian Bailey!"

The audience stood again and applauded. Youngblood quickly unsnapped the latches of the trunk and lifted the lid. Youngblood slowly reached in and pulled out what appeared to be a book to show to the audience.

Even from the back of the room, Craft saw the revulsion ripple across Youngblood's expression. The book lay limp in Youngblood's hand like a large uncooked steak.

Craft smiled, reveling in his ingenuity... the call to Bailey's hotel room the night before, inviting him out for a drink... the long drive back home, a drugged Bailey leaning against the passenger door... to his farmhouse basement to cut and print and press... twenty-six lettered copies... "covers" made of skin, sewn onto "books" made of flesh... the title, TRUNK STORIES, carved in block letters along the spine of each... placed in a large treasure chest-style trunk to be shipped the next morning to the banquet hall…

The copy Youngblood held was particularly special, for it bore the facial likeness of James Brian Bailey staring out in a terror-stricken bas-relief.

Craft at last stood, applauding in the stunned silence. "*The End!*" he shouted, with a peculiar glee.

The book slipped from Youngblood's hands and hit the stage with a sickening slap, spraying the front row with droplets of blood.

Craft continued to smile and applaud as the banquet hall filled with screams.

Nature Walk

THE SKILLET SIZZLED—onions, peppers, thick sausages glossy with grease...

Brattleboro State Park surrounded her—tall pines, wood smoke, Aunt Maggie, Uncle George, cousins Denise, Penny and Bud, Mom and Dad, and Uncle Robert. Aunt Maggie and Uncle George were underneath the awning of the camper sitting in their lawn chairs, enjoying the last of the autumn sun while the food cooked inside. Denise and Penny were helping Mom—Aunt Carol to them—with setting the picnic table. Dad was preparing the fire for when the sun went down. Bud was poking at the sausages on the Coleman stove which sat outside on a makeshift table because Aunt Maggie didn't like cooking "greasy stuff" inside the camper. Uncle Robert... well, Uncle Robert was always nearby.

"Mom, can't somebody else do this?" Bud whined. "This grease is getting to me." He coughed when he got no response.

"That's why it's out there instead of in here," Aunt Maggie reminded everyone with a point of her finger. "George, you and your sausages..."

"I just love 'em, darling... like I love you." Uncle George leaned over and gave his lips a pout. Aunt Maggie swatted him and everybody laughed.

"Ma," Bud persisted.

"*All right, all right.* Maybe your cousin, Lisa, will want to take over?"

"*Yes!*" Bud said with a pull of his fist, and jabbed the cooking fork into the top of a nearby tree stump.

"Lisa, take over for your cousin. Seeing that you won't eat meat, the least you can do is help cook it," Lisa's mother announced, a hint of disapproval in her voice.

"Now, Carol, Lisa's entitled to her preferences," said Lisa's father.

"What? Lisa doesn't eat meat?" The look on Aunt Maggie's face said, "My children eat what's put in front of them, no if's, and's or but's." She and Uncle George exchanged looks. Carol was going soft in her old age, letting her children—oops, sorry—child run the roost. But then it wasn't Lisa's fault she was an only child.

"*Lisa's a vegetarian... Lisa's a vegetarian...*" This came from Denise and Penny who sidled up to Lisa's mother as if they were all against her. Then Bud added: "*Get the veterinarian... give Lisa a Cesarean...*"

"Come on now, you're embarrassing her," Uncle Robert chimed in, and smiled at Lisa's red cheeks. Lisa got up off the rock she was sitting on, brushed the dirt from her behind, and dusted off her hands. She gave Uncle Robert a dirty look, but Uncle Robert's smile only widened. "*Heeere she is... Miss Amerrrica...,*" he sang.

Why did they have to go on this stupid camping trip, anyway? thought Lisa, as she stepped around the tree stump to stand over the sizzling frying pan. She was getting a little too old for this. She grabbed the double-pronged cooking fork and poked at the sausages, moving them around, turning them over. The smell of onions and grease engulfed her, making her queasy. She stared at the sausages, at their elongated shapes, their glistening skins. She had stopped eating meat over a year ago, ever since—

She looked up. Uncle Robert was staring at her. She stared back, unblinking. He smiled and looked away.

"Mom, can I go for a walk before supper?" Bud asked.

"Yeah, me too."

"And me too," his sisters quickly added.

"Definitely not! There're bears out there!"

"Oh, Maggie, let 'em work up an appetite. This is a vacation, remember? They're supposed to be having fun."

"Oh, all right—but supper'll be ready in half an hour. Stay together."

"Sure Mom."

"Sure Mom."

"*Yes!*" And all three were gone, down the trail and into the woods.

"Lisa, how 'bout you? Maybe a walk will do you some good. You've been sulking all day." Lisa's mother had an unopened packet of paper plates in her hand. Her eyes meant well.

"Nature walk," Uncle Robert announced, getting up. "Come on, Leese."

"Thank you, Robert."

"No, Mom, I don't feel like it," Lisa said, gripping the fork in her hand.

"Oh, come now, you and Robert used to always go for walks in the woods. Or has our little girl outgrown such things?" This was for the ears of Aunt Maggie and Uncle George.

"I'll go if Dad goes," Lisa said, playing her last card—

"Oh, no dear—"

—and losing.

"—I'm a little too pooped out. You and Robert go. Have a nice time."

"I'll try and have her back before eleven," Uncle Robert said, and they all laughed together. Uncle George, Aunt Maggie, Mom, Dad. Uncle Robert was so funny sometimes, always there to make light. Always there.

"Well, go on, Lisa. I'll keep an eye on the sausages."

Lisa looked at her mother. Why did her mother resent her so? Couldn't she see what was going on? Lisa looked to her father. *Dad?*

Lisa's father was crouched in front of the fire, snapping kindling wood into perfect lengths, arranging them in perfect order.

Aunt Maggie?

Aunt Maggie had gone into the camper to check on everything.

Uncle George?

Uncle George sat reading his Road Atlas.

"*Lee-sa!*" Uncle Robert. He had his jacket on and was already halfway down the trail.

"Lisa, don't make your uncle wait," Lisa's mother said, arranging the picnic table until it was just so.

Lisa stared at the sausages frying before her. *I wish he'd burn in hell... I wish he'd burn in hell...* She jabbed at the thick links and made them bleed greasy blood. She looked up at the tall trees that surrounded her and fought back tears. The sky was a gray overcast. The air was turning colder. It would be dark soon. *There're are bears out there.* The fork she gripped in her hand felt strong, almost a part of her.

"*Leeee-sa!*"

"I'm coming!" she yelled to Uncle Robert. "Let me get my jacket first!"

Lisa hurried into the camper, past Uncle George and Aunt Maggie, and grabbed her jacket.

"Be careful out there," Aunt Maggie said.

"I will, Aunt Maggie, I will," Lisa said. She passed by the little makeshift cooking table on her way towards the trail. "Mom, don't forget Uncle George's sausages."

"Okay."

"See ya, Mom."

The tone in Lisa's voice made her mother look up.

Lisa stood with her hands in her coat pockets; there was a nervous grin on her face. "Sorry if I've been a pain lately," she said.

Lisa's mother smiled. "Have a nice walk."

She watched her daughter skip down the trail to catch up with her favorite uncle. *Just when I begin to worry*, she thought, and shook her head, smiling to herself.

She finished setting the table, then checked George's sausages. She turned down the heat and looked for something to turn them with. She checked the table, the ground, even the tree stump, but there was nothing to be found.

"What did they use, their fingers?" she asked no one in particular and headed back towards the camper.

The Dog Park

IT WAS WIDE AND SPRAWLING, if a bit isolated. There were stand-alone trees for marking, walking trails that wound up into the hillside, and a fenced-in area to run free—to meet others, to make friends. And for the humans there were benches to sit on and spectate, while the dogs had their day.

Terry brought her Boston Terrier, Pugsly. "C'mon, Pugs," she said as she opened the car door and stepped out onto the gravel parking area. She attached Pugsly's leash to his collar and the dog jumped down, his nose automatically hitting the ground then lifting into the air.

She had left Pugsly's shock collar home. She didn't want anyone to think she was cruel. The shock collar was her husband Ted's idea. Early on, if Pugsly didn't obey, Ted would beat the dog into submission. Terry had almost left him and taken Pugsly with her, when Ted suggested the collar. It was a compromise. But still she didn't like it. At home, it was if Pugsly was in the army. Sit. Stay. Lie down. Here, at the dog park, he could just be a dog. If Pugsly liked it here, Terry might even tell Ted about it. But until then it was her and Pugsly's little secret.

For the first ten minutes Terry simply strolled along the dirt-worn pathway that circled the park, Pugsly's leash in one hand, her tote bag in the other. In the bag were bottled water and dog treats, and plastic baggies in the event that Pugsly needed to go number two. Pugsly made quick work of marking each and every tree, fountain, and garbage receptacle along the way. How such a small dog could produce so much urine was beyond Terry's understanding. *Dogs must have a reserve bladder somewhere in their bodies,* she thought, *like that extra gallon of gas that seems to sit unnoticed until the gas gauge on the car reads empty.*

Today, just a handful of people were at the park. A young couple with a Pitty pup. An older gentleman walking an old Labrador. A jogger, who didn't appear to have a dog at all. Pugsly kept his opinions to himself for the most part, and was praised for it. "Such a good boy," said Terry, stopping to pat him on the head and scratch his chin each time he didn't bark. Maybe Ted's "discipline" had paid off. But Terry wasn't about to give Ted any credit for it. It was Pugsly's smarts that kept him out of harm's way. Pugsly was the one who had learned and had adapted. Ted was too set in his ways for that.

Terry had at last circled the grounds and approached the enclosed play area. She entered through the double gate and unhooked Pugsly's leash. "Go on! Go play!" Terry said, pointing to nowhere in particular. You're free, she thought. Pugsly looked at her and began to shiver. "It's okay, Pugs, go on!" Pugsly then turned and walked away, nose to the ground. Terry sat on one of the benches just outside the enclosure. She watched Pugsly like a mother watching her child at the playground.

Only Terry didn't want children—at least not with Ted. If he treated Pugsly like an infantryman how would he treat their child?

"Boston Terrier?"

A woman had sat down next to Terry. Terry slid over slightly to preserve her space. "Yes. Pugsly."

"Cute dog. Mine's the goofy-looking mutt over there. Half-

Goldie, half-Greyhound, half God-Knows-What."

"He's not goofy-looking. He's a handsome boy."

"He's a she."

"Oh."

The two women laughed.

"Hi, I'm Anna." The woman held out her hand.

"Terry."

"First time here?"

"Yes. First time anywhere."

Anna studied her. "Don't get out much?"

"No. My husband likes me to stay put."

"I see." Anna nodded.

"I'm sorry," said Terry. "I don't know why I said that. I'm just not myself today."

"Believe me, I know what that's like."

Pugsly ran up to the half-Goldie, half-Greyhound, half God-Knows-What and the two of them froze nose to nose. The mutt's tail wagged like a windshield wiper on high, and so did Pugsly's. The mutt then ran off, Pugsly chasing after.

"Looks like Maggie's made a friend," said Anna.

For the next half hour Pugsly and Maggie played tag, and tug-o-war with a stick. When another dog was introduced to the mix Pugsly and Maggie put the new dog through a series of sniffs and submissions before it could join their exclusive club. Terry felt such joy at watching her little Pugsly so happy and free, without Ted's shadow looming, without the added anxiety of trying to anticipate Ted's bark. She checked the time on her cell phone and gasped. She popped up off the bench and entered the double gate.

"C'mon Pugsly, it's time to go!"

Pugsly peeled away from the other dogs dutifully and Terry attached his leash.

"Same time tomorrow?" said Anna.

"I don't know, maybe." Terry glanced toward the parking lot. Suddenly all she wanted to do was get home. Before she was found out.

"Well, it was nice meeting you," said Anna. She crouched and scratched Pugsly under his chin. "See you handsome boy."

Pugsly danced at the compliment.

"About tomorrow, I'll try," said Terry.

Anna smiled. "I'll be here."

"C'mon Pugsly, let's hurry home."

Ted walked through the door at his usual time with his usual attitude. If it wasn't complaints about the boss, it was complaints about the traffic. And if neither of those two were worth complaining about, he'd find something. Like tonight.

"Hot dogs and beans, again? I thought you were going to make a pot roast?"

"I didn't have time."

"Didn't have time? You're home all day. What were you doing?"

Terry paused in the middle of spooning out the baked beans onto his plate to stare at him. She had rushed home from the dog park, but by the time she had completed her chores there was little time left to make dinner. "Sorry, I got caught up in my book and just lost track." She plopped the spoonful of beans onto his plate much harder than she had intended.

Ted laughed. "You mean that romance crap you read?" He shook his head, picked up his fork and dug in... and proceeded to burn his mouth on the hot beans. "Fuckin'-A!" He dropped the fork and spit out the beans.

Terry couldn't help but let out a giggle.

"You think that's funny? I just burned my fucking mouth!"

Ted rose from the table, picked up the plate and hurled it into the sink, shattering the plate and peppering the backsplash tiles with baked beans. He grabbed Terry by the throat and pushed her up against the stove. "You did that on purpose didn't you?"

Pugsly, who was sitting in his kennel, barked.

"No, Ted, it was an accident."

Pugsly barked again.

"Shut the fuck up!" Ted let Terry go, walked over the kennel and kicked the grilled door where Pugsly was peering out. Instead of barking again, Pugsly growled.

"You're gonna fucking growl at me!" Ted struggled to open the dented kennel door, cursing again. When the door at last opened, he fished Pugsly out by his collar. Ted raised the terrier to eye-level, daring the dog to make another sound. He gripped the collar so tightly, Pugsly could barely swallow let alone breathe.

"Ted, please!" Terry stood with her hand covering her mouth, expecting the worst but unable to do anything about it.

Ted glared at her. He tossed Pugsly to the floor and told the dog to get into its cage. Pugsly obeyed. Ted grabbed his jacket. "I'm going out."

"Where are you going?" Terry tried to stop him, but he pushed past her and slammed the door on the way out. Terry watched him leave the driveway, wheels squealing as they hit the pavement.

Terry crouched in front of the kennel and Pugsly ran into her arms. "It's okay, boy. He's gone now. What a good boy."

But, as she pet Pugsly, Terry couldn't help but notice that her hands were shaking.

It was after midnight when Ted returned. Terry lay on her side, pretending to be asleep. When he crawled into bed, he smelled of cigarettes and alcohol. His stubbly chin scraped against her shoulder. "I'm sorry about earlier," he said, his body spooning her. He cupped her breast and kissed her neck. She felt him grow hard against her rump. Terry remained still, staring at the shadows on the wall. He kissed her neck again, his other hand traveling down to the hem of her nightgown.

"Ted, I'm tired," she said.

"No you're not. If you were tired you'd be sleeping." He said it as if it were a joke she was supposed to laugh at. He got on his knees and the covers sloughed away. He grabbed the band of her panties and pulled them down.

"Ted, please..."

"I said I was sorry..."

Before she could stop him, he had rolled her onto her stomach and was on top of her, pushing her legs apart, his hardness probing for entry. "I love you," he said, as he forced himself inside of her.

For two days Terry didn't leave the house. Unfortunately, what happened the night before wasn't the first time. She would have stayed in bed all day, but she couldn't stand the thought of being in that bed any more than she had to. She lay on the couch instead. She read. And when she couldn't focus on her reading, she watched television, with Pugsly at her side

On the third day she gave Pugsly a bath, got dressed, and went back to the dog park.

Anna was there, as Terry had hoped. They sat and chatted as before, while their two charges chased each other inside the play area.

"Have you been up to the hiking trail?" Anna asked. When Terry gave her a puzzled look, Anna pointed to the woods that skirted the edge of the property.

"No, I haven't," Terry said.

"It's good exercise and actually much cooler than sitting out here in the sun." Anna waved at the air to no avail. "We can keep an eye on our children, too. Want to take a stroll?"

Terry watched Pugsly and Maggie play, oblivious to the world around them. She felt funny leaving him, but these days away from the house were as much for her as they were for him. "Sure. Why not?" she said and grabbed a bottle of water from her tote.

They were on the trail in no time, and Anna was right, it was much cooler in the pines. There was a gentle breeze on the hill, blowing in from the dog park. The trail was close enough to the edge of the woods that one could still see the entire play area.

"I used to take Maggie up here," said Anna. "But I felt bad because she had to be on a leash. So now I leave her with her play pals. I figure this is her chance to run, so why ruin it?" Anna laughed.

Terry nodded. "When my husband's home, Pugsly spends all of his time in a kennel."

"Doesn't he like the dog?"

It was Terry's turn to laugh. "He says he loves Pugsly. But he's got a funny way of showing it."

"You know, I know you're not this kind of person, but some people want pets just so they can have them. It gives them a sense of power and control. I don't know if I could live with a person like that."

Terry stopped abruptly. Anna stopped too. "I'm sorry. Did I say something wrong?" she said. Terry shook her head and pointed. On the trail ahead, a coyote stood. The coyote didn't seem at all interested in them, its eyes were focused instead on the dogs running around inside the play area in the distance below.

"Get out of here!" Anna shouted, stamping her foot. She had a water bottle in her hand, cocked and ready to throw. The coyote stood firm. It even took a step toward the two women. For Terry, the look in the coyote's eyes was reminiscent of Ted when he'd had too much to drink. Meat. That's all she was to him, a place to sink his teeth into, a place to satisfy his hunger.

"Back away slowly," said Anna. Terry was about to run when a tan blur shot through the underbrush and hit the coyote blindside. It was a cougar, sleek and powerful. The coyote barely let out a peep as the cougar's jaws clamped down on its neck with a muted snap. The coyote's body went limp. The cougar eyed the two women before dragging the coyote away into the woods.

As profound as the encounter was, Terry and Anna couldn't keep their legs from shaking as they hurried back to the play area.

"We should probably tell someone about the cougar," said Anna.

Terry looked at her, her mind still distant. "No, I think we should wait," she said.

"Okay," said Anna. "Who would believe us anyway?"

Terry and Pugsly's little secret didn't stay secret for long. That night, over dinner, Ted was once again complaining just to complain. He wondered why the laundry wasn't done, why the dishes were still in the sink. Terry couldn't lie anymore.

"I've been taking Pugsly to the new dog park."

"You what?"

"We've gone twice. I met a friend there. We talk while Pugsly and her dog Maggie play together."

The look on Ted's face elicited a private joy inside Terry. She tried not to show it.

"So you're turning into a lesbian now?" Ted said with a smirk, between shovelfuls of mashed potatoes.

"No, Ted, she's just a friend."

"I don't care who the hell she is. I don't want you seeing her." Terry saw the whites of his knuckles as he gripped the fork. When she didn't say anything in response, he shouted, "Did you fucking hear me?" Pieces of mashed potato flew from his mouth.

"Yes, Ted, I heard you. I won't see her anymore."

"Damn straight. Now pass the green beans."

Pugsly didn't make a peep.

Terry knew Ted's ego wouldn't let him go to work the next day without wondering if she was going to disobey him. After Ted left, Terry cleaned the house thoroughly. She scrubbed in places she'd never scrubbed before. She washed the dishes: every spoon, every fork, and every knife. She even stripped the bed and put the sheets in the machine. When she was done cleaning, she showered and dressed, and made herself a boiled egg. While the egg cooked in the bubbling water, she dismantled Pugsly's kennel and tossed the pieces into the yard. She then grabbed her tote bag and drove to the dog park.

Anna wasn't there, but that was okay. Pugsly would just have to play with the other dogs. As noon approached, Terry kept her eye more on the parking lot than on Pugsly making new friends. As expected, Ted's car nosed into a parking space. He was so predictable, so insecure. *What did I ever see in him?* thought Anna. It didn't matter now anyway, she wasn't that person anymore.

She got up from the bench, taking her tote bag with her, and made her way to the hiking trail. From the woods she watched as Ted followed her. She hid behind a large pine tree. She could almost hear his thoughts as he walked past. She was meeting someone here in the woods. Not the "friend" she had told him about, but a lover. He was going to beat the crap out of this guy, whoever he was, and then drag Terry home and beat the crap out of *her*. Terry could smell it on his sweat, like a sixth sense. It was the scent of hunger.

When Ted was far enough along the trail, Terry stepped out of the woods and followed him. She unwrapped the knife she had stored in her tote and gripped its handle. She made sure her scent was downwind.

B — Side

WHEN BOBBY BANKS SAW THE young kid stop and hover over the used LP rack at the back of the shop, he felt like a father passing on his musical genes to a new generation. While his record store, The Coconut Groove, specialized in current imports and indie labels, it was the used LP rack that was Bobby's first love. He tightened his ponytail, adjusted his John Lennon glasses, and made his way over to the kid.

The "kid" was likely a student from the local university, nineteen maybe twenty at the oldest, but that was still a kid in Bobby's fifty-five-year-old eyes. Bobby watched him pull Uriah Heep's *Demons and Wizards* out from the rack.

"Great album," said Bobby.

The kid jumped a bit. His eyes were a pale gray. There was a shadow of a mustache forming above his lip.

"Awesome cover, that one. You a fan of the 70s?"

The kid looked at the album. "My dad used to listen to this." He put the album aside and returned to the rack.

"Was your dad an audiophile, too?"

"A what?"

"Did he have the equipment? Turntable, stereo receiver, amplifier, all stacked up like a pagoda made of brushed aluminum and wood veneer? Tower speakers? He *had* to have had tower speakers. Speakers so big and heavy they left permanent footprints in the carpet. Speakers so loud, the bass so low, the dishes in the kitchen rattled in the cabinets and the neighbors complained?"

"Yeah, I guess." The kid paused in his search, pulled another LP out, shook his head and stuffed it back. "I don't know. I only saw it in pictures."

"Pictures? No, man, you have to see the real thing. You have to hear it, feel it rise up through your bones. You know, years back, a store like this would also sell stereo equipment. They'd have special sound rooms set up with a dozen separate systems, all the latest and greatest—Harman Kardon, Marantz, Kenwood, Pioneer. The sounds just poured like freakin' honey, free for the listening. You'd slide on a pair of headphones and you'd be transported, hearing things you never heard before, stuff the car radio just can't translate... like the sound of the guitar pick on the strings... or the singer taking a breath... or harmonies you never knew existed. Pictures can't do it justice, man. It's something you have to experience for yourself. There's nothing like it."

"Sounds cool. How much for this one?" The kid held up the Uriah Heep album.

"Five bucks. What kind of turntable do you have?"

"I don't. I just like the artwork. I'm gonna put this on my wall."

Bobby rung the kid up. As he bagged the album and handed it over, he said, "Hey, if you ever want to actually hear what the record inside sounds like in all its high fidelity glory, just let me know. I've got a system at home that can register a six on the Richter Scale."

"I'll keep that in mind. Thanks."

"No problem."

Bobby watched him leave. *Maybe... just maybe*, he thought. Something skipped in his heart and scratched at his senses. He heard the tear of cellophane... smelled the sweet oily aroma of vinyl... felt the fingertip warmth of spring buttons, stepped knobs, and toggle switches. It was the summer of '73. He was sitting in his beanbag chair, headphones on, blocking out the sounds... the sounds beyond the music, beyond his bedroom door... the bass drum thumps and the guitar shrieks. *Bobby, help!*

The front door rang. Two college girls entered the shop. Bobby rushed back to the present. He felt something wet at his fingertips and looked down at his hand.

Shit!

He grabbed a napkin from the fast-food lunch he had that day and pressed it against his wrist. Blood soaked through the porous paper. *Cut your damned fingernails*, he chided himself.

"Can I help you find anything?" he called to the girls.

"Just looking, thanks," one said.

"Look all you want."

He pulled away the napkin. The bleeding had stopped. There were four half-moon gouges in the skin of his left wrist, and pale shadows of previous markings.

Bobby shook his head and began counting receipts, humming the chorus of Kansas' "Carry On My Wayward Son."

The following day, the kid was back. Bobby didn't expect to see him so soon.

"Did you forget something?" Bobby flashed a smile. The kid went straight to the LP bin again.

"I remembered another one my dad used to have."

"Oh, yeah?" Bobby left what he was doing and found something else to do closer to the LP bin. "If you give me a title, I'll be able to tell you if I have it or not."

"That's okay, I'd rather look for it."

Bobby was unable to keep his eyes off the kid's fingers as they danced across the album tops. *Dark Side of the Moon... Houses of the Holy... Machine Head...* He didn't have to see the entire album to know which ones they were.

The kid was just as quiet today. It was a curse to be shy, thought Bobby. Shy people were locked inside their own lonely room. Not until someone came knocking did a shy person ever think to open the door. Bobby looked to make sure no other customers were in the shop before focusing his attention on the kid.

"Hey, if you don't mind me asking, what's your name?"

The kid softened his concentration and turned. He looked at Bobby for several seconds before answering. "Jared."

Knock, knock... come in...

Bobby smiled again. "Jared, my name's Bobby. I got a proposition for you. You seem like you're interested in what I have here. How about you become my supplier?"

Jared stared at him, gray eyes unblinking.

"Every Saturday, once the nice weather comes, people start having garage sales. Before I opened this shop, I used to spend my weekends going from garage sale to garage sale, picking up old records. You'd be surprised how many are still out there. People have a hard time getting rid of them. They contain memories, you know? Everybody remembers where they were when they first heard a particular song they fell in love with. They never forget that excitement of waiting for a record's release and rushing down to the record store to buy it, then bringing it home and listening to it over and over again. For some, it's more than just memories. Certain songs—certain albums—changed their life. It's like hearing God talking through your speakers.

"Anyway, I'm here at the shop now on Saturdays and I can't help but feel I'm missing out on all those albums and 45s that are just going to end up in the dumpster. I could really use someone to do some scouting for me. I'll give you fifty bucks, plus I'll reimburse you for gas and the records you find, of course. I'll even throw in the added incentive that you get to keep whichever ones you want, free of charge. What do you say, Jared?"

Jared thought about it. He thumbed through a few more albums. Then it was his turn to look around the shop to see if they were alone.

"Instead of fifty bucks, can you get me some weed?"

Bobby laughed. "Jared, my man, you got a 70s soul that's for sure. You got yourself a deal."

Bobby held out his hand and Jared shook it, smiling for the first time.

For the rest of that week, Bobby had trouble concentrating on work in anticipation of Saturday afternoon. He had given Jared a hundred dollars cash to cover the cost of gas and purchases. The kid could have taken the money and never returned. But Bobby fancied himself a pretty good judge of character. In fact, Jared reminded him a lot of himself at that age—having more sense than the average kid, but quiet, introverted, almost lost. But Bobby was going to help him out, help him find his way if he could. Help him the way he wished someone could have helped him.

When Saturday finally came, each ring of the front door brought Bobby's eyes up from whatever he was doing, his heart leaping and then falling back again when it wasn't Jared. It got late, near to closing time. Bobby was on edge for most of the day, distracted, and a little bit annoyed. Did he misjudge? Was Jared off laughing with his buddies, recounting how he'd taken some old hippie for a c-note?

It wasn't a good feeling. It felt like that first skip on a record. It stopped his heart. It sent his thoughts scrambling. Back to 1973...

Useless no good piece of shit... sitting around all day playing that long-haired music...

A cold wind blew into him full of anger, hatred... and fear...

Once again Bobby didn't feel pain until it was too late. Blood welled up from the half-moons he'd made in his wrist again. He looked for something to soak up the blood. The door rang. In walked Jared carrying a large cardboard box. Bobby wiped the blood on his jeans.

"Hey, there you are. How'd you make out?"

Jared walked over the counter and set the box on top. It was heavy. There must have been fifty albums in the box, all lined up facing forward.

Bobby performed a cursory flip-through. He turned to Jared. "Un-fucking-believable. See, I told you they were out there. Was this all at one garage sale?"

Jared nodded. He handed Bobby the change from the hundred.

"No, you keep it. You earned it." He pushed Jared's hand away. The kid's fingers were warm, extinguishing the lingering iciness the flashback had given him.

"Have you got my weed?"

Bobby glanced around out of reflex. Thankfully, the customers had come and gone. "Not here. It's at my place."

Jared stared at him with those gray eyes. "Can you get it?" he said.

Bobby looked at the time. "I guess I can close up a little early today. You're going to have to follow me. It's okay, I don't live far."

It took a lot of convincing but Bobby finally talked Jared into coming inside to get his "payment."

Though his parents were long gone, Bobby still lived at home, in the old split-level ranch he grew up in. He led Jared down into the basement rec room that looked like it hadn't changed in thirty years. The floor was covered in a purplish indoor/outdoor carpet. Wood paneling ran from floor to elbow height where a six-inch shelf added space for ashtrays and knickknacks. There were album posters on the walls: Jethro Tull, Genesis, Neil Young, Fleetwood Mac. A leather couch sat in the middle of the room facing a homemade wall-to-wall shelving unit that housed Bobby's stereo system, along with hundreds of albums.

"So this is it," said Bobby, the pride in his voice unmistakable. "Hey, while you're here you have to listen to something."

Bobby jumped into action, pulling a seemingly random album out of the collection and slipping the vinyl record from its antistatic sleeve. "You see, by the mid-seventies they had perfected what they called 'the live experience.' Then the eighties came along and everything went digital, and that was that." He raised the lid on the turntable and set the LP in place, flicked a switch and slowly lowered the lid. The turntable's arm swung, and before it dropped, Bobby had the amplifier and speakers on, filling the room with an anticipatory hiss. A bass thump followed as the needle settled into the album's groove. Out of the four tower speakers, two in front, two behind, rolled the sound of the sea.

Bobby handed the album to Jared. "Quadrophenia by The Who. Tommy's good but, musically—sonically—Quadrophenia's their best. Here, sit on the couch. I've got it positioned just right so if you sit in the middle you hear everything." Jared sat and listened, holding the album in his hands. The music grew louder. Bobby sat down beside him. Jared didn't stay seated. He got up and walked over to one of the shelves. Instead of LPs, this shelf was filled with smaller records, each in their own individual sleeve. Jared looked at Bobby as if to say *What are these?*

"45s."

"Like mini-CDs?"

"Yeah, you got it." Bobby got up. He turned the music down a notch. "Oh, yeah, 45s were great. Sometimes the single was different than what appeared on the album. Like this one here." Bobby pulled out a 45 of Yes's "Roundabout." "Usually they were edited down for Top Forty airplay. Sometimes a single wouldn't appear on an album for years, only showing up in Greatest Hits collections, like this one." Bobby showed Jared another 45, this one with a picture of Elton John on the sleeve. "'Lucy in the Sky with Diamonds,' great Lennon/McCartney cover. I think Elton actually improved on the original. Same goes for 'Pinball Wizard.'" He slid the 45 back into place. "But the best thing about 45s were the b-sides. The b-sides tended to show a different personality of the artist. Stuff that didn't make it on the album because it was too dark or too weird or just too damned different. There are some really great songs found on b-sides. I like to think of b-sides as the artist just saying fuck it, I'm going to do what I want no matter what." Bobby paused as the sea sounds faded. "Sometimes I feel we all should have an outlet like that, a b-side in our life where we can just be free to express ourselves no matter what society thinks."

Quadrophenia moved onto its second track, "The Real Me."

"Can I have my weed now?" Jared said.

Bobby was standing so close to the kid his legs were shaking. "Yeah, sure, I'll get it for you."

Bobby cranked the music back up before he left the room. "Listen to that horn section," he shouted.

The sound of The Who faded as he went into the laundry room. He opened the cabinet where the laundry detergent and drier towels were stored. Up on the top shelf, his fingers found a large plastic Ziploc bag. Inside the larger bag were half a dozen smaller Ziploc bags of marijuana. Each of the smaller bags held enough to last an average toker a week. Bobby grabbed two of the smaller bags and a packet of rolling papers. *Maybe the kid will want to light one up*, he thought. When he returned to the rec room, Jared was checking his cell phone for the time.

Bobby held the bags and rolling papers up. "I thought maybe you'd want to roll one with me."

"No, I gotta go."

"Aw, c'mon, just one. I'll put on Fleetwood Mac's Rumours and we can chill." Bobby walked past him to find the Rumours album.

"Dude, I can't, I gotta go. Can I have my weed?" For the first time there was an edge in Jared's voice. An edge Bobby didn't hear due to Roger Daltrey screaming "Can you see the real me... doctor? Can you see the real me... mother?"

"But you haven't heard the sound of the guitar pick on 'Dreams'..."

Bobby was shoved from behind. He fell against the turntable, skipping the record, and dropping the Rumours album from his hand. He bent to pick it up, a little dazed.

"Just give me my fucking weed, you fucking faggot!"

Bobby looked up, momentarily seeing his stepfather's face

superimposed on Jared's body. He continued to cower, sweat now beading on his brow. "But I thought we could just hang out... I thought we could be friends... I thought you were like me."

This only seemed to enrage Jared more. The young man's face blanched and he grabbed the nearest heavy object—a lava lamp—and stood over Bobby. "I'm not like you!" he screamed, "I'll never be like you! Never! Ever!" Twice Jared came down with the lamp on Bobby's head.

Bobby tried to shield himself but the first blow got through, and the second one cracked his skull. Bobby didn't feel the rest of the blows because he was back in 1973, sitting in his beanbag chair, headphones on, summer air wafting in through the bedroom window. Only this time when he heard his mother screaming for help, he got up, crying out, "I'm coming, Mom... I'm coming..."

Lost Dog

Every year at this time, Steve Manemann has the same dream. The dream is bright and tinged with yellow like an old photograph. It's twenty years earlier, and he's only eight years old. He's sitting in a pile of October leaves that his father has just raked, the itch of grass in his sweater, the smell of decay filtering through his nostrils, potent and sweet. He shakes the leaves from his hair and squints his eyes into the sunlight. At the end of their long dirt driveway, he sees a woman.

She's wearing a long gray raincoat and holds a small paper bag in one hand, an empty leash in the other. *Must have lost her dog*, he thinks, as the woman treads toward them. But there is something about her that fills young Stevie with a mixture of curiosity and dread.

As the woman slowly reaches the top of the driveway, he notices how pale her skin is, nearly gray, and her expression matches her color. Like a stone. Not gloomy, not sad, just... determined.

"Dad?"

His father stops raking and turns to him. His father is big, and his big face looks down. Little Stevie doesn't realize it then, as he points toward the woman, but this will be the last time his father will acknowledge him.

From that moment on, the dream-that-isn't-a-dream becomes a nightmare as little Stevie watches his father greet the stranger with a neighborly, "Hello, beautiful day, isn't it? What can I do for you?" The woman approaches without a word and without a smile, and it seems as if she's pocketed the sun in her long gray coat because a sheet of gray clouds suddenly occupies the sky, and a chill runs beneath the surface of little Stevie's sweater.

As the dream darkens, so does the look on his father's face as the woman steps closer still so that little Stevie cannot hear, and his father simply nods. Stevie would have left his pile of leaves and joined his father's side, hugging his leg the way he did when he was afraid, but the tall, thin, gray woman turns to him and her eyes, which he thought were the palest of blue, suddenly turn black, and her mouth pulls down into a grimace, which stops his eight-year-old heart in his chest and keeps him huddled in the leaves, seeking the only comfort available. Little Stevie can only watch as the woman turns, and his father follows her, and together they enter the woods never to be seen again.

Every year at this time, as Steve Manemann stands and rakes the leaves from the same trees his father had raked, he remembers the horror that followed—the interrogating questions, the accusatory glare in his mother's eyes as if he were lying about the whole incident. There was no lady with the leash and the bag. His father simply swore him to secrecy. Like father, like son. For years, Steve thought his mother was jealous that he, not she, was the last to see his father. It took even longer to understand why his mother reacted with such distrust. Bits and pieces overheard from aunts and uncles—*What a terrible thing to do to his family; I hope he rots in hell*—eventually began to uncover the truth about his parents; how they had nearly split before he was born, and would have if not for the child curled inside his mother's womb; how the wanderlust in his father's eye remained even after his son had been born and continued until the day of his disappearance.

Every year at this time, Steve Manemann basks in the aloneness of his yard-work, beneath the warm October sun, working up a sweat as his father once had, standing in the yard of the house he inherited, his wife inside folding laundry or talking on the phone with friends—anything, he suspects, to keep her mind off the nagging worry that he is cheating on her. Little does she know his reluctance to come to bed has nothing to do with whether he finds her attractive anymore, or whether he has found somebody new.

Every year at this time, as he pulls at the leaves trapped in his rake, Steve Manemann's eye does wander but not in the way his wife assumes. It wanders down toward the foot of the long dirt driveway as it did on that day twenty years earlier. He's anticipating the return of the woman in the long gray raincoat, a leash in one hand, a small paper bag in the other. As she draws near, the bag appears to be damp on the bottom, soaked through with what looks like blood, heavy with a weight that betrays its contents.

Every year at this time, Steve Manemann thanks God that his wife is barren, and there will be no little Stevies playing in the leaves and looking up at him in horror when the tall gray woman comes in search of her lost dog, and his heart goes all too willingly.

Periphery

THERE IT WAS AGAIN.

Craig Jeffries sat at his desk working on his latest deadline: a website for a local laser optics company. But something had raced past the corner of his vision, disrupting his train of thought.

He stared at the dimly lit hallway that led into the kitchen, expecting to see a rat come skittering back across the floor. Six-hundred fifty dollars a month, heat and hot water—rats included. He figured as much. The apartment was all he could afford right now, what with the alimony and the child support. But it was a small price to pay. After eight years of subverting his own needs, he had finally made the painful decision. He now had a place to call his own: his own furniture, a futon for a couch, the papasan chair he'd always wanted, a stereo on which to play whatever music he wished. At the moment, Sibelius' Fifth Symphony spilled out of the bookshelf speakers. Craig surveyed his belongings and, despite the likelihood he was sharing his apartment with a rodent, he felt a serene sense of satisfaction. He had done it. Second guesses be damned.

He stared once more at the kitchen before returning his attention to his work.

On the flat-screen monitor glowed a simulated laser system. Green and red streams of light bent at right angles off a series of mirror mounts. The laser beams framed—and were supposed to draw attention to—the company's logo. But the green and red lights didn't appear as if they were actually streaming. They were throbbing instead. *A nice effect for a techno dance club*, thought Craig, *but not for a laser company*. The animation he had spent hours creating would have to be reworked.

Before losing himself in his coding, he made a mental note: get traps.

For the next three hours Craig tweaked the splash page's logo until it was just right. When he finally glanced at the time again it was 8:45. Crap. He needed to call his ex.

Rachel had chastised him the last time he'd called after 9:00 pm; by then the kids were in bed, and most of the time she was too. But then Craig guessed that was one of the reasons why their marriage had failed: she chose quality time with her pillow over quality time with him.

Rachel picked up on the fourth ring. "Yeah?" Her voice sounded impatient. Not good.

"Rachel? Hi."

"Yeah?"

"You sound mad."

"What is it, Craig?"

"How are the kids?"

"They're fine." A moment of stubborn silence. She could never stay mad at him for very long, but she was getting better at it. "Maggie's got a cold, and Kelly's being a pain in the ass, if you care to know."

Craig could hear his four-year-old singing loudly in the background. "Of course I care. Is Maggie all right? Has she been to the doctor?"

"It's just a mild cold. Her nose is a little runny. She's got a slight fever."

"How's her ears? Have you given her the nose drops like the doctor said?"

"She'll be fine, Craig. I gave her some Tylenol. Why did you call?"

Guilt. There was always guilt. He wanted to spend a Saturday alone. He needed to get the laser job done. Work all day, if necessary.

But the guilt. Rachel had the kids six days a week, how could he ask her to grant him such a privilege without sounding like the ungrateful asshole she must think he must be?

"Craig?"

"Sorry, I just called to find out what time you wanted me to pick them up tomorrow, that's all."

"The usual time. Is everything okay?" She sounded more curious than concerned.

"Yeah, why?"

"Did you want to skip tomorrow?"

How could she tell? That was another thing about their relationship that didn't sit well with Craig—the fact that on occasion Rachel had the ability to reach down inside him and turn him inside out, expose the truth. In this instance, he almost gave in, pleaded no contest. Yes, it was true, he didn't want to have the kids this week. But that wasn't the whole of it. In fact, maybe he didn't want to have the kids next week either, or the week after that, or... But that was too horrible a truth to admit. That one he had to keep so far down even he couldn't reach it.

"No, no, I just..." Frustration began to tie knots in his thoughts. "Look, I'll be there at ten; have the kids ready, okay? I'll be there."

"Sure, whatever."

"Goodnight." As he hung up the phone a pain gnawed at his insides like a small, feral beast.

The guilt. Always the guilt.

He glanced around at his apartment. He had everything he wanted, so why did he feel so shitty?

The shadows reminded him of his more immediate problem: get traps.

Get trapped.

Get trapped into living someone else's life. Fulfilling everyone else's expectations but your own. All the while convincing yourself that you're doing the right thing, the good thing. The good husband, the good father... the good lover. All of it false. Just an actor with no other role to play.

But no more.

But the pride of his resolve was short-lived. Something moved at the periphery of his vision. He turned.

Again, the kitchen was empty. Nothing but the dark. But Craig had the unsettling feeling there was indeed something there, watching, waiting for him to look away. Or perhaps it was there in the open, yet invisible, and he would only be able to see it if he knew what to look for.

The following morning Craig stopped at the local Agway before swinging by Rachel's to pick up the kids. Amid the dusty smells of feed and fertilizer, he found himself standing in the traps and poison aisle. The traps looked archaic—dungeon devices for torturing small animals. He couldn't see killing the animals: they too were only trying to find a comfortable niche in which to live. There had to be a better way, something more humane. And to his surprise he found just the thing. Tip-Traps. They looked like tiny trailers with a slight bend at the middle. All the animal had to do was walk inside, walk past the point of equilibrium, the trap tipped and down came the spring-loaded door behind it. Simple. No mess. No pain. He grabbed two and headed for the cash register.

As he put his traps on the counter, Craig caught sight of a small dog in the shadow of the stockroom doorway, a short haired muscular miniature of some kind. It ducked away before he could see what breed it was.

"Shy little fella, isn't he?"

The man behind the counter, dressed in coveralls and sporting an NRA button on the brim of his cap, stared at him straight-faced. "What's that?"

"The dog." Craig pointed toward the stockroom. "Shy little fella." Craig could see the man still wasn't getting it, so he walked over to the stockroom and leaned in.

Nothing but feed bags and boxes.

Craig walked back to the counter. "Sorry, thought I saw a small dog."

"Nope. Rat maybe. Anything else?"

"No, that will be it."

Craig took one final look at the stockroom doorway before exiting the store. He bet the guy behind the counter was pulling one over on him. He could have sworn it was a dog.

Craig's daughter, Kelly, liked sitting in the papasan chair. It was like one of those big, soft teddy bears you never win at the carnivals. Craig figured it was a substitute for his not being able to hold her. Maggie received most of the attention nowadays. At a year-and-a-half there was hardly a second she wasn't in Craig's lap or at least trying to get into it. The three of them were watching the movie, *Finding Nemo*. At the moment, Nemo was trying to explain to everyone in the fish tank why he needed to get back to the ocean. But soon it would be lunch. Maggie would go down for the afternoon, and he and Kelly would put a couple of puzzles together or color. Craig didn't mind watching the kids. He just minded the fact that watching the kids took him away from his work.

He glanced over at his desk as if to say, "This is only temporary, sweetie. Don't worry, we'll share plenty of quality time together tonight." But as he was silently lamenting his inability to get his work done, his heart did a stutter-step as something small and gray ducked behind his computer.

"Dammit!"

"What is it, Daddy?" Kelly asked, her eyes wide.

Craig lifted Maggie up off his lap and set her back down in his place. "Nothing, honey. I just thought I saw something, that's all." He cautiously walked over to his desk and began poking around.

"Is it a mouse?"

Craig turned to his daughter. "Did you see it?"

By now, Maggie had slipped off the couch and was hanging on Craig's leg. "Got get down... got get down..." It was her way of saying she wanted to be picked up.

"Daddy, I'm scared." Kelly stared at the floor, searching for anything that moved. She pulled her knees up to her chest, making her look even smaller in the papasan chair.

"It's okay, honey, Daddy's got mouse traps in the kitchen."

Kelly's gaze shifted to the kitchen. "There's mouses in the kitchen?"

Craig laughed. "No, no—"

"Got get down... get down..."

Craig picked Maggie up and walked over to where Kelly sat.

"Daddy, hold me."

"I can't, honey. Don't worry about the mice. There are no mice. What do you feel like for lunch?"

"Daddy, I'm afraid."

"Kelly, there's nothing to be afraid of. Now, what do you want?" Craig could hear his voice rising.

"Daddy, I can't eat in the kitchen."

"Kelly!"

Kelly broke into tears.

Craig couldn't deal with this right now. He was angry with Kelly for being afraid, angry with himself for raising his voice to her. In the midst of his anger, he felt a slap on his face. Stunned, he looked at Maggie, her mischievous smile only inches away. "Bonk!" she said and reared back to hit him again.

"No!" he said sternly. Maggie's innocent blue eyes stared at him before her face crumpled into tears.

"It's okay, it's okay, Daddy didn't mean to yell." Craig walked around the living room with Maggie in his arms. He stopped at the window for her to look outside. As he calmed Maggie, he asked Kelly if she wanted some Spaghetti-O's. Kelly nodded yes, focusing her attention back on *Finding Nemo*. Craig figured there were no mice in the ocean, and no insensitive fathers to raise their voices at their daughters, either.

He glared once more at his desk and swore to himself.

As he carried Maggie into the kitchen and sat her in her highchair, he made a mental note: get a cat.

That night, the phone rang. It was Rachel.

"Craig, Kelly told me a wonderful little story about mice."

"And you believed her, of course." Craig laughed, dry and humorless.

"I don't see what's so funny. I don't like the idea of the girls being in that kind of environment."

"Rachel, it was nothing. I thought I saw something and Kelly got spooked, that's all. She used to freak out if a moth flew into the house, remember?"

There was a long silence.

He should have never mentioned the house. Rachel would probably never forgive him for having to sell it as part of the divorce settlement.

"Kelly also said you shouted at Maggie?"

Craig laughed again, this time a little more sarcastically. "Nice little detective you're raising there."

"I'm teaching them to tell the truth, not to keep secrets."

"Okay, Rachel, that's enough. Yeah, so I raised my voice. Don't tell me you don't raise your voice when they piss you off."

"But you frighten them, Craig."

Craig hated that—the fact that when a mother raises her voice to her children, it means mommy's just mad, but when daddy does he's a monster.

"Okay, Rachel, you win. I'll keep it in mind. Is there anything else?"

"Yes, what was it you saw?"

"What was what?"

"You said you thought you saw something. If it wasn't a mouse, then what was it?"

It was my life passing before me, the wasted hours, the wasted moments, scurrying like rats leaving a sinking ship. Like now, this wasted telephone conversation...

"Nothing. It was just a shadow, a trick of the light, that's all. It was nothing." He gritted his teeth.

"Oh." She seemed disappointed. "You still want the girls next Saturday?"

"What kind of question is that? Of course I do. It's the only time I get a chance to see them."

"All right then."

"Okay."

Rachel hung up.

This time, when movement teased him out of the corner of his eye, Craig refused to look.

The weekend ended with Craig barely meeting his deadline on the laser job. He went to bed beat, his mind a messy blur of red and green tracers. He slept till noon the following day. He had another job lined up, a local jewelry/head shop called The Diamond Dog that wanted to go high-tech. Pipes, clips, rolling papers, and a wide assortment of handmade piercing accessories, along with more traditional rings, earrings, chains and bracelets—all with a similar Goth motif. Craig had over a hundred digital images he needed to sort through and organize. In fact, one of the young ladies who worked at The Diamond Dog loaned him a CD he had commented on while he was there. Her name was Gina. Twenty-something. Dyed black hair, chopped short; black fingernail polish; ears triple pierced. Pretty. Full face, big blue eyes, and a smile like gold. And a nice trim body to boot. It had been six months now since the divorce. It was time he thought about dating again.

But first things first. Feline companionship before female companionship. Craig drove to the city's animal shelter and found a full-grown, nearly all-white short haired female tabby available for adoption. On the ride home, he named her Nilla, short for vanilla. The cat crawled up his chest and nestled under his chin all the way home, thanking him for saving her from the dreaded needle.

"Hope you're a good mouser," he told her.

At the apartment, Nilla settled in comfortably, finding the spot under Craig's desk the optimum place to curl up. At times the cat would lie on Craig's feet, purring to the syncopation of his typing.

By the middle of the week, Craig met with the Diamond Dog's manager, Alex, to demonstrate a preliminary model of the new website. Alex loved it. Gina was also there. Before leaving, buoyed with confidence, Craig asked her if she'd like to go to dinner one night. She agreed, affording Craig the type of smile he hadn't seen in years. A smile that conveyed a genuine affection.

"Friday?"

"Sounds great," she replied.

God, even her voice was pretty.

When Craig arrived at his apartment, he found Nilla in the living room corner, her tail swishing from side to side. She looked to be chewing on something. Craig froze. *She caught one.* He approached the cat with caution.

"Whatcha got there, Nilla?"

Suddenly, Nilla rolled over on her side and began batting a paper wad between her paws, as if to say, "Want to play?" Craig noticed the wastepaper basket had been spilled over. He knelt down and scratched Nilla's head, relieved.

For a moment there, he didn't want to see what she had caught.

By Friday, the Diamond Dog site was uploaded and complete. Craig dropped by the shop at closing time and Alex gave him his check. Alex also gave him a couple leads on possible jobs. With money in his pocket and Gina at his side, he then set out on his first date in over eight years.

The first half of their date was his idea, dinner at a nice Italian restaurant uptown; the second half was Gina's. The Outcasts were playing at a club on Trumbull Street. They paid at the door, got their hands stamped like teenagers, and let themselves get sucked into a seething mass of leather, denim and sweat. For the next hour their stomachs swallowed bass and their ears defended against a barrage of growling vocals and glass-shattering guitars. Craig couldn't remember the last time he'd felt so liberated.

"Not bad." Gina took in Craig's apartment with an appreciative nod.

"You want a beer? Wine?" It was after midnight. The sound of the club was still ringing in Craig's ears.

"I'm all set, thanks." Gina slipped off her denim jacket and laid it across the back of the futon. She wore a thin black pullover underneath.

Craig went into the kitchen and grabbed a beer out of the refrigerator.

"You into Asian culture?" Gina called from the living room.

"Yeah, someday I'd like to see it all. China, Japan, Cambodia." Craig nearly tore his thumb off on the bottle cap before realizing he had bought an import without twist-offs. He rummaged through the kitchen drawer in search of a bottle opener. He finally found one and joined Gina in the living room. He wasn't surprised to see his coffee table being used to roll a couple of joints.

"I have this great CD by these two Japanese girls who rock. I have to loan it to you." She handed Craig one of the joints. She lit hers first before handing Craig the lighter. If his ex could see him now. Craig then took his first toke in years.

Seconds later, Gina squealed. "Oh my God!"

Craig's heart leaped in his chest and his mind scattered.

"What a beautiful cat!"

Nilla jumped up onto the futon and walked across Gina's lap, onto Craig's lap, and then back again. Nilla must have heard the rustle of the rolling papers and became curious.

"Her name's Nilla. I rescued her from death row."

Gina petted the cat. White hairs attached themselves to her black top. "She's beautiful." Gina looked up. Craig saw she was getting buzzed. He also saw a need, a loneliness he recognized. She reached out and gently hooked him around the neck. "My hero," she said, pulling him into a kiss. Her mouth tasted like spice. Her tongue was hot between his lips. Nilla jumped down and walked into the kitchen for a bite to eat.

Craig awoke, his head pounding slightly. It was just becoming light outside. Gina lay next to him on her side, still asleep.

He put his hands behind his head and stared at the ceiling. What a night. *I'm baaaack in the saddle agaaaain*, howled Steven Tyler's voice in his ears. The sex was great. Gina had an amazing body. He couldn't believe his hands had been allowed to explore such beautiful terrain. But there came the inevitable comparison. He thought about Rachel and how it used to be—the house, the kids. It seemed so long ago. Their marriage was doomed from the very beginning. The more he had tried to make things work, the more he seemed to alienate himself from himself, until he could no longer hold on. The kite string had gone out too far. One day, he simply let go.

Craig rolled over onto his side and Gina stirred. He nudged himself closer until his body pressed up against hers, like two continents divided and yet perfectly matched. She turned her head to kiss him. "Good morning," he said. He reached for her breast and gently played with her piercing. Her nipple hardened. "What a pleasant surprise," she said and pressed her rump against his growing erection.

With the completion of the Diamond Dog account, Craig's business took off. Word of mouth spread quickly among the counter-culture. Soon he had jobs lined up for a tattoo and piercing magazine, and one for a sex toy manufacturer. He and Gina dated now and then. No strings. He liked it that way. Nilla continued to catch wads of paper and balled-up socks, but nothing animal. As the work began to mount, his weekends became more and more valuable. For the first time, he decided to call Rachel to tell her he wouldn't be taking the girls on Saturday. But before he could tell her, his oldest daughter told him something he wasn't prepared for.

"Mommy's moving."

"What was that, Kelly?"

His daughter *tsk*ed and repeated the words as if she were talking to a child. "I said, Mommy's moving."

"Put Mommy on the phone, okay, honey?"

"Craig, hi. I've been meaning to call you."

"Kelly says you're moving?"

"Yeah, I got a job offer."

"A job?"

"It's at our western office."

"Okay."

"California."

Craig didn't know what to say. California was three thousand miles away. His feet suddenly felt numb, his ears began to ring. He imagined himself floating up toward the ceiling, out the window, into the sky, tethered by nothing but a thin, golden strand.

"Are you taking it?" he asked her.

"I don't know, yet. We'll have to talk."

"Sure, when?"

"Soon."

The silence stretched between them.

"Well, I know this is bad timing," Craig said, "but the reason I called was to ask if I could skip this weekend with the girls. I'm really swamped."

"No, it's okay, that's fine, glad to hear things are taking off. Thanks for letting me know. You want to say goodnight to them?"

"Sure, put 'em on."

The overlapping voices of Kelly and Maggie saying "Goodnight" made him smile, but his heart ached.

"Goodnight, girls," he shouted back. They sounded happy. Then Rachel was back on the line.

"I'll call you, okay?"

"Hey Rachel. Thanks." He hung up the phone.

California. He couldn't believe it.

In the days that followed, the fleeting shadows returned, becoming more pronounced, more defined, more frequent. First, there were the usual ghost blurs of movement in a room or down a hallway. But then there came the other "blurs"; the brief glimpses of substance in the mirror as he shaved; the same images reflected in the darkened glass of his apartment windows at night. At one point Craig just stopped shaving. He kept the window shades shut. And, most disturbing of all, he would catch Nilla staring up at the ceiling or into a dark corner. When he would look to see what she was staring at, he would inevitably find Nilla staring at him instead, making him feel foolish. Craig began to worry. He finally made an appointment with an optometrist. Ironically, it was on the same day he was to meet with Rachel to discuss never seeing his children on a regular basis again.

In the darkened examination room, Dr. Kim leaned in so close Craig could smell the fish the man had eaten for lunch. A bright light probed his dilated pupils. At last, the doctor switched on the room lights.

"No problems. Everything's good." Dr. Kim smiled.

Craig squinted as if he were staring into the sun.

"You have sunglasses for the drive home?"

Craig shook his head.

The doctor handed Craig a pair of cardboard cutout sunglasses. "Avoid bright lights. Two hours. Have a nice day. See the receptionist on the way out."

Craig decided to drive home and rest before meeting with Rachel. There was nothing wrong with his eyesight. In fact, his vision was slightly better than twenty-twenty. The eye drops the doctor had put into his eyes to enlarge his pupils made his eyes feel like lead.

Back at his apartment, Craig tossed the 3D movie-looking spectacles aside. The room lit up like a blast furnace. Purple halos surrounded each light fixture. And squinting didn't help. He pulled all the shades and elected to lie down on the futon. When he closed his eyes, all he could see was the doctor's bright light probing the corners of his vision. *What was he looking for? Tiny creatures? Specks of consciousness leaking out, trying to escape the vast black cavern of my mind?*

Craig opened his eyes to the dimly lit room. The ceiling crawled with black moths.

Blink. Reset.

Craig turned his head toward the stereo cabinet. From around the edge of its door, a tiny, clawed hand crept.

Craig quickly got up and went into the kitchen. He needed a beer. He opened the refrigerator and jumped back when he saw a host of fleeting images disappear into the sides of the refrigerator's plastic walls.

What is happening? Craig closed his eyes, blinked hard.

He jerked his head to the side. The kitchen cabinets snapped shut as tiny hands suddenly retreated.

"You need to lie down, rest your eyes," he told himself.

Craig put the beer back in the refrigerator door and felt his way into the bedroom. He stretched out on the bed and closed his eyes against all the blurs and disturbances swarming around him, dancing at the periphery of his vision. Maybe darkness—maybe the solitary comfort of his own private sanctum—will be enough to banish them.

But, no, they were there, too—black on black, moving, invading, settling in, making a home in his waking consciousness. He couldn't escape them.

Craig wanted to scream. He wanted to go back in time to change the direction of his life, to rethink the decisions that had brought him here to this point, to reconnect the ties he had so weakly and selfishly loosened along the way.

But they would have none of it. Not now —now that he knew of their existence.

Craig listened to the subtle hum and vibration of their activity and, at last, relaxed. And like nosey, bothersome neighbors, he slowly, reluctantly, accepted their tenancy.

In time, he hoped, he would come to see them not as some kind of enemy, but as hapless creatures just looking to find a comfortable niche in which to live. Maybe one day he would come to see them as friends.

Post Mortem

1. LOVE IS

"Do you love me?"

"Of course I do." His lips found her mouth; his fingers fumbled to undo her bra.

"I don't normally do this."

"It's okay. We deserve it."

Afraid he'd ruin her bra, he let her undo the clasp. The weight of her breasts fell into his palms. She lay back and he followed her lead. Piece by piece, clothing was shed until they lay naked together. He paused.

"Can I ask you something?"

"Anything."

"Can we hurry up and get this over with?"

"Of course. But are you sure? Are you really, really sure?"

"I've never been so sure of anything in my life."

"Okay." She shifted beneath him as she reached for the ice pick. "Now hold still."

Twice he saw the look in her eye, a moment of purity and glory so blinding it filled the room... before the ice pick stole it away and everything went dark.

The pain was surprisingly slight. A viscous fluid dribbled down his cheeks. He felt her tongue lap at the leakage as if she were kissing away his tears.

"Thank you," he said, seeing things much more clearly now. "Now where were we?"

2. IT'S NOT YOU, IT'S ME

"IT'S NOT YOU, IT'S ME," he said, as she sat on the couch beside him writing I LOVE YOU two-hundred and seventy-three times on the skin of her forearm with a sewing needle, one for each day they dated.

"Believe me, I never meant to hurt you," he added, as she tossed aside the needle and, using her slender fingers and sharp nails, gouged out her left eye, then her right.

"I just want you to be with someone who can give you the love you deserve."

He got up then to get a glass of water. While he stood at the kitchen sink, quenching his thirst, she slashed at her blouse with a razor blade. She then cut out her heart and set it on the coffee table. Her cat came over and began licking the now lifeless organ.

He turned. "Are you sure you're going to be okay?"

She nodded.

After giving her a farewell hug, he left. He took the stairs to the street. When his feet hit the sidewalk, he took a deep breath, relieved, thinking, *That went well.*

3. MONSTER

I CREATED HER. I had my hands inside of her. I fiddled with her heart. Now, she says she loves me. What am I to do?

She's a monster. She lives, she breathes, she feels. She is everything that is human, and yet she is not God's divine creature. She is mine.

I told her I was simply her doctor, and she was my patient. Anything more would be wrong. In the end, I told her I didn't know how to love. But I loved her anyway.

I kept our affair a secret. We laughed and dined while she healed. At night, I took her into my arms, careful not to reopen her wounds. It was almost real.

But my conscience overcame my will, and one day I confessed. I didn't truly love her. So I set her free.

She looked at me with utter sadness. She cried monster tears.

It's been months now since I last saw her, but I see her every day. Her blood still stains my hands. Her tears track slowly across my heart.

She's a monster.

She's a monster.

No matter how many times I say it, she is still less of a monster than I.

4. THE WOUND

HE INSERTED THE NEEDLE into his flesh. As he worked, the wound talked.

"What did I ever do except love you?"

He pulled the thread through. The knot snagged, dimpling his skin. He inserted the needle again. The corner of the wound squeezed shut.

"Please—can't we just go back to the way it used to be?"

He repeated the process. Puncture... pull... puncture... pull. The wound's voice constricted.

"I can't believe you would do this to me. After all we've been through."

He hurried to finish, feeling the muscles in his fingers weaken, along with his resolve.

"See, you don't really want to do this, do you? It's all in your head. You're just having a bad day."

He took a deep breath and sank the needle in. Three more stitches. The wound was nearly closed.

"You're crazy, you know that? I should have never opened myself up to you. You're a selfish son of a bi—"

He pulled the last stitch and tied off the thread. The wound howled beneath his skin, but the howling eventually abated. Soon, only the weeping of red tears marked the spot where his heart used to be.

5. BONFIRE

SHE STOOD BEFORE THE FLAMES, the heat washing over her in waves of guilt and retribution. The clothes he had bought her, the books—even the leaflets and ticket stubs she had saved from their handful of dates, were now heaped and burning, consumed by the fire she had built in the backyard of their dream home.

"Mommy?"

She turned to see their future child, a frightened look in the young boy's big brown eyes; a beautiful child; the child she had always wanted from the kind of man she had dreamed of sharing her life with. But it wasn't to be; the man of her dreams was just an illusion.

"Come here, sweetheart."

She clutched the young boy to her breast before tossing him onto the flames. The child shrieked and squirmed, the flames eating him up as quickly as the photographs of her imagined honeymoon.

"Don't worry, baby," she said. "Mommy's coming."

Then she too stepped into the inferno. Flames licked at her skin, peeling away layer after layer of reality, until all that was left was the essence of her desire and the black char of memory.

The Stagnant Ponds

Stillman watched as the bulldozers methodically destroyed what was left of the pond. In the spring, he had made it a habit to drive down the long industrial park road on his lunch break and pull his station wagon over into the high grass that bordered the vast expanse of algae and weeds that had found its niche along the Interstate. Stillman assumed most people thought the pond an eyesore, its slick green mire representative of the slow-moving and the unkempt. But, for Stillman, the pond was a world unto itself. He had seen flocks of birds come and go, flowers bloom, and had even caught the sight of something dark moving beneath the filmy surface, perhaps a beaver or a muskrat adopting the wetland habitat as its home. But then summer came, unnaturally hot and dry, and soon the thick water began to recede—a slow, degenerative process that, by July, had shrunk the pond to half its original size, its reedy banks draped with dried blankets of algae. It wasn't long before some keen-eyed developer noticed the dying land and wished to speed the process along.

"Vultures," said Stillman as he took another bite of his

sandwich. Fifty yards away, two mud-encrusted bulldozers dug into the still wet (still warm) clay-rich soil and pushed it towards the great black mound forming at one corner of the lot. The mound had already achieved a height above the bulldozer's cab, and a ramp had been created to pile the drying mud even higher. Stillman watched, helpless to do anything else, attracted by the strange progression of operations like some garish funereal process.

To the right of the mound, three men stood beside a pickup truck. Two of the men were dressed in white shirts; they pointed this way and that. A third man stood, hands on his hips, attention seemingly concentrated in the direction of the two noisy bulldozers. Behind them rose the steep incline of the Interstate, its midday traffic rush, which Stillman used to think of as soothing, lost beneath the guttural Sturm and Clang of the two earthmoving machines.

Stillman finished his sandwich and sat a few minutes longer before heading back to work. The bulldozers had begun a new section. Their blades lifted slightly, like medieval doctors poised before their next incision, then down they fell, sinking deep into the black mire. Stillman could almost hear the ground cry out as the blades nosed forward, furling the wet earth into thick folds, like stripping the flesh from a patient not yet deceased.

Over the next several weeks Stillman watched in abject fascination as the two bulldozers went about their daily routine. For the short time he spent each day observing, he had never seen the drivers separated from their machines, and had come to consider them as one, their torsos pinned to the black interior of the cabs, arms attached to the knobbed drive levers of their cockpits. Even their heads appeared mechanically operated, swiveling from side to side, encumbered by headphones that matched the color of the bulldozer's framework, their eyes masked behind black reflective sunglasses.

The two supervisors came and went with efficient regularity, while the lone foreman wandered the now desolate parcel of land in search of... In search of what? Stillman wondered. Dead fish? Indian arrowheads? Empty beer cans? Perhaps the stripping of the pond bed had uncovered some underlying guilt in the foreman, Stillman theorized, guilt that urged him to make peace with the land that he was party to destroying. Perhaps not. Perhaps the foreman was merely killing time, stretching his legs between coffee breaks, thinking of this weekend's barbecue or last night's baseball game. Perhaps no one else felt the same about this small area of wasteland as Stillman.

Stillman shook his head and brushed breadcrumbs from between his legs onto the floor-mats. He sipped his soda and checked the dash clock. To his surprise, today's visit had taken him fifteen minutes beyond his usual hour.

He quickly started the wagon and backed out of the high grass, halting at the edge of the road. He looked both ways then stopped again to watch, drawn to the changing landscape and its clattering architects.

One of the bulldozers had crawled up the steep incline that led to the top of the still-growing dirt mound. It was now near thirty feet high, and when the bulldozer reached its summit, the soft soil underneath its front tracks gave way slightly. The heavy machine tipped forward. A dark plume of oil smoke exited the bulldozer's exhaust as the driver worked frantically to pull the twelve-ton leviathan back onto firmer ground. Finally, the machine lurched to safety, its payload unreleased. The bulldozer sat idle for a moment, as if to catch its breath, before tipping its bucket in what had now become a ritual cascade of black humus.

Stillman had to leave just then, but that image of the bulldozer's sudden desperation had left him feeling... *exhilarated*. As he raced up the speedway-like S curves of the industrial park drive, on his way towards a certain reprimand, his face held an unaccustomed smile.

By the end of August, the thick layer of plant matter and underlying top soil had been completely stripped, and an area the size of several football fields was laid barren, its uneven surface an odd patchwork of brown silt and gravel, splashes of powdered stone, and long, sinewy roots that lay like dehydrated serpents awaiting burial. The dirt mound had attained a height that was nearly level with the towering Interstate, and appeared the perfect companion piece—a Mayan-like temple to worship the Gods of the Highway. Meanwhile, Stillman sat in his usual place, waiting for the new phase of operations to begin, anticipating its arrival with a mixture of dread and curiosity.

It came in the form of sand.

The bulldozers were replaced by two massive dump trucks, each carrying enough sand to fill an average-sized swimming pool. The trucks thundered in and out of the access drive nonstop, collecting their loads from a sand and gravel pit that was less than a mile away, along the same route Stillman traveled to work.

Running late, Stillman found himself caught behind one of these sloth-like machines, their backs filled to overflowing. He used caution not to follow too closely, for each dip in the road produced a cascade of sand and pebbles from the back of the truck. *Perhaps it's leaving a trail to follow in case it gets lost on its way back to the gravel pit,* thought Stillman derisively.

The dump truck pulled off and Stillman drove past, eyeing the progress that had been made since the day before. Row after row of sand mounds waiting to be leveled stretched across one end of the open acreage. Soon to be buried beneath it all was the memory of the sadness Stillman had felt when the pond first began to dry, the weight of its canopy too heavy to stay afloat—a memory that was now linked to a feeling that somehow the pond had let him down. Stillman also remembered the pain as the bulldozer's blade first ruptured the ground's soft skin, and the almost audible cry that had accompanied the breach of land. And, finally, Stillman relived the exhilaration he had felt witnessing the lurch of the bulldozer the day it had nearly tumbled off the dirt mound, as if the earth itself were trying to shake it off its back.

Something had to be done, Stillman decided. *But what?* He turned onto the industrial park drive. The entire process seemed unstoppable. And then a thought occurred, and a smile once again inhabited his face. His heart matched the speed of his vehicle as he raced up the long, winding hill to work.

The night was clear, the air cool and crisp. The stars were like tiny chips of glass scattered across the flat black surface of the sky. The bulldozers were where the workmen had left them, their buckets down like the heads of large animals tucked close to the ground, fast asleep. The single chain guarding the entrance to the open lot was easily bypassed. Light jacket, boots, garden gloves with holes in the palms from too much use.

A car rushed by on the Interstate, headlights chasing the open road. A tractor trailer truck. Two more cars, one passing the other.

The metallic beasts sat along the edge of the lot. The intruder approached them with the caution they deserved. A hand ran along one of the beast's flanks, up and down until it had found its Achilles heel.

The hand reached inside a coat pocket.

Another car rushed by on the Interstate, its high-speed whoosh like a sigh of relief. And in the momentary illumination a knife dug deep into the soft jugular of the beast's neck—the hydraulic cable that provided movement to its head. The first in a series of small wars had begun.

Three more cables, three more puncture wounds, the same treatment for its twin, and Stillman pocketed the knife and walked back to his car, leaving the yellow-skinned monsters' viscous blood pooling beneath the moonlit night.

The following day Stillman drove down to his usual lunch spot. A police cruiser was parked on the lot. A policeman was talking to the workmen. There would be no work today while the hydraulics were repaired. It looked like the mounds of sand would have to wait, considered Stillman, as he bit into his sandwich, eyeing the frustration evident in the foreman's demeanor.

Stillman watched as the policeman took notes. Damn kids, he could hear the foreman say. But before he settled into his cruiser, the policeman glanced up to where Stillman sat in the high grass overlooking the lot. The policeman pulled out. Stillman watched him. The cruiser turned his way and pulled up alongside.

Tall, deliberate, the officer got out and walked around to the driver's side of Stillman's car. He eyed the construction lot below, then turned his gaze on Stillman.

"Excuse me, sir. I'm Sergeant Riley of the State Police barracks in Danielson. Can I ask your name?"

"Arthur Stillman."

"Mr. Stillman, the workers down there say you sit here almost every day."

"That's right. I eat my lunch. I like the view. Am I trespassing?"

"No, you're fine. I want to know if you've seen anything out of the ordinary recently. Strange vehicles. Teenagers."

"Why, what's going on?"

"Someone vandalized the equipment below."

"No kidding. Is that why things aren't moving?"

"Probably just some local kids. So, nothing comes to mind?"

Stillman thought for a moment, shook his head. "Sorry, Sergeant. I wish I could help. I'll keep an eye out."

The officer handed him a card. "Please call this number if you see anything. Thanks for your time."

"Sure thing."

The officer got back into his cruiser and left.

Stillman finished his sandwich, sucked his soda dry, enjoying the straw's gurgling sound, like the death throes of a blood-let animal.

By the middle of the week, the crew was back to work, the dump trucks dumping, the bulldozer's bullying. Stillman watched. Sunday night, Stillman drove his car to work and parked in the empty parking lot. Under the silent panorama of stars, he walked down the industrial park drive, then crossed the road and entered the construction lot. Two of the mighty dump trucks sat side-by-side on the hard-packed, oil-stained soil. Stillman slipped between the trucks and, like a mouse removing a thorn from a lion's paw, cut the valves out of their massive tires.

For the next three days it rained. August was nearly over, its previous weeks of heat giving way to skies saturated by the summer build-up. The lot turned to mud again. There were standing puddles of water, which pleased Stillman. The air smelled raw, damp, pregnant with life. But soon the skies cleared, the sun resumed its hot and humid onslaught. The workers returned to their duty.

Stillman returned to his.

This time it was the electrical systems. Battery cables severed like spinal cords. Ignition covers removed and multi-colored wires shredded like nerve endings laid bare.

This time Sergeant Riley didn't waste his breath.

"Arthur, I ran your license." The policeman stood over him, eyes masked behind dark glasses. "In August of 1996 you were charged with negligent homicide, but the count was later dropped."

Stillman bit into his sandwich. Pieces of tuna fell onto the wax paper in his lap. The sergeant continued.

"Your wife and child were both killed in that accident." The sergeant crouched to the level of Stillman's window and took off his glasses.

"Arthur, that's tragic about your family. It must be very painful for you. But these are hard-working men; there is no need to take it out on them..."

The sergeant's voice began to fade and Stillman began to

tremble. Not because he was afraid of being arrested. But because the memories began to trickle back, like water through cracks in a well-fortified dam...

...Impatient shuffling of cars... Fourth of July weekend traffic... Massachusetts disappearing into the trail of headlights left behind... wife by his side, dozing... son asleep in the backseat. Alone, it seemed, in the dark coffin of his car. He could have been at home, sitting in a room, surrounded by the glow of a television set. Or in a movie theater, acting out a life through the images on the screen. Or watching the stars from his front porch, trying to pinpoint his place in the universe. He could have been asleep, in a dream about driving home from his wife's parent's house... Fourth of July weekend... traffic thick and claustrophobic... not noticing the red lights tripping like warning flags... brake lights blooming in the night like the reflective eyes of hungry animals possessed by extra-sensory vision... the night coming to a sudden, irretrievable standstill up ahead... a tractor-trailer truck laying on its side like a prehistoric beast shot for trespassing across eternity... his leg reacting too slowly and punching ineffectually between accelerator and brake... the screen of red lights coming up too quickly, sharp turn to the right, away from the herd of automobiles and pick-ups and sport utility vehicles, into the thin cables of the guide rails... up and over and down into the high grass, hitting his head on the windshield, his chest on the steering wheel, stars in his eyes and his breath taken... his wife suddenly in his lap, her face awash in dashboard green, her skin opened along the seam of her forehead, consciousness stolen... his son just a sound like wood tumbling off a neatly stacked pile... then whoosh, a buoyant, free-floating feeling, like death, like sleep, like the final scene in a play about memory as the curtain falls and leaves the calming hush of contentment on your skin as you leave the theater... the water cold and thick with alien life... and a sinking feeling, as metal and glass and rubber descend in a slow-motion gurgling exercise in futility... into the depths of the reservoir, claiming his wife, claiming his child... and the silent screaming soul of a man whose life has been forever altered...

The workers got one of the bulldozers going. Black gouts of smoke coughed from its silver throat. The air filled with the roar and rattle of its metallic tracks. Its blade lowered and dug into the sand.

Stillman turned toward the police officer. "Sergeant, am I being charged with a crime?"

The sergeant put his glasses back on and stood. He folded his notepad and slipped it back into his belt clip. "Have it your way." He nodded towards the workers below. "They asked me to tell you not to park here anymore. Now, there's no law that says you can't. But a word of advice, Mr. Stillman. These guys don't like their equipment being fucked with, and if they decide to take matters into their own hands, I won't be here to stop them. Now, you have a nice day."

When the cruiser pulled away, Stillman meticulously unscrewed his thermos and poured a cupful of chicken noodle soup. He eyed the construction workers as he drank the scalding hot liquid. A single tear ran down the slope of his cheekbone and dropped onto his collar.

Two days later, Stillman was let go from his job. He didn't mind all that much. In fact, it gave him more time to spend down by the roadside overlooking the site, calculating his next move. He couldn't let the crew finish filling in the lot. Each truckload of sand was like a shovel full of sterile earth tossed upon the open grave of his memories. A sense of urgency gripped him. As he sat with his lunch in his lap, the debris of that morning's breakfast littering the dashboard, he decided it would be tonight.

Stillman wrapped up his half-eaten sandwich and started his engine. Down below, the crew was gathered in the shade of one of the idle bulldozers, eating their own lunches. They nudged each other, drawing their attention to Stillman's movement. They watched his departure. Stillman drove away, silently bidding farewell to his captive audience.

Hot August night. The sky rumbled with sheet lightning. Stillman abandoned all pretense of disguise and pulled his station wagon directly onto the lot. Lights off, engine off, he rolled to a stop.

The highway loomed in the near-distance, traffic floating on an invisible cushion of black. On the seat beside him, four five-pound bags of sugar, one for each of the beasts' bellies—a sweet snack to put each to sleep for good.

Stillman could feel the victory of this moment welling up inside of him. One large payment of restitution for all the defeats he had suffered at the hands of a cruel and imponderable fate.

He walked beneath the cloak of night, under the eyes of the stars, toward the tall, dark shadows of the machinery, the sugar bags like babies in his arms about to be delivered to their respectful mothers. But a sudden blinding light caught him mid-stride. A voice shouted. "Hold it right there!"

Stillman froze, unable to see beyond the bright spotlight perched high atop the bulldozer's cab, pinning him in place. He dropped the sugar bags into the sand and they broke open at his feet. Footsteps and whispers began to surround him. "Okay, boys, get him!" a voice said, and Stillman ran.

He ran toward the light, his shoulder knocking someone out of his path with a winded "Oof!". Disoriented, Stillman found himself running across the open, arid landscape of the empty pond bed. His feet dug into the soft sand that had replaced its once verdant life. The crew chased after him, but Stillman knew his feet were carrying him across a more familiar landscape, having chased his dreams on countless occasions across the ruins of his nightmare reality. Calls for him to stop went unheeded, as thunder crashed overhead. Stillman winced, recalling that awful thunderous sound as his car collided with the guide rail, sending him up and over and down into the oblivion of his loneliness.

Stillman chased after the memories of his wife and child, as the shouts for him to stop eventually trailed away like ghost voices in the wind. Traffic rushed by along the elevated Interstate, a blur of white and red lights like a busy airport runway. He had made it across the pond bed and had entered the woods that bordered the empty lot. He heard the rhythmic chitter and thrum of insects, the intermittent gulp of frogs and other wetland life. Branches... then shrubs... then weeds. The sky opened up and the sounds of life surrounded him. His shoes sank into the soft mud and the cool thick water of a new landscape, a more welcome environment— another pond he never knew existed, hidden by the trees, perhaps formed when the other pond was taken by the sun.

Stillman waded in and splashed like a child under the night sky. The stars danced like flecks of glass scattered atop the pond's rippled surface. Stillman rejoiced in his newfound habitat, a place only he could appreciate for all its rich and hidden worth. His wife, his child, the life that was lost on that terrible night—he knew they were here.

Head down, Stillman kicked up his heels and dove into the center depths of the pond to find them.

Thirty-Two Scenes From A Dead Hooker's Mouth

THIRTY-TWO

A FLY TIP-TOES IN AND OUT of the half-open orifice. Back alley, brick wall backdrop. Early morning sun creeping down, waking garbage stink from cold scum. Slow swarm of uniformed legs, black leather shoes, the squawk of police band radio. A face leans in. A photo is taken. "Damn shame. I wonder who she is?" Another click, whirr, high-frequency whine of battery recharge. "Was," says a voice flat as city pavement. The fly crawls in, disappears down a slippery slope.

THIRTY-ONE

NIKKI STUFFS THE MONEY in her skirt and begins to undo the

guy's belt. "Now, let's see what we have here." The guy isn't saying much. They seldom do. It's just as well. The heroin is humming its feel-good song in her ears. Not a whole lot matters after that. She feels for the guy's cock but a pudgy hand pushes her away. "Nicole, stop." The guy's voice cuts through the cotton candy spinning in her brain. She lifts her head. "I still think you're the prettiest girl on the planet." In the lights on the dash, the guy's face is so serious, so sincere. It's like staring at a photograph. But she can't quite remember when it was taken. And then she hears the words she hates. Words that slice through the meat of her heart. "I love you."

THIRTY

THE GUY'S EYES WERE constantly on the move. He was either strung out on meth or this was his first time looking for kicks along the curbside. The eyes light on her mouth. Nikki's used to this. They can't help it. She walks over to the dark blue Plymouth, smiles. The john is awestruck. "How much?" he stutters, eyes once again darting across the neon-lit traffic rush. "Depends what you want." The guy was definitely new at this. He stares at her mouth again, entranced. She taps her heel, impatient. "Blow-jobs are fifty," she says. She doesn't even ask if he's a cop. She can tell. The guy's just too weird. Like the smell of his car. A caustic, ammonia-kind of smell that makes her nostrils flare. The guy nods and reaches to open the door. "Sorry, I don't ride with strangers. Pull into that alley over there. I'll be right over." The guy does as he's told. Nikki walks to the corner thinking *Fifty bucks!* She checks her pocket for a condom.

TWENTY-NINE

"COME ON," SHE PLEADS, "just till I get over." Her teeth feel like aluminum foil, gums like Silly Putty. Electricity wired throughout.

Coming down hard. Manny keeps staring, eyes focused on her soft lips, the wet interior of her mouth. A dealer's gaze, that black sparkle in the eye when the money's not there and yet payment can still be extracted. "Anyone ever tell you you have a beautiful mouth?" The guy places the nickel bag in his shirt pocket like bait in a bear trap and sits back. Nikki can see the outline of his stiff cock beneath his jeans. Her teeth chatter. Her gut cramps and she tastes bile. She imagines the rush, the sweet sui-slide into oblivion. She drops to her knees and pretends she's kissing some boy at her junior prom.

TWENTY-EIGHT

NIKKI WRAPS HER LIPS around the end of the pipe and inhales her last piece of heaven. She eases back onto the pillow and imagines Andrea lying beside her. She can almost smell her shampoo. Sometimes she hears Andrea call her name. Funny how each day it seems her reality chips away like the polish on her fingernails. She pictures Mojo and the other girls as balloons. Mojo is a shiny balloon, black as an oil slick, trapped in a police cruiser. The girls are just a handful of badly tangled but colorful balloons cut free to float among the city's shifting air currents. She watches them scatter as a little girl in a blue jumpsuit, skipping playfully down the sidewalk, jumps up and grabs one of the balloons and darts into a long, dark alleyway, never to be seen again.

TWENTY-SEVEN

THE JOHN'S CAR SUDDENLY speeds away, spinning Nikki back onto the sidewalk, snapping the strap on her pink vinyl mini-handbag, as cops fly in from all angles, lights a kaleidoscopic snake charmer's trance. Mojo doesn't run. He simply grins, arms raised, cell phone held high, as two cops flash their badges and a pair of cuffs. And for the first time since Andrea's death, Nikki smiles a genuine smile, her lips chapped but the pain feels good, the pain feels real. But the relief is only momentary as the police cruiser whisks Mojo away like some kind of celebrity, his cat-confident eyes locked onto hers as they drive by.

TWENTY-SIX

"DID YOU HEAR?" This time it's Sandy, another one of Mojo's girls, but the look of horror and fascination on the girl's face is the same as the last time Nikki heard those words. It's as if they've all become zombies and when one of their own goes down, they just keep on walking. Nikki waits to hear the name, but in her gut it's as if she's already been told. Sandy speaks the name but it doesn't seem real. *No, not her. Not now.* "Where? Where is she?" Sandy recoils as Nikki grabs her by the shoulders, her nails digging in. "Let go, bitch!" Sandy pulls away and points. "Two blocks down. Just look for the crowd. Psycho." And Nikki runs, as best she can in three-inch heels. She has to make sure Andrea's not alone. It was her job to watch her back. She finds the crowd and threads her way through. The alley is taped off. A twisted body lies in a puddle of blood and filth. Cops circle like vultures. Taking notes, so nonchalant. "Okay, back it up." Nikki feels the pavement grow soft beneath her feet. Andrea will never forgive her. Nikki will never forgive herself.

TWENTY-FIVE

A FLASH OF BLONDE HAIR, a blue jumpsuit. Nikki's eyes follow the fleeting image as it threads through the sidewalk's nighttime body traffic and disappears into the mouth of an alleyway. "Hey, where you going?" Andrea's voice trailing as Nikki rushes toward the spot where she last saw the little girl. She pushes past the stares and the whistles and the crude comments to reach the alley, and to her surprise the little girl is there, kneeling on the wet cement where a splinter of light shines down from above. Nikki feels her heart pounding because she knows she's seen this girl before. Not as a street runaway, or a picture in a magazine, but in her own memory. She approaches the kneeling child. The girl's head begins to twist around to see who's sneaking up behind her. "There you are!" Andrea's voice echoes down the alley. Nikki turns. "You okay?" And Nikki shows Andrea what she's found, but the splinter of light now shines down upon nothing. Her eyes search the darkness. Only shadows. "Sorry. I felt like I was gonna puke." And she does. Nothing but clear bile and a couple undigested cheesy fries. "C'mon, we better get back before Mojo sees us gone." She follows Andrea back out onto the street, back to their place on the corner to wait for their next trick, all the while thinking it's got to be the drugs, or the lack of sleep, there's no way the little girl was real, because the girl looked exactly like *she* did when she was that age.

TWENTY-FOUR

A YOUNG ANOREXICALLY-THIN blonde hangs on Mojo's arm as if to keep from floating up into the night sky. "Who's the stick?" Nikki blows a jet of cigarette smoke out of the corner of her mouth. "Her name's Sandy. Mojo's new girl. Don't he know guys like women with meat on their bones?" Andrea reaches down to squeeze the skin above her hips to demonstrate, but realizes the fat that used to be there has long since wasted away. Nikki shakes her head. "I give her a week before she runs home to mommy and daddy." Nikki feels Andrea's arm snake around her shoulder. "Hey, you're not still stuck on him are you?" Nikki finally stops staring at the new girl and laughs like it's the most ridiculous thing she's ever heard. She drops her cigarette butt on the sidewalk and grinds it under her toe. "Don't be stupid, Dre. Mojo's bad mojo. You're all sweetness and nice. And you taste good too." Andrea smiles. A smile that was once beautiful perhaps but now her upper lip carries a deep crease from being split open by a drunken john. Some of her teeth are missing and the ones that are left are a permanent yellow. "Friends to the end." Nikki puts her hands on her ears and winces. "Stop it! I hate that voice!" And the night brightens for just a second before the darkness settles back in upon them.

TWENTY-THREE

ANDREA ARCHES HER BACK. "Yeah, that's it... right there..." She grinds her clit against Nikki's tongue. "Mmmm…" Nikki uses the head of her piercing as a prod. Andrea's thighs begin to tremble, Nikki can feel it through her jaw. The taste of her lover becomes more electric, spiking through the Captain Morgan sweetness still on her tongue. "Oh, God, yes…" Hands grip the back of her head, fingernails dig into her scalp. Nikki rides the wave of spasms until Andrea's hands let go, then draws her face up towards another set of lips. Gentle kisses, strokes of affection. "I love you to death, Nik. Don't ever leave me, okay?"

TWENTY-TWO

"I THOUGHT I TOLD YOU, no fucking shit, and for fuck's sake, no fucking rock!" Andrea runs for the bathroom. Mojo grabs her by the hair and she squeals. "How many times, huh? How many times? That stuff will kill you!" He spins her around and punches her in the stomach. Andrea folds and a white spew jets from her mouth. "Last time. Now get yourself cleaned up and out on that street. You look like shit." Andrea stumbles into the bathroom and shuts the door. Nikki sits on the bed watching it all like a bad dream. And the dream just gets worse. "Who's selling her that shit? Manny?" Nikki's silence says it all. "That piece of crap Puerto Rican, I'll bust his fucking head for fucking with my girls." Mojo looks at her like she's the most vile thing on the planet. He picks up the ashtray containing the crack pipe and hurls it toward her. Nikki ducks and the ashtray shatters against the wall above the bed, showering her in a spray of jagged pieces. She feels one flick across her cheek. Her hand comes away red. The pain is dull, like the rest of her body. The blood seems to calm Mojo down. "Let me see." He squeezes Nikki's face. "It's nothing," he says. "Now clean up this place and get to work." Nikki reaches for him, but he turns and leaves, glass crunching beneath his heels. She can hear Andrea sobbing in the bathroom. Nikki wants to cry, but her eyes are defiant. She hasn't cried since cancer ate her mother up. Nothing seemed worth it since. Not even this.

TWENTY-ONE

"DID YOU HEAR?" Andrea's eyes are as wide as searchlights. Nikki shakes her head. She had just finished her third customer of the night and was enjoying a cigarette break. She smoked pretty regularly now. "You know Marcy, right? One of Big John's girls? They found her all cut up and shit over on Ketchum Street. Dead. The cops hauled Big John's ass downtown, but he says he didn't do it. That's messed up, ain't it?" Andrea's about to cry and Nikki gives her a hug. Andrea's shaking. Probably more to do with the meth she's been taking to stay awake at night. "Don't worry, Dre, I've got your back." Andrea stares at her. Her eyes look as if they want to swallow her up. She gives her a peck on the lips. "I love you, Nik." Nikki grins. "Can I finish my cigarette now?"

TWENTY

THE FREAKY GUY IS BACK AGAIN. But he has the green, and Nikki needs her daily pick-me-up. "What will it be this time, Killer?" The man pulls a rubber dong the size of a wiffle bat out of a paper bag and lays it on the passenger seat. "Is that for me?" Nikki asks playfully. The man shakes his head. "Why don't you get in?" Nikki pulls the gum out of her mouth and tosses it in the gutter. "Back in fifteen," she tells Andrea and slips in alongside the john.

NINETEEN

THE HOT SMOKE ENTERS her throat like a wool mitten left on the radiator too long. Except this mitten unravels the moment it hits her lungs, sending out a network of fine pleasure-tendrils to every inch of her body. Scintillation crisp. Soft burn. Slow melt. She lies back on the couch and nestles her head next to Andrea's. The smell of Andrea's shampoo is like a garden full of roses. "Jesus fucking Christ!" is all she can say, her tongue suddenly gone lazy in her mouth. Andrea nods her head. "I told you it was the best."

EIGHTEEN

SHE SITS ON THE EDGE of the bed in the hotel room. Her nerves are only slightly dulled. Mojo had let her smoke some weed beforehand just to mellow her out. There's a knock on the door and her stomach floods with acid. "Come in," she says, holding her voice firm. A middle-aged man enters the room. He's wearing glasses. He's wide but not very tall. His gut hangs out over his belt. He appears to be just as nervous as she is and this somehow sets her at ease. "So you're the big winner," she says. The guy grins slightly. "Come here." The man walks up and stands before her. She pauses before reaching up to undo his belt. The pants drop to the floor with a jangle. "You don't waste any time, do you?" The man's cock bulges against his briefs. She pulls the briefs down and smiles. It's a fake smile, but it's supposed to make them feel happy, make them feel big. She opens a condom and places it in her mouth, a trick Andrea taught her. She winks a "now you just hold still" wink, then bows her head, slipping the condom onto the man's cock in one smooth practiced stroke. He doesn't say a word during the whole two minutes it takes for him to shoot his load. When he's done, he hurriedly pulls up his pants and leaves, but not before he hands her a hundred dollar bill. "Thanks," she says. Her first john.

SEVENTEEN

"HERE, TAKE THIS." She holds the small white tablet up to her face. "What is it?" It has a dollar sign imprinted on one side. Mojo grins. "You never had X before? Oh, you're in for a treat." He hands her a half-empty bottle of ginger ale gone flat. She swallows the pill in one gulp. "You're so beautiful. That mouth of yours is gonna make you top girl." Nikki doesn't mind hearing the beautiful comment come out of Mojo's mouth. This is a new day, a new life, she's an empty void just waiting to be filled. Mojo leans over and kisses her again. His tongue feels warm in her mouth. His eyes never close. They watch her as one watches something precious, something desired. His hands tug at her tube top and he slowly lifts it up past her small, firm breasts and over her head. Her blonde hair falls back across her shoulders like a caress. She can't tell if it's the drug he just gave her or the fact that she never knew her own father, but she has never felt so comfortable in the arms of another man, so *protected*. Mojo drops his head and takes one of her nipples into his mouth, gently sucking until it aches. Tiny frissons cascade down her body. Mojo smiles, then scoops her up off the couch and carries her into the bedroom. He lays her down. She watches him as he removes his tank top. The room becomes a dark, velvety backdrop. The city is miles away. Mojo unzips her skirt and slides it down to her ankles and off her feet. He cups one of her legs and kisses her calf, all the while his gaze unbroken. Nikki isn't wearing any underwear. Mojo kneels on the bed and leans forward between her legs. He cups her ass with his hands and gently raises her up. His mouth connects with her wetness and her head floods with a sensation she's never felt before. Every movement, every gentle nip, every flick of his tongue, coats her nerves with a delicious warmth that intermittently numbs and electrifies. She gasps and gives in wholly to the moment as time stands still and Mojo eases himself into her and their bodies merge in a seamless complement of arms and legs and soul and love and comfort until her void fills to overflowing. "I love you, Mojo," she says afterwards. Mojo caresses her cheek with his finger. "I love all my girls." And she didn't care if she was just one of many. As long as Mojo was there when she needed him.

SIXTEEN

MOJO EYES HER AS IF he's seeing her for the first time. He even takes his sunglasses off. A grin paints his face like a wicked thought. He doesn't say a word and takes her by the hand and leads her away. "Want me to join you guys?" Andrea offers, left stranded. It's the middle of the afternoon. "No, baby, this is a private party. You just make Mojo some money." Nikki looks over her shoulder. Andrea appears hurt, but then she smiles. *I told you*, she mouths, happy for her.

FIFTEEN

THE GUY WITH THE FULL-BODY tattoo and the silver septum dangling from the middle of his nose turns, needle in hand and says, "You ready for this?" Nikki takes a deep breath. "Just do it, okay?" The tattooed man nods appreciatively. "A sweet angel like you. It will be my pleasure." He locks the clamp tight on her tongue. Nikki closes her eyes and pictures her Uncle Martin's cock as the needle pierces through.

FOURTEEN

THEY STEP OUT OF THE clothes store and onto the sidewalk. Nikki is dressed in a yellow spandex tube top. A black vinyl skirt terminates mid-thigh and hugs her ass. She walks comfortably in her brand-new second hand three-inch heels. "You look like you've done this before." Andrea can't stop staring at her. "I was a model once. It's easy. I'll teach you." Nikki spots a guy walking on the sidewalk on the opposite side of the street. She stares the guy down. He nearly walks into a pole. They both laugh. "God, wait till Mojo sees you. I bet he'll want to do you right there." They pass by a tattoo and piercing shop. Nikki stops. "Hey, I have to do something first." Nikki grabs Andrea's hand and pulls her into the shop.

THIRTEEN

THE SHOWER HITS HER skin like a thousand hot needles. She shivers at first, then lets the water blanket her head and shoulders. Her mind races as she washes the dirt from her skin. She can't stop the flood of images. The look on her mother's dying face. Uncle Martin's sickening smile. The shadows in the alley. All of it leading up to Andrea's outstretched hand. And Mojo. She lets the water wash it all away. All except Andrea and Mojo. She can still feel his touch. Her nipples harden. She rinses off and steps out. Andrea is there, sitting on the toilet seat. She was watching her the whole time. "You're so beautiful." Nikki turns. "Don't say shit like that!" Andrea looks as if she's about to cry. "Sorry, I just never seen anyone on the street that looks like you. You could be a—"

Andrea's voice echoes with a hundred other voices Nikki's heard over the years. *You could be a model. You could be a movie star.* That's all they see. That's all anyone ever sees. Nikki looks in the mirror and the anger goes away. That's all in the past now. "I didn't mean to yell. Sorry?" Andrea's face brightens. "Friends?" Nikki holds out her hands. Andrea smiles. "Friends to the end." She tries her best Chucky the doll voice. "Eww, I hated that movie." They both laugh. Nikki hugs her. Andrea's skin is hot to the touch.

TWELVE

"NIK, THIS IS MOJO, Mojo this is Nikki." The guy in the muscle T and the tattooed arms clicks off his cell phone and pockets it. His eyes start at the bottom and work their way up. When they reach her face, they slide back down to her mouth. "I've already explained the deal to her. She doesn't have a problem with it." Andrea steps back as Mojo circles like a tiger. "Is that so?" He stops, his nose just an inch away. His eyes penetrate her. Nikki admires the way his hair catches the light, slicked back and tied into a ponytail. He smells like one of those magazine swatches. His hands grab hold of her hips and slowly slide into the curve of her waist, then on up to her breasts, where they pause, thumbs prodding gently. "You have a problem with this?" he asks. She can feel her nipples harden. She shakes her head. "Good." He raises a hand to her chin and kisses her. She can feel the tip of his tongue and the brush of his thin mustache on her lip. She sucks it deep into her mouth. He tastes like hickory smoke. For a moment, the world seems to disappear. The street sounds, the endless night, her whole miserable existence—gone. His kiss is like a drug. She awakens to his voice in her ear. "I'll take good care of you, as long as you take good care of me," he whispers. "If I wasn't busy, I'd take you upstairs right now and show you how good I can take care of you." He kisses her again, more lightly this time, a promise of things to come, then reaches into his jeans pocket and pulls out a fifty. He hands it to Andrea. "Take her back to your place. Get her cleaned up, and tomorrow take her shopping." Andrea smiles a "He likes you" smile as they hurry away giggling down the sidewalk. Nikki runs her fingers across her lips. She can still taste him. She thinks she's in love.

ELEVEN

"HEY, WHAT'S YOUR NAME?" Nikki looks up, eyes blinded by the corner streetlight. The girl with the four-inch heels and the short leather skirt standing before her crouches down. "Hey, you all right? Want something to eat? I'm on a break, you want something? There's a place right around the corner that makes the best cheesy fries. C'mon." Nikki looks around. The alley reeks. There are shadows within the shadows. "Why are you being so nice? You don't even know me. I probably look like shit." The girl smiles. There's a glint of braces. "Naw, you're beautiful. Let's just say I've been there." She holds out her hand. "My name's Andrea." Nikki looks around again. The shadows have moved. "I'm Nikki." She shakes the girl's hand. "C'mon, Nikki, let's get you fixed up."

TEN

SHE HAD TO KEEP MOVING. Shadows. The shadows seem to follow her wherever she goes. The night never sleeps. Nikki crouches in the alley, wedged between a stack of cardboard boxes and two large garbage bags that smell like a sun-baked salad bar. A splinter of light shines down from above on a patch of wet cement like a tiny island amid all the black. A bedroom night light for runaways. She tries to make herself invisible. But still she senses they can see her. They could be just tricks of the light, false movements created by street signs and store awnings shifting in the warm, gritty breeze.

Or they could be real. The homeless. The hungry. Following her like dogs on a blood scent. Street people longing for company, or worse. Watching her every move. Waiting until she falls asleep. Waiting until she finally gives in to the night. Waiting to take her to the most vile place on the planet. Where she belongs.

NINE

THE KNOCK COMES AGAIN, and this time Nikki hurriedly stuffs the last of her belongings into her backpack. "Come on, sweetie, open the door. Aunty Sue won't be back for at least a couple hours." She glances around the room a final time. "Don't you want to play, Angel Eyes?" There's a framed photo of her mom on the dresser, when she still looked pink and healthy. Nikki grabs it quickly and slides it into the backpack. "Uncle Martin isn't feeling happy tonight. Come on, honey, don't you want to hear Uncle Martin laugh?" The air is cool upon her face as she crawls out the window into the night. She realizes her cheeks are wet with tears. She hurries away down the sidewalk, beneath the streetlights, toward town.

EIGHT

NIKKI SITS IN THE FRONT seat of her date's Buick Skylark. Her prom dress feels like a plastic bag against her skin. Her date's pudgy hand falls on her shoulder. "I think you're the prettiest girl on the planet." His face is so serious, so sincere. His cheeks dimple into reservoirs of pure adoration. And she can't help but laugh. "So, now what, you wanna fuck? And here I didn't think you had the balls to make a move." Adoration turns to shock, then to pain. Which makes her laugh even more. The boy recoils. She reaches for his crotch. "So, c'mon, let's see what we have here." He pushes her away. "Stop it. That's not what I want." His voice sounds strangled. "Oh, come on, with a line like that? Unless you're not that way." Tears glisten at the corners of the boy's eyes. "Why are you doing this? I love you." And there it is, a real emotion, an honest truth, pulled from one heart and offered to another, bloody, raw. It fills the car. Nikki feels like she's about to suffocate. She has to make room to breathe. "Seems to me you love ring dings more. Now, be a good boy and take me home and I won't tell everyone how pathetic you are." She faces forward, relieved, not expecting him to reach across and open her door and shove her out onto the parking lot, where she falls hard on her rump and bites her tongue. For a moment he stares at her. Stares as if she's the most vile thing on the planet, before spinning the tires of his parent's car and taking off into the night. And she just laughs. Laughs until her sides hurt.

SEVEN

"LET ME SEE MY BABY." Nikki stares at the woman in the hospital bed. *That's not my mother*, Nikki keeps telling herself. The woman's hair is gone. Her skin looks like pissed-on underwear. She smells funny. Nikki can't move. She can't breathe. She feels tears welling to the surface of her eyes and wants to run. She wants to get high. "Mom?" The woman reaches out. "Yeah, it's me, baby." The woman pats the bed. "Come sit." Nikki sits uncomfortably near to the ghost that's talking to her. "I have something real important to tell you. I've always tried to do what's best for you. You know that, don't you? That's why I've made arrangements. After I'm gone, I want you to go live with Aunt Sue and Uncle Martin. They'll take good care of you." And Nikki bites her tongue. Sinks her teeth into the hard pink flesh and feels the pain spike through her. "Okay, Mom, whatever you say."

SIX

"WHY DO YOU HAVE TO GO and screw everything up?" Her mother looks at her as if she's the most vile thing on the planet. "Don't you see I'm trying to do what's best for you? That photographer was the best in the business. And you had to go and throw your body at him like a whore!" Nikki doesn't understand. It's all business, you give a little to get a lot. That's what her mother had taught her. "You said to be nice to him." Nikki begins to chew on her lip. Her mother's face relaxes a bit. "My baby. What man wouldn't be attracted to you. But you're still only twelve years old. Besides, he's a married man." Her mother laughs. A joke between two women. A bond. For the first time, a bond stretches between them. "Uncle Martin is married." And the bond suddenly snaps. "What's that supposed to mean?" Once again she's the most vile thing on the planet. "Nothing, Mom, you wouldn't believe me if I told you." Nikki gathers her clothes and walks out.

FIVE

"YOU'RE SO PRETTY. You could be a model." She hears it so much she could scream. And when she does, a hand arcs out of the cigarette-laced air and slaps her across the mouth. "Apologize to your Uncle Martin!" Her mother grimaces. And Nikki runs into her bedroom, the taste of blood on her tongue.

FOUR

IT'S UNCLE MARTIN'S turn again. If she makes him laugh it will be her turn. She likes it when it's her turn. Uncle Martin always seems to find a place where she's ticklish. It makes her skin all icy. He's wearing those Hawaiian shorts again and he keeps saying, "Keep looking, keep looking." Until she starts tickling his stomach, only it's not really his stomach. It's not soft like his stomach. It seems to move beneath her fingers like a kitten beneath a blanket. "Right there," he says as he closes his eyes. "That's getting ticklish. I think I'm gonna laugh." And her little hand keeps tickling like a tickle bug because she wants to hear Uncle Martin laugh. She loves it when Uncle Martin laughs.

THREE

"SMILE, SWEETIE." The photographer's flash blinds her momentarily. "Oh, she's a natural. A real doll. You sure she's only six." The man laughs. Nikki yawns. "Hold still!" her mother says. Her mother's teeth grind, her lipstick twists into a squashed butterfly. "Smile pretty for the man." Nikki wants to laugh, but she smiles instead. And the two of them melt. Like Silly Putty.

TWO

"WHAT A BEAUTIFUL LITTLE GIRL! What's her name?" Tucked behind her mother's fishnet legs, she looks out from behind. The lady with the shopping cart simply stares, smile plastered like a cartoon face. "Nicole, smile for the nice lady." She feels a pinch on her arm. "Smile, honey." The pinch grows sharper, nails entering her skin. And she smiles, mouth shaped into a perfect angel bow. And the lady with the shopping cart gasps in awe and delight.

ONE

UNIFORMS. WHITE. Nothing but white. Heads, shoulders. Faces. Faces without mouths. "Clear the airways." A disembodied voice.

Fingers poke and prod. Rough penetration. Suction. Dry rush. Gasp. Taste. Swallow. "Time: 2:47. Nicole Elizabeth Branford, welcome to the world."

Lump

W_HEN C_RAIG H_OENIG_ WOKE UP this morning and stepped into the shower, he wasn't thinking anything in particular, other than preparing for another workday ahead; a routine he found comforting in the aftermath of Benny's death. He soaped his underarms, his legs, his groin. He paused at a spot just below and to the left of his naval, in the midst of pubic hair where his scar lay hidden. A lump.

He forced a cough and the lump bulged beneath his fingertips. A dull ache followed.

Again? he thought. That thought was followed by *Fuck me!* Craig didn't want to go through another hernia operation. Especially now that he was living alone. And reaching out to Claire was out of the question.

So he did what most men do—what he did when it happened the first time—he ignored it.

Maybe it's not what he thinks it is. Maybe it's just a muscle pull, a strain. It will mend on its own. Time heals all, he told himself: wounds, bad feelings, that awful haircut you thought was a good idea at the time. Just give it some time, whatever it is, and everything will be back to normal again.

With Benny, however, he was still waiting.

And now this.

Fuck me.

Finding peace after the death of a child is never easy. Nor should it be.

Benjamin Brian Hoenig was born on February 7, 2015. For Craig and Claire Hoenig, he was their pudgy little beautiful boy. Craig called him Lump. Aside from being a bruiser—outgrowing his onesies faster than they could buy them; dimples marking his thighs, elbows and the backs of his hands—he was a lump of joy, a gift for Craig and Claire to build a world around.

Craig put Benjamin to bed one night with an extra blanket. There was a chill in the air and Craig thought nothing of it. What he did think was he wanted to keep his son warm, to protect him like any good father would. He kissed his son goodnight, told him he loved him, and shut off the bedroom light.

After Benjamin's death, Claire blamed everything. God. The crib manufacturer. The blanket. But mostly she blamed Craig. Craig believed it was because he was the last to see their son alive.

For Craig and Claire, the death of their son became like a cancer between them, a lump of grief no amount of counseling or time could overcome. Claire shut down emotionally and Craig drank too much. They were separated within a year. Craig got an apartment closer to his job, while Claire stayed in the house until the divorce finalized.

Craig missed his little Lump. He missed the little boy he would have become, the teenager, the man. He missed the whole lifetime of what could have been. All Craig had of him now were memories of his first eighteen months. And a scar.

A surgical scar from the hernia operation Craig had shortly after Benny's first birthday. Add the combined weight of Benny and the gargantuan car seat he filled, and the act of lifting it awkwardly into the backseat of their SUV, and voila. Something had to give. Craig had discovered an egg-sized lump in his groin the following day.

But Craig knew aches and pains were all part of being a parent: the headbutt to the chin, the inadvertent poke to the eye, the stepping on small plastic toys with bare feet. And, yes, sometimes minor surgery. But how many of us would gladly accept this pain over and over again to have your child back?

Craig went to work as planned, but not without a little medicinal help. A shot of Irish whiskey in his coffee did the trick. His job was one of those plug and play professions: quality control engineer for a major circuit board manufacturer. He'd been performing the act for so long now, half the time he was on autopilot. Dave, his boss, had been pretty lenient since Craig lost his son. The two of them would go out for drinks now and then. Dave had no children and had been twice divorced, so he couldn't offer advice. And that was okay with Craig. It probably took the pressure off Dave, too.

But Craig's job required a lot of sitting, and by the end of the day the dull ache in his abdomen, that had been minimal that morning, had blossomed into a gut-punch that, at times, made him nauseous.

Craig left his miniature city of resistors and semiconductors and went into Dave's office. "I gotta take off. I'm not feeling well."

Dave gave him his usual look of concern. Craig could almost hear Dave's thoughts thumbing through the hit list. Was he coming down off a bender and, once he left, was about to get back on it? Was he depressed? Or was he simply telling the truth?

Dave nodded. "Go home and get some rest. You look like shit."

"Thanks," Craig said. "See you tomorrow."

Craig couldn't wait to get home to see what the fuck he'd done to himself.

The pain, however, didn't prevent Craig from making his usual pit stop at the liquor store on the way home. He needed to stock up.

By the time Craig walked through his apartment door, he had to rush into the bathroom. To say he puked his guts out would be an overstatement. It was nothing but coffee and bile. This wasn't a drunken heave but a pain threshold one. Apparently Craig had reached his limit. And the retching didn't help.

He undressed. The mere act of unbuttoning his jeans was a relief. He stood in his shirt and underwear in the harsh light of the bathroom and was astonished by what he saw.

The bulge, which he could only feel that morning, was clearly visible: an egg-shaped rise on top of the old hernia incision. Foolishly, he pressed on it and doubled over in pain. Bile rose again to the back of his throat, but after a couple deep breaths the pain subsided.

What the fuck?

Not today. I can't deal with this today, said the weaker Craig inside his head. *It can wait till tomorrow. Tomorrow, first thing, I'll call the doctor who performed the original surgery and make an appointment. Something's screwed up. Maybe there's a warranty on surgeries. Once they fix something, it should stay fixed, right?*

He treated his empty stomach to some scrambled eggs and toast, and washed it all down with a healthy dose of whiskey, no ice. By late afternoon he was passed out on the couch.

Craig dreamed he and Benny were playing on the living room floor of the home he and Claire once shared. Craig would lie on his back and pretend he was sleeping. Benny would crawl onto Craig's stomach and Craig would 'wake up' and say, "It's the baby monster! Oh, no!" Benny would giggle till he drooled as Craig tried to get away. But Benny would always catch him, because he was one smart baby monster.

A cell phone was ringing. It brought Craig up out of the dream into a darkened apartment. He fumbled for the phone and finally answered it. It was Claire.

"I called your work and they said you'd gone home sick. Is everything okay?"

"I had an upset stomach, that's all," he said, and right away Claire picked up on the slight slur in his speech.

"Are you drinking again?"

"What do you mean 'again'?" he said, a touch of sarcasm in his voice.

"That's right, from what I hear, you never stopped."

"Is that why you called, Claire? What's the matter, you needed someone to kick and no one was available?"

He heard Claire take a deep breath. "I scheduled a memorial service for Benny. It will be two years tomorrow. I thought you might want to be there."

It was Craig's turn to take a deep breath, and with it came an excruciating stab that was accompanied by a wave of nausea.

"Craig? You sure you're all right?"

"I'm fine," he said through gritted teeth. "I gotta go." He ended the call.

It was an odd thing to say. He clearly wasn't going anywhere. He just needed the conversation to stop, for the memories to stop. The dream he'd had kept resurfacing, becoming more real than Claire's voice.

Two years. It was hard to believe. Benny, dead longer now than he had been alive.

Craig pulled himself into a sitting position, leaned toward the end table and switched on the lamp. The pain in his side was still there but it had become less focused, spreading now from navel to groin.

Tears wet his face as he reached for the whiskey. *Straight shots from here on*, he told himself. The sooner he reached oblivion the better.

That's when he felt the first movement.

It was an odd flutter beneath the skin, as if he were being caressed from the inside. He looked down and watched as his abdomen rose, deformed, then returned to normal—normal being a now tennis ball-sized bulge where his hernia scar was located. He leaned over for a closer look.

The bulge moved again, only this time he saw what appeared to be the profile of a miniature face.

"Lump? Is that you?"

His heart beat so heavy he thought it just might stop in his chest. As crazy as it sounded, Craig believed his boy had come back to him.

"I'm so sorry," he said, fresh tears streaming down his cheeks. He tried to cradle the swelling but only managed to induce more pain. He watched the lump rise and fall, each time appearing to settle slightly larger than before. It was growing fast.

Craig didn't know what to do. He could go to the hospital, but they'd likely treat it as a hernia, or even worse, a tumor and cut into Benny—kill him without knowing. Craig had to protect his son, make up for the way he hadn't protected him that night in his crib.

He eyed the bottle of whiskey. He had his own anesthesia. He had steak knives in the kitchen. He had plenty of clean towels. He even had a soldering iron to cauterize the wound—part of a soldering station he had set up at the apartment for his own electronics projects. He never thought he would need it for surgery.

Benny pushed against his skin, restless. Craig had made up his mind.

He gathered everything he could think of and brought it into the bathroom. Extra lighting. A mirror. Knives soaking in a tumbler of whiskey. Soldering iron plugged in and smelling of burned plastic. Craig stripped naked and sat on a bed of towels, his back against the tiled wall. He even shaved the hair surrounding the previous incision. Then he waited for the contractions to begin.

"It's okay, Benny, I'm here for you, now," he said, gently caressing the ever-expanding growth in his side. The pain was now secondary to the nervous excitement he felt.

By the time Benny was ready, Craig was pretty well anesthetized. The skin over the lump was stretched taut, shiny like the surface of a balloon. From his vantage point, Craig thought the previous scar looked like a white landing strip on a flesh-colored hilltop.

Craig lifted one of the steak knives from the tumbler and placed the knife edge on the scar. He took a deep breath, let it out, and began moving the blade gently back and forth. He didn't want to hurt Benny. Not again. Although the coroner had said he had likely felt no pain. The blanket had slowly choked off his air supply while he slept. Benny simply lost consciousness and never woke up.

Again, the tears were back, clouding Craig's eyes. He began to sob, recalling those early days. The raw sensation of grief that tore at both he and Claire. How they couldn't look each other in the eye. How Benny's death had drained the life from them and dried up any life-sustaining cord that connected them to each other. Two deaths occurred that day. Benny and the love he and Claire had shared. Benny's was merciful. Theirs was not. It was slow and painful, a punishment, no doubt, for their carelessness.

But all that was about to change.

Craig must have at last broken through the skin because the flesh-colored hilltop was now spilling tiny rivers of blood. A dark gash had appeared where the white scar had been.

Craig dropped the knife and pulled at the edges of the incision with his fingers. He had washed his hands as best he could, and probably should be wearing rubber gloves, but infection was the least of his worries.

He pried the incision open and there he was. Benny's head moved beneath his fingertips, struggling to get out, struggling the way he imagined Benny had struggled as the blankets cinched tighter around his neck, regardless of what the doctor had said.

"It's okay, Benny... Everything's going to be all right... I've got you... Daddy's here..."

Craig pulled harder at the edges of the incision and, using his abdominal muscles, he pushed. He felt the pressure build. He pushed again, crying out as the skin tore. Benny's head crowned. With one final push, he was through.

"There you are," said Craig, cradling his son in his bloodied hands. "I've got you, my little lump."

The joy Craig felt was the ultimate anesthesia. It didn't matter that Benny didn't look like any newborn he'd ever seen. It didn't matter that blood as thick as chocolate syrup was pouring from the self-made incision. All that mattered was that he was able to hold his son one last time.

THE GOLDEN DOOR

There is a home that lies beyond
And past its golden door
Awaits the one who's now away,
Not lost—just gone before.
And in that home that lies beyond
The Master will prepare
A place for you,
And when He calls
You'll meet your loved ones there.
—Author Unknown

ONE

AS I LIE IN THIS BED that isn't my bed, in this house that isn't my house, listening to the wind push against the eaves searching for weaknesses in its hundred-year-old frame, I have come to believe I am supposed to die here.

It's okay. If I do, I won't be alone.

I've spent the last thirty years married to a beautiful woman. I witnessed the birth and growth of our two daughters, who now have lives and families of their own. I've been fortunate enough to be employed during that entire time, earning enough to live comfortably in a fine house on a nice country lot. I've lived a good life. Why then did I go and throw it all away?

I'm not about to detail the slow, degenerative process that led to my wife and I divorcing. What matters is one day I found myself wanting out—wanting a cessation of the pain, disillusionment and disappointment of a life I believed was no longer in my control. I saw a bruised and battered marriage that could not be saved, no matter how hard I tried. So I simply let go.

Room for rent. Old home. $450.00 per month.

The instant I saw the ad, my heart began to race. I wasn't looking for much, just a place for my reading chair, my piano, and enough shelf space for my books. Not only was the price more than affordable, it was closer to my work and in the same town, Columbia, where I spent my childhood.

I called.

Imagine my surprise when the address given to me was on the very same country road I grew up on.

I took an extended lunch away from the office that day and met with who I believed to be the owner of the house. He was an older gentleman, white haired and heavyset, but active-looking based on the flannel shirt and jeans he wore and the 4x4 vehicle he drove. "It's not much," he said as he gave me the tour of the aging colonial. He showed me the kitchen, living room and upstairs bedroom—furnished with bed, dressers and end tables. There were two other spare rooms upstairs, empty, one with homemade bookshelves along one wall. I asked about the rooms and he said, "Sure, take 'em if you need 'em."

I did. I had the first month's rent in my pocket, cash. He gave me a key and introduced himself. "Just call me Woody." We shook on it. I moved in the following week on the first of September.

I hardly saw Woody after that. He retired to his downstairs bedroom by 7:00 pm most nights and was gone to work when I got up for morning coffee. On the rare occasions we crossed paths, I learned that he had recently been divorced, worked in construction, and was responsible for supplying sand for the DOT trucks for the eastern half of the state. The owner of the construction company Woody worked for had bought the old house specifically for the property and had built a multi-million dollar home in the wooded acres out back. When Woody needed a place to stay, the owner offered him the job as caretaker for the old dwelling.

Needless to say, it was surreal driving through town each morning on my way to work. These were the roads I used to bicycle as a kid. Swimming in the lake at the foot of the hill was almost a daily ritual in the summertime. There were a few new additions, of course—a development here, a renovation there—but for the most part the town of Columbia was as familiar as old clothes. Even the old house I now rented from. It was known as the Kulgren House when I was growing up. One summer, my brother was hired by the elderly couple who lived there to mow the lawn. Mrs. Kulgren would let my brother and I hunt butterflies in the field out back, which was now grown in. She would let us pick from the black raspberry bushes that grew along the path that led into the woods, a path now gone, absorbed by undergrowth. There were snow apples in the winter, crab apples and quince in the summer. The trees were still there, but had since been overgrown by poison ivy and no longer appeared to bear fruit. Mrs. Kulgren used to offer us oatmeal and raisin cookies and slices of spiced bread as snacks. Mr. Kulgren was a mysterious gentleman, tall and quiet with a deep, grumbling voice. His most prominent features were his eyebrows, which grew wildly above his cold, gray eyes. Most of the time, Mr. Kulgren stayed in his workshop—a separate building that sat beside the carriage-shed-style garage—where he created pewter plates painted with enamel.

It's odd, I know, but from the day I moved in, carrying my boxes of books up the narrow stairway to the spare bedroom, I was comfortable here, as if I were home again. Odd, because my real childhood home had been just down the street; a home that burned when I was eight years old. The house that replaced it was still there—a house we had lived in for only a few years before my parents separated and the bank took it back—but I had never thought of it as *home*. Home had turned to ash and cinder. Home had joined the sky in the form of heat and smoke, like the spirit of a loved one, never to return.

Until now.

TWO

MY WIFE AND I MARRIED YOUNG. Too young I must admit now. But youthful ignorance has its benefits. When we bought our dream house, we dove-tailed neatly into our respective roles. I worked long hours, and when I was home I worked outside maintaining the yard. There was always a project or two pending, a stone walkway here, a garden fence there. While I was outside, my wife took care of the inside: painting, stenciling, the selection of home decor, the constant rearranging. She cared for the children. She washed the clothes. She cooked the meals. She bought the food. So, when I left my beautiful wife and fine house, I needed to assume both roles.

I had never lived on my own, and had to learn to do all the things one does when one lives alone. For the first time in my life, I shopped for my own food. I made my own meals and washed my own clothes, folded my own shirts. My days were filled with a comfortable routine and a pleasant randomness. There was a genuine feeling of independence that relaxed and re-energized me. I hated to admit it, but leaving my beautiful wife and fine house was the best decision I had ever made. There was, and always had been, a sense of artifice about who I was there. But here there was no pretense, no subtle battle of wills, no more lies. I was, at last, free.

But I was alone. And sometimes that was palpable. The quiet was much quieter. The echoes louder. At times, I could almost hear my own thoughts.

Sometimes, I voiced those thoughts aloud... and sometimes the house answered back.

It answered in the form of the rattle and hiss of the radiator; in the creak of the floor boards. At times, the window frames shuttered and shook as if besieged by a sudden chill. House noises one would expect. But there were other noises I couldn't quite identify but attributed to one aging mechanism or another. Noises I grew accustomed to hearing and ignoring as the days progressed. It helped that I was a sound sleeper.

I didn't begin to suspect that there was something "other" here until October, when Woody began to spend his weekends in Maine, leaving me in charge of the old colonial.

It began simply enough. The long weekends home alone had me puttering about, sweeping floors, washing laundry, cooking meals for the week ahead. A box of spaghetti, a half-pound of ground beef, and a jar of tomato sauce provided lunch and dinner for days. A large can of baked beans and a six-pack of hotdogs provided the rest. It was cheap. It was easy. And, with the right amount of seasoning, it was good. But even with the television on, I would hear things. Rumblings. The sound of footsteps where footsteps should not be. There were also sightings. Sudden movements that disappeared when my eyes flicked in their direction. Early on, one of the strangest occurrences was me waking one morning to find that a stray cat had crawled beneath my bed covers and was nudging its wet nose against my face. The slam of a door downstairs and a man's deep voice cursing "Damn cat!" caused the stray to dart out of the room. When I got out of bed to tell Woody the cat he was looking for had been in my room, I realized the house was as silent as ever. There was no cat. No

Woody cursing it. No slamming door. Woody wasn't home. I was alone.

The funny thing was that the cat was gray—all gray but for white boots and a spot of white on its chest. It also had green eyes. Funny because, growing up, I had a cat that looked exactly like it. A cat named Smokey.

But it was just a dream. An odd waking dream, but a dream just the same.

In my mind's defense, I had never known this kind of isolation and had become more liberal in my acceptance of the tricks one's mind might play. I thought, so this is what desert wanderers experience when they see an oasis where there is only endless sand. This is why long-haul truck drivers crash, avoiding phantom objects in the road.

Of course, I could have called my wife, to ease the silence (after all, we had separated on good terms), but I didn't know what we would have talked about. We had barely communicated when we were together, so why begin now? I had my work and the people I worked with. I was content. I was, at last, solitary—a state, perhaps, I had been destined for all along.

THREE

As WINTER NEARED, there were entire weeks I wouldn't see Woody at all. When I'd come home from work, his watch and pocket change would be on the kitchen counter near the door; his coat and work shirts draped on the back of the dining room chairs. Unless I opened his closed bedroom door (which I never felt compelled to do), I had to assume he was sleeping soundly on the other side.

I would eat quietly, watch television with the volume turned low, and wash whatever dishes needed washing before heading upstairs to bed. I tried to make as little noise as possible. Not only was I respectful of Woody's presence, I had become respectful of the house itself, as if it too required a certain behavior to be maintained. Respect the house and the house would respect me, I believed.

It was a silly thought, I realized, but as October carried into November, I had begun to think of the house as more than just an aging structure. Its outer walls were its skin; its windows, eyes. The rooms were like the separate chambers of its heart. The house breathed. It was alive, much the same way Woody and I were. And like any old home, I thought, having been abandoned, left empty for so long, it had almost died. But Woody's presence, as well as my own, had breathed new life into its cracked skin and creaking bones. It once again had a life all its own, and yes, even an emotion, albeit temperamental. An emotion that was on display one Sunday morning after a night of fitful sleep.

Again, I was awakened. This time, the noises didn't emanate from downstairs where Woody would have been; they came from upstairs, just down the hall: heavy footsteps, slamming doors, and what sounded like voices engaged in an argument.

Initially, I was held captive in my bed, frozen like the little boy I remembered, up in my attic room in the childhood home that had burned, gripped with fear as my parents argued, my father's voice booming, my mother's shrill. But, on this morning, the noises dissipated just as quickly as they had come, vacuumed from the present into some dark past memory.

Had I imagined it?

With the fuzzy residue of sleep lingering in my head, I left my bed, opened the bedroom door, and peered into the hallway.

The light from the bathroom window gleamed along the wood railing at the top of the stairwell.

I stepped out into the hall and the floor immediately creaked beneath my feet. I glanced down the stairwell to the first floor. There were no sounds. No Woody puttering in the kitchen, humming to himself, making breakfast. No television drone. It was Sunday. Once again, he was gone for the weekend.

The spare bedroom door was closed. I approached it and eased the knob in my hand. I had to apply more pressure than usual to force the door open. It had been shut all the way, wedged tight where the warp of the door met the jamb. At last, I freed it.

Sunlight filled the room's three plastic-covered windows. The two windows directly ahead looked out, over bushes, onto the road. The window to the right offered an unobstructed view of the driveway. I stepped over to this window and confirmed that Woody's truck, usually parked on the grass, in a nook next to the overgrown shrubbery, was absent.

I looked both ways, my nose pressed against the plastic, the warmth of the sun on my face. I shook my head and intended to walk away, wash up, go downstairs and make some coffee, but a loud thump overhead stopped me in my tracks.

I stood in front of the attic door. I had yet to explore the attic, not knowing if spiderwebs or hornets or mice were present, and with no desire to find out. But I found myself reaching for the doorknob... the knob turning in my hands. I stepped back as the door creaked open on its hinges. A steep, rough-cut set of stairs shot upward. Sunlight poured in through the small window at the peak of the house—the same window I would catch myself staring at after retrieving the mail at the end of the driveway, as if expecting to see a face staring down. Nets of cobwebs hung from the eaves. Aside from the webs, however, the attic was relatively clean.

The stairs were as steep as a ladder; I expected to hear the thump again as I pulled myself up. I was surprised that the attic had a floor. It was a large space, and it was virtually empty; nothing but old slats of wood and window screens stacked neatly against the eave. It wasn't as drafty as I had imagined. The heat of the house rose into the crawl spaces and warmed the air. In fact, a good vacuuming and a braided rug, an easy chair and a television would have made for a nice getaway, I thought. Add a mini-fridge and it could be a party for one.

But I already had all the privacy I could ever want. Too much, in fact.

I approached the large central chimney and searched beyond to see what could have made the noise I had heard. I came to the back window that looked out over the woods. Through the treetops, I could see the deep blue of Columbia Lake at the foot of the hill. I looked down. The canopy of vines below had lost most of its leaves. Beneath a particularly dense clot of vines and briars, I spied a small wooden structure.

A well house.

It was a feature of the property that my brother and I had never seen during our childhood visits. Looking out the attic window, I was confident there were other features of the property, as well, that had gone unseen, unexplored.

The wind howled just then and something thudded against the roof overhead. The big oak tree that grew alongside the house shedding a piece of rotted branch, I assumed.

Satisfied, I made my way out of the attic and went downstairs.

FOUR

LATER THAT MORNING, my mind still buzzing from discovery, and feeling the need for some fresh air, I donned my winter coat and went outside. At first, I walked around to the back of the house and located the old well I'd seen from the attic window. I pushed my way through the undergrowth and parted the canopy that clung to the well's miniature roof. The rope around the winding barrel looked frayed. There was no bucket (perhaps fallen down the well's throat ages ago), but overall the well was still in good condition, perhaps preserved and protected from the sun all these years by the ever-thickening canopy of vines.

I leaned over the ledge and peered into the cool black void. Instead of making a nuisance of myself and shouting, as one would in a cave to hear one's echo, I bent to the ground and picked up a fist-sized stone. I dropped it into the well and listened.

A long, silent second passed before I heard a heavy *kerplunk!*

I smiled.

Feeling enervated, I decided then to take a walk.

Over the years, if I had been driving in the area, I always made it a point to detour past the "old homestead," as my father liked to call it. Perhaps, I was hoping the house that had burned would still be there, that it had all been one fantastic dream. That those memories of a warm June morning in 1972, when I was awakened by my mother screaming for us to "Get out!" along with what sounded like clapping noises, had been a figment of my childhood imagination. But, no, the house that was built in its place was there instead, standing like an imposter. As the years went on, I had stopped taking the detour. I guess I had finally given up hope.

As I walked down the road, past the old homestead, the property appeared very small. There were two cars in the driveway, a utility shed to the right that never used to be there. Bushes now blocked where my brother and I used to ride our bikes, playing chicken at night, my brother taking off in one direction around the house while I rode in the opposite direction, my heart pounding at each blind corner. The front yard looked too short for the football scrimmages our dad used to run with us. "Go out for a pass!" My brother and I would run, each clamoring for the ball.

I could see my mother working in the garden in the back (now a well-manicured lawn). My mother had also played badminton with us kids, my two sisters on her side, my brother and I on the other. We would play until the bats came after the birdie, swooping so low we feared they might hit us.

It didn't seem possible three of them were gone: my mother and father dying years ago, my brother recently passing from a heart attack at the age of forty-eight.

I walked to the end of the road and turned around. This time I didn't look at the old homestead as I passed by. I kept my eyes straight ahead, recalling the not-so-special times. The times my brother had teased me until I cried. The times my father had terrorized the household with his loud voice, penetrating eyes, and his angry hands. I remembered my mother crying in her room.

And when she wasn't crying, she was distant, an overwhelming sadness draped about her like a shroud. I remembered it all and grew tired. When I returned, I needed to rest. I made myself a cup of tea, turned on the television, and reclined on the small sofa. I found a movie on one of the independent stations, a murder mystery. I was asleep before the first commercial break.

FIVE

I'M WALKING AMONG the ruins of our burned down home. Except I'm not eight years old, I am the age I am now. The smell of damp char permeates the air. My brother is there, my mother, too, picking through the ashes in search of memories. I find the microscope I received for Christmas; its wooden box is scorched, the microscope inside ruined, its plastic eyepieces heat-deformed. What remains of the house is nothing more than a few standing support beams and a fireplace chimney. The roof had collapsed and the piles of debris are difficult to delineate. I stumble through what was once my bedroom, smudging my sneakers black, when a gray streak darts out from under the rubble and runs toward the woods.

"Smokey?"

It's our tabby cat, left behind, no doubt scared and confused by the sudden change of landscape.

Smokey stops atop the stone wall and stares at me, his green eyes wide, as if I'm a stranger.

"Here Smokey," I call, abandoning the pile of ash, my hand outstretched.

Smokey turns and bounds into the woods...

I awoke to the sound of a fork scraping across a dinner plate. I lifted my head. Woody sat at the dining room table eating a plateful of roast beef, boiled potatoes, and carrots. I sat up quickly, embarrassed for having taken up the sofa, which Woody usually sat on while eating dinner.

"Sorry," I said, "I guess I fell asleep." I rubbed my face, still groggy from the mid-afternoon nap.

Woody smirked. "This is your place, too. I made a plate for

you. It's on the counter." He gestured toward the kitchen.

The local weather was on the television, the forecast calling for heavy snow. Woody's rheumy eyes stared at the map of Connecticut and the approaching storm front. "Looks like I'm working tonight." He gave his head a brief shake. "I should have retired when I had the chance." He ate the last bite of his meal and stood. "Ah, well." He went into the kitchen and washed his dishes, while I watched the weather. Five to six inches were expected, with a Nor'easter to follow. Woody put on his boots and coat.

"Okay, Graham, you have a good evening. Remember to turn down the heat before you go to bed."

I assured him I would, and he was out the door. Moments later his 4x4 left the driveway.

I wouldn't see him again for another three days.

The weathermen were right: a Nor'easter did follow, but no one predicted just how bad it would be. The night after Woody left, the snow turned hard and steady as the Nor'easter churned up the coast. The lights flickered with each wind gust, threatening to blink out. I lit some candles in the spare bedroom where my piano sat. The weight of the accumulated snow and ice on the rooftop added new sounds to an already full repertoire of creaks and rumbles. The furnace labored under the cold. As if believing I could soothe the storm, the candles providing a soft ambiance, I began to play.

My father played piano, a kind of ragtime jazz he had learned by ear, mimicking the 78 rpm records his parents listened to. It was the only time I ever saw my father completely in his element. His heavy hands and thick fingers would skip lightly across the keyboard, his foot rising and falling on the sustain pedal. As I grew older, I also learned to play piano by ear. Like my father, I found in it the same solace, the same emotional outlet that my temperament required.

As I sat in the candlelight, I began with classic holiday songs: The Christmas Song, Ave Maria, and a slowed down waltz-styled version of Jingle Bells. This would be the first year I would spend the holidays away from my family, and the sadness of that realization imbued my playing.

The wind howled.

My hands began to find keys and chords that were unfamiliar but reflective of my mood. I improvised. I was feeling both solemn and nostalgic, and the music my fingers produced provided a wistful soundtrack to my thoughts.

It was then the wind outside died down and the house seemed to settle into a quiet I had never heard before. For a moment it felt as if the house were listening, as if I had an audience. I felt a presence in the shadows behind me, beyond the stacks of unpacked boxes, just out of reach of the candle's wavering flame. I played on.

Call it wishful thinking, but I was reminded of when I had first learned to play and I could hear the creak of my mother's footsteps as she listened from just outside the doorway. I missed her attentiveness. I missed her kind, giving heart. She was the light in an otherwise dark universe when I was growing up. And though her light dimmed from time to time, eclipsed by forces she could not control, I still missed her.

A loud thump gave me a start, and my fingers stopped mid-key. It sounded as if a heavy boot had stomped on the floorboards in the attic overhead. The wind had picked up and again I assumed the sound had been just an errant branch hitting the roof from the large oak tree.

The mood broken, I stopped playing, brushed my teeth and went to bed.

SIX

THE STORM LASTED THREE DAYS, dumping nearly three feet of snow on most of Connecticut. The plows carved out what they could, creating snow banks higher than the stone walls in places. The local news stations began urging people to dig out their mailboxes because the undelivered mail was piling up at post offices as deep as the snow itself. As I made breakfast on my second morning home from work, unable to get out of the driveway, the owner of the property, who up until now I had never seen, came by riding on his monstrous snowblower. Great white fonts shot up into the trees and broke like waves over the bushes. In a matter of minutes, as if by magic, the driveway was clear. But the mailboxes remained buried. So, with nothing better to do, I grabbed the shovel from the mud room and made my way down to where the mailboxes were last seen.

It was the first break in the skies in over a week, and my neighbors were outside clearing their driveways and cleaning off their vehicles. The morning sun cast a warm glow on the wintry surroundings. It was quite beautiful and serene. Using the shovel's blade, I sliced away the snow bank, letting the chunks fall at my feet. The snow was heavier than I'd anticipated, and soon my arms tired. I leaned on the shovel to let my muscles relax. Perspiration dampened my forehead and my temples pounded lightly to the increased tempo of my heart. Across the street, a middle-aged woman and her two teenage boys freed their pickup truck from the ice and snow. She backed the pickup out onto the road. I recognized the guttural rumble of the truck's motor, as I'd heard it on many occasions roaring to life and taking off down the street like a jet plane. I waved, like I usually do when encountering strangers, and the truck pulled up next to me, the window rolled down.

"I've been meaning to stop and formally introduce myself," she said. "I'm Carol." The woman smiled and held out her hand; I removed my glove and gave her hand a gentle shake. "It's nice to see the old place lived in again."

Based on the age of her children and the style of her hair— blonde, short and permed—I guessed she was in her late thirties, perhaps older.

"Graham," I said, "I'm renting the upstairs. I actually grew up here in Columbia. My parents owned one of the houses just down the road." I pointed in the direction I was referring to.

"And now you're back," Carol said.

She was all smiles. It was hard to tell if she was hitting on me or just being neighborly. It was probably obvious that I was a single man, my graying, solitary manner something only a woman would recognize. If I had been of a different mind, I might have adopted a more suggestive tone and said something like, "You should still drop by sometime. I'll show you what it looks like on the inside." Or "Your smile is the highlight of my day, so far." But I just didn't have that kind of male egotism inside me anymore. I was more concerned with clearing the mailbox of ice and snow than getting into bed with another woman.

"It's kind of strange," I said. "My brother used to mow the lawn for the elderly couple who once lived here. The Kulgrens?"

"Then you must have known the Harrisons—Jan and Derek?"

"The name sounds familiar," I lied. She was obviously mistaking me for someone much younger, someone closer to her own age.

There came an awkward silence then. She looked in her rearview mirror. "Well, I better get going before a snow plow comes along and hits me. You take care."

"It was nice meeting you," I said.

She smiled and drove off, probably thinking how sad I was, how broken. If so, she would be wrong. I was now more accepting of life than I had ever been. I believed life had no intent on making us sad, or breaking us. Things just happened. It was up to us whether to invite that sadness, or brokenness, inside.

I finished the rest of the shoveling, clearing enough snow so the mail carrier could pull up and pull away with ease. As I walked back toward the house, I glanced up at the attic window. A figure stood staring down at me. My temples still pounded from the exertion and my head felt a little light, but I could swear that what I was seeing was real. My footing slipped and I glanced away for just a second. When I looked back, the figure was gone.

SEVEN

THE ARRANGEMENT WOODY and I had was unusual in this day and age. There was no lease, no legally binding commitment on my behalf, just an inherent trust that, in his absence, I would take care of things.

Which I did. Faithfully. I made sure to never let the furnace run for too long, and never to leave the lights to burn unnecessarily. I made sure the kitchen was tidy at all times—dishes washed and put away, refrigerator free of spoiled food. I swept when the floors needed sweeping, cleaned the bathroom sink and mirror when it needed cleaning. On the first of every month I would leave a rent check on the counter before heading off to work; that check would be gone when I arrived home. Between the weekends in Maine and the winter storms that churned like clockwork up the coast, Woody had become more specter than landlord. Only the occasional plate of food left for me (like one would for a stray cat) or a hastily-scribbled note stating the day of his return, provided proof he existed at all. One day, perhaps to test the theory of Woody's existence, my curiosity got the better of me and I found myself standing outside Woody's bedroom door.

I knocked first. Even though his 4x4 was absent from the driveway, I wanted to be able to show that I had made every attempt not to trespass.

I even called out. "Woody?"

I paused long enough before turning the knob. The door was unlocked. It swung open freely. "Woody?" I said again, entering the room.

Inside was an old bed and a dresser with a lamp on top, nothing more. The bed was made and looked as if it hadn't been slept in in quite a while. On the wall, beneath the window that faced the driveway, the plaster was crumbling; a patch of white flakes littered the hardwood floor. I walked over to the dresser. At the base of the dresser lamp were a few coins, a book of matches, and a pen with advertising on its side. My ears were sensitive to any car sounds in case Woody should arrive home unexpectedly. I reached up to open the topmost dresser drawer but hesitated. I felt as if I were being watched. Entering a room was one thing, but peeking into private belongings was a much greater offense. Besides, I thought, what if the drawers were empty? What if the Woody I had been seeing and had talked to in fact did not exist?

A chill ran along my arms and I fled the room. I convinced myself later that my sudden exodus was because I didn't want to get caught, and not because I was afraid of what I might find—or not find—in those dresser drawers.

EIGHT

DURING THIS TIME, my work was inconsequential. It was a job like any other, a means to pay the bills. With my newfound bachelor status, I was in no rush to get home at night. In fact, some nights I'd continue to work after everyone had left for the evening, enjoying the solitude I had grown accustomed to. A week after the Nor'easter was one such night. It was nearly nine o'clock when I locked the company doors behind me and stepped out into the parking lot. A light snow had begun to fall and I drove cautiously. Five miles of back country road that usually took me fewer than ten minutes to travel took me twenty. Eventually, I made it home and pulled into the driveway, the snow crunching underfoot as I walked from the carriage shed to the front door.

The temperature had dropped during the day and the house was cold. I raised the thermostat and put the teapot on the stove. The house grumbled and stirred as if waking from a long sleep. I changed into my flannel PJs and, tea in hand, I unwound in front of the television set, the familiar sounds of the programs providing a mind-numbing comfort that had been a frequent retreat during my married life. The house warmed around me, radiators whispering for my attention.

My cell phone rang.

The lights were off and I was bundled in a blanket on the couch. Woody was gone, having left earlier in the evening in preparation of another storm, I assumed. I got up and sought out the phone in the dark.

My winter coat hung on a hook in the entryway near the washer and dryer. At last, I pulled the still ringing phone out of one of its pockets.

"Hello?"

My voice must have sounded strange because my wife was unsure it was me.

"Graham?"

"Oh... Hi." I returned to the couch and once again wrapped myself in the blanket. I hadn't spoken to my wife since I'd left. Our divorce proceedings were still pending a court date.

"Do you have a minute to talk? I don't want to bother you?" she said.

I detected a hint of sarcasm in her voice. Perhaps she had called out of loneliness. Or perhaps she had been drinking. I had to stop myself from speculating. I was done speculating; done guessing what motivated her actions. "No, no bother at all," I said. "What is it? Is everything okay?"

There was a long pause, long enough for my mind to be distracted by a sudden gale outside that blew ice pellets against the side of the house. I was about to say "Hello" again, thinking we had lost the connection when she spoke.

"I just want to know one thing. Why?"

"Why what?" I said.

"Why did you leave?"

The question caught me off guard. *Why?* She had to be kidding. After all this time? *Why?*Anger welled inside of me. "So you want to have this conversation now?" I shook my head. "Why do you think I left?"

"I don't know. I want to hear it from you."

"Okay, let's see. I didn't want to be there anymore. I felt it would be better if we were apart. And, to be honest, we don't love each other, so what's the point?"

An edge had entered my voice. I knew my words could be cruel at times; when angered I hurled them like throwing knives. She responded in kind.

"'Honest?' Since when have you ever been honest, Graham? You don't know the meaning of the word. Everyone is asking me what happened. What am I supposed to tell them?"

"Is that all you're worried about? Appearances? Tell them whatever you want, I don't care. I'll take the blame. I'll be the bad guy. I really don't care."

I didn't want the conversation to turn into a shouting match, so I hung up. It felt good to be able to just shut her off with a press of a button. The phone rang seconds later.

"What?" I yelled, perhaps too loudly.

"Graham, don't hang up. Don't hang up, okay?"

"What?" I said more amenably.

"Why are you so angry?" she said.

I laughed.

"You think this is funny?"

"No," I said, "I think this is ridiculous. You just don't get it, do you? That's what makes me angry."

"Get what?"

I laughed again. But in truth I wanted to cry. I wanted to release all the tears I held trapped inside, fueling the hurt and resentment I harbored against her. And what hurt most was, even now, she was too stubborn to say "Graham, I love you. I want you to come home. Let's work this out." No, she always had to have the upper hand. I always had to be the one to succumb, to expose my weaknesses. But no more.

I listened to the storm raging outside and felt those tears crystallize inside of me. I felt my heart grow cold, and before it could shatter, I let go of everything—the pain, the hurt, even the love I once felt for her, no matter how undeserving of it she was. I heard the house groan just then. The floorboards creaked, and something in the attic thumped. My voice achieved a passionless tone I had never heard before.

"It's over," I said. "Don't call me again. I won't pick up. Goodbye, Kate."

She had tried to interrupt me, but I had said all I needed to say. I hung up and put the phone aside, as if it had been a wrong number, and went back to watching television. I don't remember when I fell asleep, but I slept peacefully that night for the first time in quite a while.

I spent the following day, Saturday, unpacking the boxes that had sat stacked in the spare bedroom for the past four months. My collection of books, mementos of places I'd been, pictures of my family. I put them all out, filling every available space on the bookshelves in both the spare bedroom and the reading room.

I made lunch and ate in solitude. When the sun, at last, broke through the clouds, I went outside and shoveled a path to my car. The trees sparkled and the branches creaked at the slightest breeze. Six inches of fresh snow blanketed the ground, with a layer of ice crystals on top. The sound of neighboring snowblowers cut through the afternoon calm. As I cleared my car, I saw a gray cat stalking the property behind the carriage shed, near the stone wall. I stepped into the snow to get a better look, but the cat bounded into the woods.

"Smokey?" I called. "Here, Smokey..."

I waited. I heard a single meow. I smiled.

It was absurd, I know. Because if indeed the cat I saw was Smokey—*my* Smokey—he would have been over forty years old. But what was once absurd was now merely a stretch of the imagination. And whether it was the relentless snow and cold of winter contributing to a desire to return to a sunnier time in my life, or whether it was the extended leave from my family, which fostered a distance, both in my mind and in my heart, that stretched further and further with each passing day, I had become more receptive to the unimaginable. I had reached the conclusion that whatever was happening to me, whatever strange and surreal occurrences the house was allowing me to experience, were real.

And I welcomed them.

NINE

THE HOLIDAYS CAME and went. For Thanksgiving, my older daughter and her husband dropped by with a plate of food. They were either concerned that, now that I was living alone, I wasn't getting the proper nutrition, or they were simply fact-finding, my daughter acting as emissary for her mother. To gauge my mental state perhaps. After a brief tour, I sent them on their way with a thank you and a smile. I kissed my daughter on the forehead to demonstrate her old dad was doing just fine. For Christmas, both my daughters visited. They brought gifts. I had gifts of my own to give them in return. The visit was awkward. They appeared confused that I was happy, that I didn't ask how their mother was doing. I could see the question in their eyes. When was I coming home? How could I tell them that I *was* home?

TEN

I FEEL MY WAY THROUGH the darkness, my bare feet on the cold hardwood. I hear music drifting through the air, originating from one of the rooms above. I pass through shadows into a deeper dark. I reach out and grab the banister and pull myself up the steep stairway. The music carries a lilting melody familiar to my ears, but I just can't place it. I reach the top of the stairs and see a light at the end of the hallway, a golden frame limning the entrance to the spare room; I move toward it. My hand reaches out. The music swells as the door pushes inward and a blinding light fills the dark...

The light dimmed as I awoke.

Another dream. I half-expected to see a feline shape sitting on my bed, staring in anticipation of me getting up to feed it or pet it, or both. But I was alone.

Outside, the wind blew against the windows. There was a dull gray light beyond the plastic.

As I lay in bed, the melody of the dream lingered. I suddenly remembered where I'd heard it before. It was a song I had composed when I first learned to play piano. It was more of a finger exercise than a real song, a free-spirited warm-up before the dour and the morose claimed my mood, and my fingers. My mother loved that song; when I played my impromptu recitals, she always requested I play it. Perhaps she believed there was enough sadness in the world, and a happy song, no matter how simple, could beat back the gloom. It made her happy. And it made me happy to see my mother smile.

As the long, cold nights continued, I began to play my music more, conjuring the spirit of my mother, feeling her as she looked on, proud of the kind and gentle soul I had become. I ignored the thumps and noises in the attic, likening them to misbehaving children running about, throwing tantrums. After all, my mother's whisper had always tended to soften the jaggedness of my father's brutish ways.

With the January thaw, the layers of snow receded, allowing the grass and leaves to once again surface. On warmer days, I would climb the ladder into the attic and stand in front of the cracked and cobwebbed window, staring down upon the road and the neighboring houses like an eagle perched on the uppermost branch of a tree. I watched people go about their lives, husbands leaving for work with a honk of their horn, housewives waiting with their children at the end of the driveway as the school bus rolled up and carried them away. Leaving. Waving goodbye. *So much of life*, I thought, *is about leaving and saying goodbye, distancing oneself from the ones we love, from the ones who love us.*

One day, from this vantage point I thought I saw a teenage boy trespassing on the property. The boy carried a butterfly net and was walking along the path leading to the field out back. The field that was no longer there. It was the middle of January, and the boy was dressed in shirt sleeves. The boy had black hair like my brother.

By February, I saw Smokey regularly. He was there in the morning when I stepped out into the winter air to warm up my car in preparation for my drive to work. He would keep his distance while I scraped the ice and snow from the car's windows, but always ran —a stone-gray blur—when I tried to get near. Perhaps he would always be unforgiving, forever distrustful of the humans who had abandoned him among that landscape of smoldering ruin.

My brother paid me another visit. This time he was playing a game of hide and seek.

I was in the kitchen making breakfast when something hit the door with a thud. I stepped out and noticed the remnants of a snowball still clinging to the door's windowpane. I looked in the direction from where it could have been thrown and found myself staring at the workshop. The door to the workshop pulled shut, as if someone had just entered.

I had inspected the workshop when I first moved in, remembering how Mr. Kulgren would climb the shop's short steps and disappear into its mysterious confines. What I saw then was a building in disrepair, gutters hanging, windows cracked, a place relegated to storage.

I walked outside without a coat. *Just a quick check*, I thought. This wasn't my property but I felt every bit the steward. It was my obligation to investigate anything suspicious.

The sun worked to keep the winter chill from my bones as I approached the workshop's wooden steps. There were no footprints in the snow leading up to them, but I climbed them anyway, clearing the steps with my boots.

I tried the doorknob, testing its resolve, the metal bitingly cold in my hand. Of course, it was locked. Secure. Unopened in months, if not years.

I leaned out from the steps and peered in the front window. The wood creaked under my weight. A sudden movement inside, a shifting of light into dark, startled me and I nearly lost my balance. I heard a mischievous giggle and a thump inside, as if someone had quickly hid from view.

My brother always won at hide and seek. As kids we'd play in the backyard at night with only the light from the back porch guiding the way. I'd stand with my face toward the big maple tree and count to ten. I'd hear my brother take off, his footsteps fading into the grass and leaves. At the count of ten, I'd turn toward where I last heard him and cautiously move in that direction. Sometimes he'd be lying in the grass, like a snake, not far from home base and I'd walk right past him, my attention focused too much on what was ahead of me. Once I was past, he'd pop up and run for the maple tree, giggling. "I win!"

My brother was sneaky and sly, and inherited a cruel streak from our father, which he inflicted on me from time to time. But he was my brother. He was family. He was my childhood.

A high-pitched chirp cut through my reverie and I realized it was the kitchen's smoke alarm. My eggs were burning.

I left my brother to his silly game and headed back inside.

ELEVEN

I SELDOM RECEIVED MAIL, but I checked the mailbox every day when I arrived home from work. Most times the mailbox contained flyers and pamphlets addressed to 'resident'. Woody got an occasional statement while I received nothing. It was as if no one knew I lived there, an anonymity I secretly enjoyed. But I was still looking for something, and it arrived at the end of February. I stood at the end of the driveway holding it in my hand as a cold wind rattled up the hill from the lake. A letter from the State of Connecticut. Windham County Superior Court. Inside was notification of my divorce date.

I closed the mailbox, leaving the junk mail for another day, suddenly aware of the rumbling behind me. I turned. Carol had pulled up in her pickup truck and stopped, window down.

"Hello again!" She was all smiles and eagerness, so full of life. Her hair was different. Shorter, I believe.

I summoned a smile. "Hello."

"I just have to ask... Is that you I hear playing the piano?"

"Yes, I play now and then."

"It's beautiful. You play beautifully."

"Thank you." The letter in my hand felt as if it was going to cut into my fingers if I didn't get inside and open it.

Carol's brow suddenly creased. "Were you here earlier today?"

"No. Why?"

"I didn't think so. It's funny but I thought I heard you playing."

I knew I shouldn't ask, I should have left it a mystery, but a part of me still wanted to know. She could have heard music from a car radio carried on the wind. "What did it sound like?"

"I don't know. Kinda jazzy. Up-tempo, like music from an old black and white movie where everyone's dancing in a speakeasy."

My heart seemed to stall in my chest. It then beat more heavily as if to make up for lost time. I cleared my throat. "That's weird."

"I know, huh?"

Again, the awkwardness descended. But Carol pressed on. "Hey, if you ever need anything, I'm right across the street. Drop in for a cup of coffee, or just to chat. We're neighbors, you know. You shouldn't spend so much time alone." Again, the smile.

"Thanks, I'll keep that in mind." I turned to go.

"Looks like another storm is coming."

I checked the sky as if I hadn't seen it for myself. "Yes, it looks like it."

"Well, stay warm. Bye!"

Carol waved as she sped away, the breath of her truck's exhaust trailing like a dragon's tail behind her.

I walked up the driveway, then looked at the attic window. The figure was there again, staring down. I held up the letter as if to say I've got good news. The figure stared a moment longer, then turned away.

Carol was wrong. I wasn't alone.

TWELVE

THE FOLLOWING DAY, Woody was waiting for me when I arrived home from work. He was sitting in the living room in his easy chair, watching the news, something he did from time to time when he had the time to relax. But another storm was coming. I was confused.

"Hi, Woody," I said as I was about to climb the stairs to my room.

"Graham, can I talk to you for a minute?"

"Sure," I said.

"I've got good news and bad news," he said. "The bad news is I retired and I'm moving to Maine."

"I thought you'd be happy about that," I quipped. I knew he had planned to retire; I just didn't know when.

He chuckled. "I am. It's bad news for you, though. It means you're going to have to find another place to live."

"But I really like this place." I looked around at the sloping floor and the slanted ceiling. "Maybe I can talk to the owner."

"To be honest, Graham, I don't think you can afford to stay here by yourself. Besides—I didn't want to tell you this when you first moved in because I was afraid you might not take the room, but—the owner told me he has plans to tear the place down this summer."

For a moment I couldn't breathe. The house seemed to shudder under my feet. But I realized it was just my legs: they were shaking.

"The good news?" I asked.

"The good news is I'm paid up through the end of next month, so you've got time. Sorry it's such short notice."

"No, no problem," I said. On the television, the weather chimed in with a satellite picture of the impending storm. Woody and I stared at the screen for a moment. "You're not on call tonight, are you?"

"Nope, I'm done. The guy I trained can handle it. But I am leaving before the storm gets here. Just wanted to pick up a few things before heading back to Maine."

I nodded.

"There's a plate in the refrigerator for you. I didn't want to leave it on the counter."

"Oh, okay, great. And thanks, Woody. For everything."

"No problem," he said.

I headed up the stairs to my room.

That night, after Woody left, I had a feeling that it was the last I'd ever see of him.

Winter came back with a vengeance that night. The news had cautioned people to clear their roofs. Despite the warming spells, the accumulated weight of ice and snow had caused roofs to cave in. So far the misfortune had been limited to shopping centers and old barns. But I had begun to notice the ice that had formed on the section of the house above the kitchen. The roof there was less steep and the layer of ice beneath the snow was at least eight inches thick above the gutters. I feared if there was a weakness in the house, it would be there.

After Woody left, the snow began in earnest. I made a cup of tea, and while dunking the tea bag to extract every last drop of flavor before tossing it into the garbage, I heard a few creaks and groans above my head. I resigned to stay up in my room for the rest of the night. If there was a cave-in, at least I wouldn't be caught beneath it.

I read a little, while the wind occasionally shook the window frames and pelted the glass with pellets of sleet. At last, I turned off the light, expecting to not have electricity in the morning, and went to sleep. I didn't think about the events of the last two days—news of my court date, and the eventual demolition of the very home I lived in. Instead, these two pending occurrences seemed to coincide. The death of my marriage and the death of this house. In fact, with my recent encounters with Smokey, my brother, and the palpable presences of both my mother and father... I had more in common with the dead than the living. And I was not in the least bit disturbed by this thought. So, while outside the storm raged, inside my sleep was surprisingly peaceful.

Until the noises began.

Apparently, my father didn't share the same nonchalant attitude toward the news that the house he now inhabited was set for demolition. I awoke to what sounded like a tree slamming one of its branches against the roof as if demanding to be let in. I got up and entered the spare bedroom. I opened the door to the attic; the sound multiplied in volume. I left the door open and sat at the piano. I played the only thing that came to mind—O' Holy Night. Almost immediately the banging lessened. "It's okay," I said, "everything is going to be all right." I continued to play. I played until all I heard was the wind outside, and what sounded like a gentle sobbing emanating from the attic dark.

THIRTEEN

I HOLD THE CANDLE in my hand as I climb the attic stairs. My heart quickens because I know what awaits me. The candle light blossoms as I step up onto the attic floor. I turn and I see them: my mother, who appears to carry a light of her own; my father, who appears to absorb that light, turning it to shadow; and my brother, dancing, giggling, flickering in between. I set the candle down and embrace them. Their touch is warmth and cold, light and shadow. I am both elated and frightened because I know what this means. I hear a soft crackling sound and am not surprised when I look to see that the candle I had set down was placed too near the stack of wood slats. The attic is on fire. Soon curtains of flame surround us. The four of us join hands and close our eyes as the light consumes us.

I wake. I've overslept. I lie in bed—this bed that isn't my bed, in this house that isn't my house. This may not be my house, but it is my home.

The storm from the night before is gone; gone but for the wind that still gusts now and then, pushing against the attic eaves.

Outside, the sun is shining. I hear noises outside my window. I get up and peer through the thin plastic.

Below, I see my brother. He's at the well house, clearing away the snow. He looks up at me and smiles, before climbing in. A golden glow follows him, lighting up the well.

He wants me to come outside and play.

I head for the stairs, barefoot, with an anticipation in my chest I've never felt before.

My brother's very good at hide and seek.

This time I'm going to find him.

About the Author

KURT NEWTON'S writing has appeared in numerous magazines and anthologies over the past thirty years. He is the author of two novels, three books of short stories and nine collections of poetry. His fiction tends to lean toward illuminating the dark side of human behavior. A lifelong resident of Connecticut, he now resides in what is called the "Quiet Corner." There he lives with his wife and young son.